Two Men—Two Paths

AND AN AMERICAN EXPERIMENT FOILED?

C. Mary Finn

PublishAmerica
Baltimore

First printing

This is a work of fiction. Names, characters, places, and incidents either are the product of the author's imagination or are used fictitiously. Any resemblance to actual persons, living or dead, events, or locales is entirely coincidental.

PublishAmerica has allowed this work to remain exactly as the author intended, verbatim, without editorial input.

ISBN: 978-1-4489-6177-1
PUBLISHED BY PUBLISHAMERICA, LLLP
www.publishamerica.com
Baltimore

Printed in the United States of America

I dedicate this book to my grandfather,
who emboldened my mother to retain her spunk and spirit
and
to my mother for passing this adventurous nature on to me
and encouraging my inquisitiveness by answering every "why?"

Table of Contents

Chapter 1: The Story of Sudra 25
Chapter 2: William Meets His Traveling Companion 32
Chapter 3: William Chronicles His Travels Through South Africa. 37
Chapter 4: Traveling to a Changed Africa 47
Chapter 5: Grandmother's Story 53
Chapter 6: William Hooks Up with P.J. 63
Chapter 7: Research in Nairobi 66
Chapter 8: On Their Way to the Plantation 73
Chapter 9: Leaving Nairobi 75
Chapter 10: Arriving at the Plantation 80
Chapter 11: William Meets Turko 82
Chapter 12: Two Men Meet in Chicago 84
Chapter 13: Catherine 87
Chapter 14: Circumspection 91
Chapter 15: Home Sweet Home 97
Chapter 16: The Story of Tera 99
Chapter 17: Ida the Calf 104
Chapter 18: Two Men 106
Chapter 19: The Story of Nora 109
Chapter 20: Different Paths 113
Chapter 21: The Story of Nora II 117
Chapter 22: The Depression 122
Chapter 23: New Deal 124
Chapter 24: The Story of Jemeya 126
Chapter 25: The Story of Tera II 127
Chapter 26: American Hero Perishes 130
Chapter 27: Willy Arrives at His New Home 134
Chapter 28: A Plot Hatched 137
Chapter 29: No Roots 140

Chapter 30: The Story of Jemeya, II 142
Chapter 31: 22nd Amendment 145
Chapter 32: Junior Achievement......................................147
Chapter 33: Korean War 155
Chapter 34: The Story of Tera's Son 158
Chapter 35: Tom Minoya 160
Chapter 36: The Story of Jemeya III 162
Chapter 37: Willy Makes a New Friend 168
Chapter 38: Minoya Meets Theodore 171
Chapter 39: The Story of Anah 174
Chapter 40: Theodore Takes Two Trips 181
Chapter 41: The Story of Anah II 183
Chapter 42: The Story of Bella 188
Chapter 43: Celia 192
Chapter 44: The Story of Anah III 194
Chapter 45: The Story of Bella II....................................200
Chapter 46: A False Security 203
Chapter 47: The Story of Jemeya V 205
Chapter 48: Bad Times Ahead 209
Chapter 49: The Story of Anah IV 212
Chapter 50: Chautauqua Revisited 219
Chapter 51: Non-violent Demonstrations 222
Chapter 52: The Story of Bella III 226
Chapter 53: More Change..229
Chapter 54: The New Bella 234
Chapter 55: Kogelo..236
Chapter 56: The Story of Bella IV 240
Chapter 57: Sudden Departure 243
Chapter 58: The Story of Bella V 245
Chapter 59: The Analysis 248
Chapter 60: Love Rekindled 250
Chapter 61: The Story of Bella VI 252
Chapter 62: Closer to the Puzzle 256
Epilogue 261

TWO MEN—TWO PATHS

And An American Experiment Foiled?

Prologue

The history of our grandparents is remembered not with rose petals but in the laughter and tears of their children and their children's children. It is into us that the lives of grandparents have gone. It is in us that their history becomes a future.

~Charles and Ann Morse1

In early 1999, I began preparing for my mother's 90th birthday celebration. My siblings and I had decided that it would be held in a rustic resort in central Colorado, where my dad and mother loved to trout fish. While preparing a video for the celebration, I discovered much about myself and my family. I had a wealth of information available; grandmother's autobiography, letters that my great grandfather, Elisha Peairs, had written home to his family during the Civil War and all the letters that my grandfather William Allen Peairs had written to his parents, when he traveled around the world for a pharmaceutical company from 1881 through 1890. I read through the letters so that I could get bits and pieces to include in the video I was preparing. I also felt this video would be a picture into the past for my children and their children.

My mother was born in 1909 to William A. Peairs and Catherine Gissing Peairs. My mother always bragged that she was conceived in Australia, but born in Des Moines, Iowa. My grandfather and grandmother moved to Iowa after my grandfather asked if he might become district manager of the pharmaceutical company for which he worked. He had been traveling for the company since 1881 to all parts of the United States and around the world at least three times. He had traveled to Hawaii, Australia, India, Africa and many parts in between. He was tired of traveling and wanted to settle down and raise a family, which he managed to do having 9 children.

I recall my mother telling me that she thought that her father favored her because she had a spirit that maybe the 4 other girls in the family did not have. Girls were not suppose to climb trees, get into mischief or disappear when it came time to do woman's chores. She was sent at seventeen to Switzerland to go to a private school. Maybe that was to feminize my mother, who by the way was one good looking, sexy female and very lady like when I knew her. She loved her one year experience in Switzerland, learning how to ski and traveling around Europe. I am not sure that this is what my grandparents had in mind when they sent her there. My mom always said that her father and mother tended to be at odds about her spirit.

My mother hyphenated her last name when she got married and that was in 1932. I can remember my mother taking my sister and me on a trip to California in 1951 to visit my grandmother when I was ten and my sister was two. When we were to return, the airlines were on strike and only a few planes were flying. My mother made such a commotion about her need to get back home that the pilots agreed to let us fly in the cockpit. It wasn't until I was preparing my mother's celebration nearly 50 years later that I learned of my mother's reason for her trip to California. She wanted to discuss her breast cancer with my grandmother, and the reason she had to get back home so quickly was that her mastectomy had already been scheduled. That is how I remember my mother, always thinking of her family before anything else, remaining positive and upbeat. She always let me spread my wings trusting that I would do what was right. I had always thought her unfettered trust was because she was oblivious to what was going on, but as my own daughters sought their independence, I saw that she was just letting me find my way, quietly setting limits and teaching me the values of life through her example and encouragement— the very same values I uncovered in the letters of her parents and grandparents.

Looking through my mother's memorabilia, I found the following. Her brother had sent it to her right after their mother died in 1977, at the age of 105. He had found it among my grandmother's belongings. He included a note to my mother: "This is your mother and from my casual observations I think it is you also." The love my grandmother received from her children and the paths which they followed are testaments that she believed and followed the tenets in this prayer:

> *O heavenly Father, make me a better parent. Teach me to understand my children, to listen patiently to what they have to say, and to answer all their questions kindly. Keep me from interrupting them or contradicting them. Make me as courteous to them as I would have them be to me. Forbid that I should ever laugh at their mistakes, or resort to shame or ridicule when they displease me. May I never punish them for my own selfish satisfaction or to show my power.*
>
> *Let me not tempt my child to lie or steal. And guide me hour by hour that I may demonstrate by all I say and do that honesty produces happiness.*
>
> *Reduce, I pray, the meanness in me. And when I am out of sorts, help me, O Lord, to hold my tongue.*
>
> *May I ever be mindful that my children are children and I should not expect of them the judgment of adults.*
>
> *Let me not rob them of the opportunity to wait on themselves and to make decisions.*
>
> *Bless me with the bigness to grant them all their reasonable requests and the courage to deny them privileges I know will do them harm.*
>
> *Make me fair and just and kind. And fit me, O Lord, to be loved and respected and imitated by my children. Amen*

After finding this prayer, I could confirm my uncle's assessment of my mother. I was hoping that my grandmother had written that poem because it was so like her, but after goggling part of the poem, I found that this was written in 1941 by the founder of Highlight magazine, a magazine for children.

Preparing the video, helped me understand why I had a certain restlessness and curiosity, traveling to Europe twice and Asia, starting up several businesses, organizing community sporting opportunities for girls and my constant researching a gamut of topics: as a high school student, my final research paper was on communism. In 1959 communism was our worst fear. In my social studies class my freshmen year of college I did a project that covered man's progression, from his discovery of fire, how and when he acquired the ability to communicate through language, and why there was always a need for some form of spirituality—everything in order to find the true meaning of our existence. Getting ready for this 90th birthday piqued my curiosity—Is the way we live our life and the views we express influenced by the path followed by the ancestors who have preceded us?

It wasn't until many years later that I actually decided to delve into the lives of my ancestors and the times in which they lived to answer that question. By 1990 my aunt had gathered all of my grandfather's letters and put them in boxed folders by year, cataloging each letter according to date and place traveled. At that time, I was too young to appreciate what she had done. What is it about getting older that makes one interested in their genealogy? I had never thanked my aunt. I am sad about that. Celia, another aunt and the youngest daughter of my grandfather, had combined all the letters that my great grandfather had written home to his wife during the Civil War. I failed to thank her also.

This narrative is not about my mother, it is about my mother's parents, my grandparents and anyone's parents and grandparents and the influence they have on their progeny. It is a narrative told through my eyes looking back into the past of my ancestors by incorporating the wealth of information that I have found about them and using a historical time line of important events of our country through which they lived. I have used this information to create an imaginary, but plausible, story of two men who chose to follow different paths.

As William Martin, the author, has said

"The historian serves the truth of his subject. The novelist serves the truth of his tale. As a novelist, I have tools no historian should touch: I can manipulate time and space, extrapolate from the written record to invent dialogue and incident, create fictional characters to bring you close to the historical figures, and fall back on my imagination when the research runs out."

The main characters in this story are my grandfather, William A. Peairs (1862) and his traveling companion. It is through this story that you will come to understand how past generations can leave a character imprint engrained on each future generation. As you read, you will see how each of these men will come to have an influence on their children and their children's children, and their country. It is also the life-stories of 6 women of Kenyan decent who had come into contact with these men and their descendents. The politics and economics of an era that spans between 1894 and 2016 will take these two men and their progeny down different paths. The story line leads to a scenario that might show what the future could be at the end of each path. The study of my grandfather's traveling companion and his descendents take shape as my grandfather's family story is told.

To understand my grandfather, it helps to know his heritage.

****

My grandfather, William A. Peairs was born in Duncan Falls, OH, February16, 1862 to Elisha and Celia Peairs. Of course Elisha also had a father, a grandfather, a great grandfather, a great, great grandfather…

Peairs' Genealogy

Charlemagne was born thirty-four generations ago. It is his military accomplishments, his curiosity and his quest for knowledge that found their way down through each future generation that followed.

"He sent to England and elsewhere for books and teachers, and soon the palace school was an active center of study, of the revision and copying of manuscripts, and of an educational reform that spread throughout the realm…Among the pupils were Charlemagne, his wife Liutgard, his sons, his daughter Gisela…Charlemagne was the most eager of all; he seized upon learning as he had absorbed states; he studied rhetoric, dialectic, astronomy; he made heroic efforts to write." (http://www.chronique.com/Library/MedHistory/charlemagne.htm)

The English progeny embraced his military accomplishments; his American descendents embraced his curiosity and quest for knowledge.

Ten generations later, Jocelyn de Louvain (b. 1121), a direct descendent of Charlemagne and half-brother of the Queen of Henry I. asked for the hand of Agnes Percy, who happened to be the sole rich heiress of the noble Percy House of Yorkshire. Her father, not wanting the name of Percy to be lost, put forward these conditions

"*This Jocelyn…wedded this dame Agnes Percy upon condition that he should be called Jocelyn Percy, or els that he shold bare the arms of the Lord Percy; and he toke the councell of his syster, and he chose rather to be called Jocelyn Percy than to forsake his own armies (which be feld ore, a lion rampant azure); for so shold he have no right title to his father's inheritance, and so of right the Lord Percy shold be Duke of Brabant, tho they be not so indeed.* (Whitby MSS) And in his Rhyming Chronicle the good friar Peeris tells us that: "Therefore in con-clusion, he chose to holde hs owne armys styll, And to take the name of Percy at the saide Lady Agnes'wil'" (*A history of the house of Percy By Gerald Brenan, William Alexander Lindsay)*

This began the long line of Percys (Pearse, Pearce, Peairs), with a history that went from building castles and abbeys in Yorkshire to those at Alnwick and wars fighting to keep both intact. It was said that there wasn't a Percy" that died in his bed."

The Percy that had the first name change was Richard Percy (b. 1525), whom in around 1550 founded Pearce Hall in Yorkshire, maybe to deflect the Percy name, which had been in disfavor to many around England because of the Percy's questionable and changing allegiances . It may have been this disfavor that drove his son Richard Pearce Sr. (b. 1563) to Boston, Massachusetts in 1632. He and his two sons boarded the boat "Lyons," which was captained by his son William, who in 1639 produced the 1st Almanac in North America. He married, but had no children. The house that he and his wife built in 1637 still stands, being the oldest house which has been lived in continuously in the nation. His brother, Richard Jr.(b. 1590) settled in Rhode Island and he began the next generation of Percys (Pierce/Pearce/Pearse, Peairs) in America.

The Ohio descendents began four generations later when Joseph Peairs (b. 1760) acquired land in Zanesville, OH. During the Revolutionary War, on April 2, 1778, he was commissioned a Second Lieutenant in the Fourth Company of the Fourth Battalion of the

Westmoreland County Militia. After the war he was provided lands near Zanesville, Ohio as bounty for participation in the Revolutionary War.

Joseph came from the New Jersey area with his parents when he was about 16 years old. He immigrated with his father to the vicinity of Redstone, Fayette, Pennsylvania. His future wife's family, the Allens, fell into company along the way. Susannah Allen was 12 at that time and the Allen and Peairs families settled in the same neighborhood. The Allens were from the Faggo Manner Church, Pennsylvania. Joseph and Susannah were married in their Presbyterian Church in 1783. They had eleven children by the time he died in 1807.

He served in the military from 1778-1783, and then purchased a farm in 1783 in Fayette, PA, becoming a part-time farmer as well as a captain of the Ranger at Forks of Yough where he died April 3, 1807. (The Youghogheny River flows into the Monongahela at McKeesport which is now in Allegheny County just north of Washington Co. This location, referred to early as "the forks of the Yough," was important in the early days when pioneers followed the river Valley through southwestern Pennsylvania toward what is now the Pittsburgh area.)

In 1806, Joseph had registered the land at Zanesville, Ohio that was patented to him after the Revolutionary War, but never lived there. On March 10, 1807 in Allegheny Co., Pennsylvania, he signed his will. He had an estate probated on April 28, 1807, in Allegheny Co., Pennsylvania.

Joseph was 47 when he became ill and his will was like a "last letter" to his family. It seemed that he had not discussed his wishes with his sons or his wife, probably because he didn't want them to know how sick he was or because he was a very private man. It was a sad "letter," trying to squeeze into one letter what he wanted for his family if he had lived to see them grow up to be adults. He had 3 under 7, the youngest being 3, when he died.

"I give unto my well beloved son Elisha Peairs (b. 1785) all and entire the Mantion Farm that I now so live. And upon the following conditions to wit, in my will is that my young family shall be raised together on the farm, he shall be bound to live on the farm until the youngest of the children come to

age and be as a head to the family…he shall cause any five younger boys to wit, Joseph Jr., John, Allen, William and Isaac to be instructed to read, write and figure as far as the double rule of three. And further, that my young daughters shall be instructed to read and write…

"*Notwithstanding, I direct that the first cash that comes to hand shall go to the discharge of the small debts which I cue in the neighborhood and to the purchasing of such clothing as the family stands in present need of and further that my four daughters to wit, Betsy, Nancy, Susanna and Polly, shall at any time after the correct age be entitled to receive the following articles to wit, a bed and bed clothes and decent wearing apparel, the quantity and quality of these things to be at the discretion of their Mother, besides one horse and saddle, one spinning wheel and one bureau, two cows. Likewise, such pots and dishes, furniture as their Mother shall choose to give.*"

…likewise, a sufficient work horse with saddle and bridle, two cows, and bed and bed clothes, and a good falling ax, one pot and some Drefour furniture" for all 5 other boys."

The property in Zanesville was divided amongst the sons.

In 1813, four of Joseph's sons, David, Allen (William's grandfather), Joseph Jr. and John moved their families to the land in Zanesville, OH. The four ranged in age from 14 to 27.

The youngest sons, William and Isaac, were 13 and 11 and remained on the farm in Pennsylvania with Elisha. They did move to Morgan County, Ohio when they were older but were regarded as slightly apart by the Muskingum County Peairs because the Morgan County branch included some Democrats and many Methodists. The younger boys did not remember their father as did the older boys who moved to Zanesville, Muskingum County, Ohio 6 years after their father died. They left the younger children in the hands of their oldest brother, Elisha, who after a few years took on his own family. Their mother remarried a few years after the older boys left and after Elisha, the oldest son, married. It seemed that the younger two boys became estranged from the rest of the family either out of their own choosing or because the other four brothers did not share in the land in Zanesville—probably a combination of the two. Politics and religion often drove families apart.

Allen (b. 1798) had 5 children, Elisha (b. 1825) was the oldest and was

William's father and my great grandfather. Allen died when he was quite young, just like his father Joseph. He was only thirty-four.

My Grandfather's Parents

Elisha (b. 1825) was only 7 at the time of his father's death. He was raised by his mother with the help of his uncles John, Joseph and David. Like his father, his mother was a big influence in his life.

Elisha Peairs and Celia Joseph were married Nov. 10, 1853. Celia Joseph's family set foot in America in 1685, dispersing throughout the U.S., and Celia's father took his family to Zanesville, Ohio. Recounting her family history, Mary Joseph, Celia's aunt:

> *"there have been no great or distinguished ones among us—a few preachers of the gospel and still a less number of doctors, lawyers, or other professional men. As a rule they have been farmer people owning the land they tilled, and with a strong aversion to working the land of other people. There may have been many mechanics, in almost every handicraft. So marked the third degree who was not skillful with tools; so also it may be said, the mathematical faculty runs like a thread through the whole tribe. I have never known one not strongly marked by this faculty while many may have been, considering their meager opportunities, very remarkable."*

After Celia and Elisha married, they moved into a house where Elisha had a workshop, specializing in carriage building. They had lost two of their children in 1859, so it must have been difficult for Celia to see her husband going off to war leaving her with the responsibility of a young baby, fearing the same fate. Elisha had enlisted in the 122nd Regiment from Ohio. Except for the time confined as a prisoner at Richmond, after being captured at the Battle of Winchester, he faithfully wrote home to his wife and two children, trying to keep involved in their day to day life. His letters are a window into the feelings and thoughts of a man who leaves his family in order to fight a war between his own countrymen and often brother against brother. In his letters we learn his philosophy of life through the way he deals with marital responsibilities, child rearing and constant loneliness.

March 19th, 1863:

Yours dated the 15th was received this evening and its contents were eagerly devoured. I was as usual very glad to hear that you were all well. Am getting along right. I see you received the rice I sent you, also the bread and crackers. I believe Jim Lunsu put the bread in, I put in the crackers myself.

Keep as much as you need and sell the rest as it is higher than I thought it was, but no matter so much the better for you. Let Williamson have some. It will help you get other groceries.

You may sell all the lumber you can. These pieces downstairs are worth 25 cents. The plank is worth $1.25 per hundred feet. If you sell any of it, get someone who understands measuring to attend to it. I think the lobster stuff is upstairs. They are worth 12 or 15 cents offering. I believe Bailey will do right with that wagon, in owing you have a place to use it. I would like to have that wiped out as soon as possible...

I believe you are improving in writing. Still I can read your letters without trouble. Little Eva's letter was very nice. I am glad to receive a letter from her. I feel proud of her. Do not let her get vain.

Your letter in the box was rather distressing. I had to read it over several times before I could get my mind fixed on it and realize it. I see by the last one that you are in better spirits. Cheer up, and always look at the brighter side. I think the dark cloud is moving at present.

If I had been at home, I do not think I would have consented to your hair being cut off. It was so long and nice, but it is not my place to dictate in everything, as it would be commonly for me to do.

Yours truly, Elisha

Winchester VA, May 15th 1863.

"Dear Wife—Do not let little Willie get ahead of you for it will be hard matter to conquer him until you get order. You can tell that by others, that have been let go too far when young. Always bend the twig while it is tender and there will be no stiff branches to lop off in anger or sorrow. A few slight reprimands in the start may save many an anxious hour of suffering in after years. Do not let your love for him cause you to neglect him in the least particular. Think you better wean him. I don't think it will hurt him."

Yours in love and affection, Elisha

On April 18th, 1864 Elisha writes to his daughter: At the time Elisha had been given the position of "nurse" in the US General Hospital Emory, Washington D.C.

Dear Eva, This evening being all alone I thought I would try and converse a little to you with pen and paper. The reason of my being alone is this. All of the men of our ward were transferred to another in order that we could have ours whitewashed and fitted for the summer.

This cleaning up and whitewashing is necessary to conduce to the health of the patients. Our nice and obliging little Ward master has stepped out on some wild good chase for a little recreation. He is now able to attend to the ward himself which takes the responsibility off of my shoulders. But I must say that I can attend to it with the best of them now. I have kept my eyes open and learned what the duties are so that I am now qualified to run such an institution myself, if the necessities of the case should require it.

I am the only one the Ward master retained in the ward with him.

Eva, little Gomy as we call him is a nice little fellow and is liked by all hand. But Eva, there is no trouble for anyone to have plenty of friends. The only way to do is to treat all with kindness and love on all occasions. Although at times it is hard to bear up under all circumstances but finally in the end it is much better. Could we at all times smother down the angry feelings that at times take possession of our minds, our pathways through life would be much brighter. And when we are called to bid the world farewell we could depart in peace, provided we had chosen that better past that cannot be taken from us. Eva, you are yet young in years but useful and religious instruction received at your age will be of lasting benefit to you in after life. There is no one but our Maker knows what positions of usefulness we may be called to fill before we are called to that long home from whence there is no return. Then oh how much better it is to be ready and prepared. In saying this to you I do not wish to wound your feelings and cause you to think that you are any worse than others of your tender years. But it is a Father's advice to you such as every father should give to his dear little charges that have been given to him to cherish and provide for, and while provision is made for their bodies, the imortal part should not be neglected.

Yours in love and affection, Elisha

He writes to his daughter Eva again April 1, 1864.

Dear Eva: Your kind and welcome little note enclosed with Momma's was duly received and appreciated. I am so well pleased with the progress you are writing. Eva, it is my wish that you may become a good scholar for there is nothing equal to it. It enables you to move in all respectable society when other accomplishments accompany it. I do not wish for you to overtax your little mind to accomplish this end but be diligent at all times.

...Also, you will find a piece of poetry that I very much admire. I hope you will also admire it for it contains so much sentiment when rightly studied.

Yours in love and affection, Elisha

March 17, 1865 to his wife Celia

"...But your letter almost gave me the blues. I do wish you would not become too dispirited and downhearted. It is only hurrying you to your grave. There is nothing so good as a cheerful spirit. Still at times it is almost impossible to bear up under everything that crosses our paths...You have a comfortable little home, 2 sweet little cherubs still to cheer you up and employ your mind and hands to make them comfortable and happy."

When reading his letters, one feels the angst that envelopes him when he writes about those who chose to stay home, the pain and suffering of his fellow soldiers, the destruction of the farms and meadows as he marches 20 to 50 miles a day, and the contempt he has for those who brought his country to such a tragic war.

Dear Celia: "Some of our boys get letters from home which are written in rather a discouraging mood. It is not right for them to do so. It only worries the boys. If they were here in Virginia, they would have something to complain over. Here there are thousands of acres turned loose without a single rail to enclose them again, and the nice stone fences broke and damaged in all ways, orchard nurseries and nice growth laid waste first by one army, then another. Let them complain about high prices and hard times if they will, but they know nothing about it. It is here where they are feeling the evils of their folly. You may travel for miles and you will scarcely see anything to eat either for man or beast. But send out the forage master and he can find it, but he must hunt either the cellar or garret to find it. They have all their grain hid. Just think of a large farm with all that is raised on it having to be hid. Just let the poor dastardly coward who talks about secession and abolitionism prate away. They do not know what they are coming to, could they but follow a few of the little armies that are ransacking their beautiful valley and see the damage that is done. They would forever shut their foul mouths and let the soldiers and their leaders alone. But no they cannot; they must be continually sowing the seeds of discontent broadcast over this already distracted country, here where the monuments of destruction meet your gaze at every turn you take. Could the armies that are now at variance with each other be called home in then days, 2 generations would scarcely see this country in the prosperous condition it once was.

"Oh shame on such men as you have at home that will try to make every excuse they can rather than go and lend a hand. My honest wish is that there may be another draft and it may fall on some of them, especially to let them rave and rant as they will their day is coming."

Elisha's family and his country seemed to be his whole being. On the surface Elisha appeared to be a domineering father and husband and a person of high self esteem, but between the lines we find a lonely man devoted to his family and country, trying to be the best he could be for both. Absent a father during his formative years, he wasn't sure what role he should play. One thing we learn for sure in his letters, he believed in discipline and a good education.

We find he was neither a secessionist or an abolitionist. Through Elisha we get an insight into why so many young men left their families to fight in a war that they didn't quite understand. For Elisha, the reason was his unflinching respect and loyalty for President Lincoln. We are made to realize the tight rope the President had to walk dealing with abolitionists, secessionists and those who were neither. We saw the sadness Elisha felt when his President was assassinated and the display of emotions from the "throngs of people hanging from verandas, sitting in tree tops and lining the streets as the funeral procession made its way to the rotunda."

Elisha summed up the war:

"This cruel war is making a great many cripples for life, also, many a sweet little family without a father to look up to for their daily board. I think

in the day of final reckoning those who were the aggressors in this deadly carnage will have an awful account to settle."

He gives us a view of the times in which his son, William (1862), began his life. The next 10+ years of reconstruction would also have an effect on William's views of how society should evolve and the politics that would decide it. He was a Northerner and so was his father.

As was stated in William Allen Blair's book, *Cities of the Dead,*

'Northern White people wanted reunification with the white South—urgently and more rapidly than the supporters of the Confederacy. This was the war aim that brought together Democrats and Republicans alike. When Grant, a Republican, assumed office in 1869, he stressed peace between the sections in his inaugural address. Even the many Republicans who championed antislavery often took this position to validate the ideals of free labor and representative democracy rather than because they shared priorities with black people. Many were nation builders who bid good riddance to slavery because it had propped up a planter aristocracy, demeaned the dignity of white labor, held down the wages of working men, limited the advancement of poor white people in general, served as an antiquated and immoral system that prevented the country from achieving its full potential, or made American claims for freedom appear hypocritical in the eyes of the world. Reaching across the bloody chasm to white ex-soldiers had been a continuous part of the northern psyche from 1861 on. A peaceful, reconstructed South provided the capstone of the northern war effort—proof that a democracy could survive.

Also in Blair's book,

"One of the most prominent northern Radicals/Republicans who advocated reconciliation with former Confederates may be one of the least appreciated in this regard. Salmon P. Chase, former secretary of the treasury under Lincoln and chief justice of the Supreme Court in Reconstruction, had been an influential reformer and antislavery advocate from the antebellum period. He had pushed Lincoln for emancipation and counseled President Johnson to support black suffrage. After the war, Chase hoped for restoration of political rights for former Confederates and regretted that the Fourteenth Amendment had disfranchised rebels who might be "serviceable candidates and efficient helpers." His leniency toward white southerners had conditions. They needed to accept the end of slavery, allow for universal education, grant suffrage to black people, and operate an impartial judicial system. They could not work against the government, discriminate against black people because of race."

When Grant was running for President, the Northern Democrats believed they might be able to beat him with the help of the south. In Blair's book the Confederates/Southern Democrats stated:

"…best course for restoring southern peace and prosperity lay with restoration of the white leaders who had prevailed before the war. The North could leave southern affairs safely in the hands of the old guard because they accepted the end of slavery and it was in their best interests to promote peace. The group admitted it opposed political power for African Americans but attributed this to the belief that black people were not ready to exercise the franchise. Lee and his comrades claimed that they only wanted a "restoration of their rights under the Constitution,": "relief from oppressive misrule," and "the right of self government."

It goes on to say that Reconstruction did not include the blacks as much as the blacks had hoped. Both parties, but especially the Confederates/Southern Democrats, took on a "paternal" attitude toward the African American.

Elisha returned home from the war, happy that the war had ended and that the south had agreed to stay with the Union, but troubled by the bitterness that the southerners had for the northerners. When William began his travels, often traveling to the south, the bitterness was still there.

Through Elisha's letters we got a glimpse of the influence Elisha had over all major and minor decisions from rearing the children to all things financial. Without reading the letters that his wife Celia wrote to Elisha, we learned a lot about her through Elisha's remarks to her, either through his answers to her questions or the scolding she received for being apprehensive and not more upbeat in her letters. She appeared to be shy, a woman with little self-confidence and a woman soft and gentle with her children, and yet knew how to best handle her husband. She learned a lot about him in his letters. When the men from the war returned, they often found their lives and role in the family may have changed dramatically.

With so much of the responsibility falling onto the wives of the soldiers, they surely became more independent women, as did Elisha's wife. Even though Elisha wrote home telling his wife how to handle the renting of his workshop and a few rooms of their home in order to bring in extra money, his wife still was the one who had to make any final decisions. Letters were the only means of communication and often were received many weeks after a decision had to be made.

Elisha talked about finding other work then his workshop in the home, but wrote that due to the uncertainty of the reconstruction, he would just stay doing what he was doing. Obviously, Celia had suggested in a letter that he might find more lucrative work. After Elisha died in 1904, because Celia was left with little income, William built a small cottage for Celia on the property where he lived with his family. The main house was called Wellwood and was the home of William, his wife Catherine and their 9 children. Celia lived there until she died in 1918. She had a great influence in William's life.

William's letters to his parents when he was traveling showed the closeness he had with his mother. He acquired her softness, tolerance and tact, but it was probably through his father that he acquired the curiosity of new ideas and adventures, the duties of citizenship and fatherhood and a love for chronicling the places he had been. When Elisha was in Washington, Maryland and Virginia during the Civil War, he wrote home excited about what he saw. His son, who crossed the globe several times, was enchanted with each place he went, often taking time to look around the corner for his next new encounter.

(Historical Events 1773-1894—Aside 1)

The past often repeats itself, always advancing forward building on what has happened before. It is important to look back every once in a while in order to see how we got from there to here, and then decide where you want to go.

(All asides are found at the end of the book.)

Chapter 1

The Story of Sudra

Spring was late in coming to the highlands. Sudra sat in the dry grass at the top of her favorite little knoll. The morning sun inched its warmth over the top of the higher mountains to the east. This is the homeland of the Jo-Gen clan of the Luo tribe. Her thoughts were buzzing in her head like the honey bees which soon would be sipping the nectar of the flowers which would cover this grassy respite.

She thought of her family. The culture of her clan like most in Africa was strictly paternal. Her father, Odera was a ruoth (leader). This gave her increased stature in the social hierarchy, but only made the subservience of women in this male dominated world more difficult to endure. She was very introspective and had difficulty equating her mental keenness and absence of influence in any decision that was to be made. Her past, present and future was totally controlled by men. Her life of eighteen summers, at times other than these stolen moments, seemed to be predestined. She had no ability to affect its outcome except in her reverie.

She thought of her husband of one year—him, a tragic figure of a man, his entire family slaughtered in a skirmish with a neighboring clan. She did not understand how a seemingly minor thing like a small plot of grass could be more valuable than human lives. Their marriage like all events in her short life was not of her choosing. There was no affection or communication. Her role was to fulfill his physical needs. Her only rewards being his grunting during their coupling and his gaseous emanations after a dutifully prepared meal. The fact that the union had not produced children only added to the futility she was feeling.

From her sanctuary she could see the village of Kisumu, home for one hundred families. The yellow light of the rising sun seemed to be awakening the village and erasing the shadows of the dark night. Her family's small enclave was on the western edge of the village. The customary three small buildings, one each for the men, women and children; home for Sudra, her husband, father and mother, two brothers and their wives, and her paternal grandparents. The constant coming and goings offered no hope for privacy or a space to call her own. These private musings were her only chance to feel a sense of individuality.

She thought of a time of happiness. She had lived ten summers when the missionaries came. Her father, having a high regard for the British education and industry, allowed her to attend the mission school for a short two years. Her father's fascination with the British came from his seeing the commerce that seemed to grow like weeds, needing little external nurturing. The small school led to opening roads, the link to Mombasa, the ocean and the entire world and all it had to offer. She was absolutely enamored with learning, and the few books she was exposed to showed her there was a wonderful world beyond her village. A world she could only visit in her imagination.

Odera had shown the newly arriving farmers how to terrace the land. Together their efforts fostered a thriving agricultural community. The products of which not only improved the diet of the locals, the excess could be sent to Mombasa for sale and exchanged for items never before seen in the village.

One such family who profited from Odera's help was the Porthouse's, Jonathon and Beth. They had a small plantation on a remote hillside about an hour's walk from the village. Jonathon had come to live with Beth and her family when he first arrived in Kenya. He had agreed to help out on the plantation in exchange for a place to live. Beth's parents died suddenly in 1892, leaving Beth, who was only 16 at the time, in charge of the plantation. Jonathon agreed to stay on and help her. They married in

1893. Both having the British sense of industriousness decided to revive the old plantation and make their life in Africa. They knew they needed help, and Odera became their chief advisor. The relationship was perfect, the Porthouses received the advice they needed to survive and prosper and Odera received further knowledge of their western ways.

This union led to what had become an oasis in the bareness of Sudra's life. Since she had yet to conceive, her husband considered her something less than an asset, and his attentions had seriously waned. His neglect although hurtful was also a welcome relief—less time tending to his needs led to more time available tending to her own. Out of kindness, Odera facilitated an arrangement with Jonathon and Beth where Sudra and her grandparents would spend Saturday through Tuesday at the plantation helping with routine household tasks. In exchange Beth would continue Sudra's education. Jonathon and Beth's youth and total lack of experience doomed the Plantation's failure without intervention. The relationship between the two families had steadily grown to where Beth thought of herself, Jonathon and Sudra's family to be one in the same.

Sudra cherished these days away from her dire existence in the village. A smile crossed her lips on this Saturday morning. She rose from the grass with her heart warming, just as sun warmed the land she stood on, knowing she would be returning to her personal paradise within the hour. Little did she know that this week would be so wonderfully and confusingly different.

The dusty road, little more than a path seemed to be especially long this morning as Sudra rushed ahead of her grandparents. Would she ever get there? As she opened the gate Beth rushed to her. Beth's normal welcoming embrace was hurried. She was very excited; the plantation was to have guests and there was so much preparation to do.

The guests arrived just before night fall on Tuesday, after much prepartion. The three men were: an American named William, who was there to explore a market for his healing drugs and elixirs—a quiet and stoic man who had little to say, but acted as a perfect gentleman; the most engaging was named P. J. O'Mera a very energetic charming American who was there to hunt big game and in his words "enjoy all the area had to offer"; he was accompanied by a British man that he called his guide.

The group decided that after a long day of travel, an early dinner would be in order. Sudra was tasked to serve the dinner.

Sudra most admired the gentle and tender attention Jonathon routinely showed Beth. She assumed that when P.J. displayed some of the same behavior towards her, as she waited on the group, that this was normal in western culture. She had never experienced any of this from the men who had been in her life. She found it very comforting and gave her feelings she did not understand, but she wanted to continue. It felt like a cold dark hole in her self had been filled with light and warmth. Sudra's husband was never tender or affectionate toward her. There was no meaningful communication, and the only touching came during their coupling which was rather short, and ended with him wordlessly leaving the room to join the men in their quarters. After dinner the guests retired to their room and Sudra and her grandmother were left to restore order to the house. Beth scurried about chattering that it was so wonderful to have guests and to receive news of the outside world.

It was only a short time later that P. J. requested some more of the wonderful port that had been served after dinner. Beth asked Sudra to take it to him. Sudra was both apprehensive and excited. She softly knocked on the door and P.J. bade her enter. The room was dimly lit by a kerosene lantern whose smell intermingled with that of his cologne. P. J. stated he always had a glass of port upon retiring with a book of poetry or a novel. He asked Sudra if she read. She was ashamed to say that she did not know how to read very well, and that her home contained no books. In truth if her husband knew she could read she would have been severely chastised.

P. J. asked if she would like to read with him. They spent what may have been the most wonderful hour in Sudra's life, listening to P.J. read poems so beautiful that the words seemed like the most vibrant flowers or the most succulent candy to the senses. At times their hands would brush as they reached to turn the pages. Sudra stated she must leave because she would need to be up early to help her grandmother prepare breakfast. As she rose to leave P.J. took her hand and rose with her. He kissed her on the cheek and said he hoped they could do this again when she returned on Saturday.

Sudra returned to her quarters. Her heart felt too big for her chest and her mind was churning. She had enjoyed his companionship. Her life was changed by this brief encounter. How could she ever be satisfied with the nonexistence of existence that her life had been. Another person had listened to her and was looking forward to being with her again. She had difficulty falling asleep, but when she did she was sure she was smiling.

Sunday seemed to be much longer than any day Sudra could remember. The clock seemed to catch its breath between each tick of it progress to 6 PM, the agreed upon time for dinner. Around the table the atmosphere was more relaxed due to the fact the guests and the Porthouses were more comfortable with each other. The talking was loud and punctuated with laughter, agreement and argument. This was surely aided by the liberal amounts of alcohol that was consumed. Sudra thought the dinner would never end. Her spirits soared each time P.J. stole a glance at her and nodded. The gentlemen retired for cigars and port while Beth and the servants cleared the table.

Shortly after the day long wait was brought to an end and P.J. had requested his glass of port, Sudra entered the room; she was surprised to see P.J. was already in the bed. He said they would be more comfortable reading there rather than the straight back chairs they had used before. Sudra felt she could not refuse the guest nor did she want to. She eased herself next to him and the readings were just as beautiful as before. As he read to her, P.J. placed his arm around Sudra and drew him to her for a kiss. This was all new to Sudra, and she was certain the warmth she felt was as it should be. She knew at this moment she must give herself to P.J. Undressing her was a simple matter as she only wore a single piece of clothing. The cotton dress was slid over her head with little effort. P.J. asked her to stand before him naked which she did. Sudra was tall and slender. Her breasts were small and firm and her stomach flat. He noticed a small red beauty mark, hardly noticeable, on her neck. As was the custom her hair was very short and tight to her head. P.J. was breathless gazing at her natural beauty. He motioned for Sudra to lie down. He touched her as he kissed her. He took her breast into his mouth gently. Sudra moaned softly. He continued down, kissing her belly and when he reached her womaness he was very surprised to feel the outer lips were not as he expected. Sudra pulled him away and started crying. He asked what had happened. She explained that all girls of their clan were circumcised a few days after birth. This was to prevent women from enjoying coupling and thus keep them faithful to their husbands. P.J. pulled her to him and gently rubbed her back as her sobbing subsided. He continued with their love making and entered her gently. They moved rhythmically. As P.J. climaxed he held Sudra very tightly. She had feelings she had never experienced with her husband. She giggled inside at the thought of the mutilation of her sexuality. If that procedure was supposed to take the pleasure away she could now testify to its futility. She stayed at P.J's side until the regularity of his breathing told her he was a asleep. Sudra and P.J. continued meeting each day during the week until she was to return to her village

Sudra woke up earlier than usual. Her head was full of the memories of the nights before. She dreaded her return to the village today. During breakfast P.J. shared that he would remain at the plantation for another few weeks. He wanted to hunt and explore the surrounding area. William said his business was almost complete and would be returning to Mombasa soon. He was scheduled to meet a ship and go to Great Britain before his eventual return to the United States. Sudra received the joyful news of P.J.'s extended stay with the glee of an infatuated young girl. Her ecstasy would go on for a short while longer.

The next few weeks were like heaven for Sudra. Wednesday through Friday was spent at her village performing her duties to her spouse and extended family. Her morning reverie on her grassy knoll was filled with thoughts of the coming days she would spend at the plantation. Working, reading and sharing the bed with P.J.

The times at the plantation were more fulfilling than she could ever imagine. P.J. became even more attentive and thoughtful. Her title had changed from wench to dearest. They read every evening and made tender and passionate love. Both were avoiding the subject of P.J.'s upcoming departure.

The time passed quickly and the day of P.J's leaving arrived. Due to the surreptitious nature of their relationship, their public good-bye was only a plutonic hug and thank you from P.J. The evening before they had not made love but just held each other. P.J. gave Sudra the favorite book they shared, the love poems of Elizabeth Barrett Browning, and tucked inside the cover were 20 ten dollar bills. He promised she would always be in his thoughts and that someday he would return. Sudra in her stoic and prideful way could not cry, belying the tears and emptiness of her heart.

Sudra returned to her non-existence and cloistered her memories in a secret place. She could return there in the few peaceful moments her life allowed. Her mornings had become less restful of late. Each morning she awoke nauseous. This passed in a few weeks. She was naïve to the fact that growing in her womb was a lifelong manifestation of her time spent loving P.J. O'Mera. There would be a child to whom she could read the poetry.

The following year, 1895, Sudra had a baby girl. Sudra's husband, having no suspicion it was not his own, was not happy it was a girl. He could not understand Sudra's exuberance, for he knew that she would not get the same adulation for having a girl as if she would if she had had a boy. She named the baby Tera, after P.J. O'Mera.

Chapter 2

William Meets His Traveling Companion

The 1880's was an era of prosperity in the United States, due to the eruption of the building of railroads and new inventions: electric lighting, gasoline-powered automobiles, phonographs, steel-frame sky-scrapers. This was the boom of the 19th century. They called this the gilded age of industry.

The world's fair in Chicago in 1893 was an opulent affair exhibiting many of the new inventions and railroad dominance. The railroad brought in people from the north and east as well as many from Europe.

However, by the 1890's, times were becoming less jubilant. It was also an era of over speculation. In 1893, the New York stock market dropped sharply and panic selling caused the stock market to collapse. Unemployment had spread until at least one in 6 American men lost their jobs, 16,000 businesses failed, 156 railroads had failed as well as nearly 500 banks. This panic lasted for almost 4 years. Many businesses were looking outside America to find more opportunities and to expand the markets.

William was only 19 in 1881 when he began selling for the pharmaceutical company. Before finding his niche in sales, William was a dentist. Obviously, education wasn't a requirement to become a dentist, because immediately out of high school, he apprenticed for a year with a dentist and then opened up his own office. He came down with typhoid fever, which affected his eyesight, forcing him to discontinue his practice of dentistry. Looking for a new job, he read in the Zanesville paper that a pharmaceutical company located in Des Moines, Iowa, was hiring men who were willing to travel throughout the US to open new branches of the company. The development of the railroad allowed businesses to expand in all directions in the US. Because William's father was having trouble making ends meet, he applied for this position in order to help support his parents and his 2 younger brother and an older sister. He was single and willing to travel; he was hired.

William began traveling around the United States in 1881 finding his way to Denver, CO, San Francisco, CA, and to the frigid tundra of Northern Minnesota, and later venturing into the overseas market. He first went to Hawaii, followed by trips to Alaska and Mexico and later into India, Burma, Siam, Java, Sumatra, China and the Philippine Islands. His travels into South Africa proved to be the most momentous and profitable, but the trip to Eastern Africa took twists and turns that he could never have imagined, nor did any of his immediate family members. The last member and the youngest of William's children passed on in 2008.

We often forget that Africa is a continent and not a country. We tend to view their struggles, politics and culture as one. That is like viewing the struggles, politics and culture of Mexico, Cuba, and Canada as the same as the United State's. When in reality Africa is more than safaris and tribal discontent. Kenya, Egypt, Liberia, Libya, etc. are all part of Africa with different struggles, politics and culture. It seems that the parts to which my grandfather traveled were portrayed as parts of Africa standing still in time, until 2009 when things began to change.

1894

Working out of Australia, which had become the company's headquarters, William (b.1862) was heading for Africa, starting his travels from Sydney and winding up in Cape Town, South Africa. Because of this depression, one of many during the 19th century, many companies were broadening their scope of possible business opportunities. Britain was also going through a depression, moving into India and Africa.

William knew that the British had already set up businesses in Cape Town, so he was not feeling very apprehensive about traveling there, but he was not looking forward to the long and tedious travel by ship to the Cape. He arrived at the port of Sydney to board the boat "Moor." He was surprised to see so many women and men traveling to Africa. This seemed to reinforce the idea that he was going because his company had seen growing business opportunities. The British had already found their way into East Africa. Much had been written about South-East Africa by Frederick Selous, who had been to Africa on several hunting expeditions at least 15 years prior to William's trip to the Cape.

There seemed to be a class of wealthy men and women traveling to Cape Town; two people in particular stood out—a man of great stature, dressed as if he were going on a safari and whose name William did not know at the time—another who boarded was a soon-to-be retired politician from Massachusetts by the name of P.J. O'Mera (b.1858).

Because P.J. was traveling alone, William and P.J got together and had many heated discussions about the pros and cons of capitalism and the economic situation in the US. Both respected each other's business acumen and always left after a day's discussion on good terms, looking forward to the next day's banter—that was when William could break P.J. away from the women passengers. Early in the trip William wasn't sure why P.J had gotten on the boat in Australia, but later learned after getting to know P.J. better, that he was doing some personal business in Australia that had something to do with liquor exports. P.J. had made his fortune in the liquor business, as well as banking. William found out, after a few glasses of port and a little coaxing, that P.J.'s trip to South Africa had something to do with W. Jennings Bryan. Bryan aspired to be the 1896 Democratic nominee for President .

In many of their discussions, P.J. often called William "Yankee" and even called him a "Know Nothing." William had heard that many Irish Catholics felt themselves excluded by upper-class Northerners. William thought it funny that P.J., who was a "wealthy Northerner" didn't put himself into that category. His calling William a "Know Nothing" made William realize there was still a lot of bitterness in his family. The Know Nothing movement was an American political movement of the 1840s and 1850s. It was empowered by popular fears that the country was being overwhelmed by Irish Catholic immigrants, who were often regarded as hostile to U.S. values, particularly temperance, and controlled by the Pope in Rome. They were semi-secret and when asked about their activities, they were to reply "I know nothing." William asked P.J. why he seemed so bitter and revengeful. P.J. was very talkative after he had been drinking and proceeded to tell William about his family.

P.J. told of the oppression in his family six generations long on the same family farm in Ireland that was handed down from father to son. His own grandfather (b. 1770, d. 1840) inherited the farm he grew up on from his father and life had not gotten much better for them even after the Penal laws, which limited the freedoms of Catholics, were repealed in 1829. Being educated in the Hedge schools was so demeaning. William was curious about these schools because he had never heard of them. P.J. told him that they were called hedge schools because the schools had been conducted by priests in ditches, basements or someone's backyard. Catholics were not allowed to be educated in public schools.

Because of the famine and knowing that his future looked bleak if he stayed in Ireland, P.J.'s father moved to America at the suggestion of his friend, who had owned a brewery in their home town. His friend, who had also emigrated to the U.S., immediately opened a Brewery when he arrived in Massachusetts. P.J.'s father had worked for this man in Ireland and had been trained in the field of coopering, used in the brewery business. This man's female cousin came a year later and was married to P.J.'s father. P.J.'s father passed away in 1858, right after P.J. was born. His mother went on to buy a stationary/notion store with the help of her cousin who had brought P.J.'s father to America. This man converted the newly bought store into a grocery/liquor store. That is how P.J. got into the liquor business.

Many Boston Irish became active in the Democratic Party, which at that time was more influential in the South than in the North. During the reconstruction era after the Civil War, many northern democrats sided with the confederates/southern democrats who were not abolitionists. With a few exceptions, most Irish—Americans were hostile to the antislavery movement. Most Irishmen associated abolitionism with the worst excesses of European radicalism, distrusted it for its connection both with anti-immigration and with temperance reform, and they were suspicious of the close connection between British and American antislavery leaders. (American Immigration, Madelyn Jones)

Through their conversations, William discovered that P.J. was in awe of W. Jennings Bryan, a fellow Irishman. Both were so called Silver Democrats. Bryan was of Irish descent and was born and educated in Illinois. P.J's parents had settled in Massachusetts. Many Irish either settled in Boston, Massachusetts or Chicago, Illinois. Even though the Irish were often considered lower class and were prejudiced against because they were Catholics, they did have an advantage that other ethnic groups did not have. They spoke English and were familiar with the English system of government. Byran was not a Catholic and his parents had been in the U.S. for at least 100 years, but Irish blood runs deep, especially among politicians, so being of Irish descent did help get William Jennings Byran's father elected to the State Senate in Illinois, and even though William Jennings Bryan lived in Nebraska when he entered politics, the Irish connection in Illinois helped promote his political aspirations. The Democratic convention was going to be in Chicago in 1896. P.J. was excited that he was going to be a part of that convention.

P.J. O'Mera was married with a 6 year old son, coined J.P.(b. 1888). William was single because he hadn't found the right woman and his traveling with the pharmaceutical company would interfere with being a married man and a good father. He loved his job and traveling and wasn't quite ready to give it up.

After they left the ship, they didn't see each other until William ran into him accidently in Mombasa.

Chapter 3

William Chronicles His
Travels Through South Africa.

William arrived in Cape Town, South Africa, in 1894, to open up a distributorship for the Pharmaceutical company for which he had been working. He had already shown how profitable it was in the United States because he had covered almost every state setting up distributorships as he traveled by rail and buggy to the largest cities in the U.S. There were no railroads yet; East Africa was not as developed as the southern part, He thought he may be able to establish the first pharmaceutical company in the virgin market in East Africa. He stayed in Cape Town for 7 days, where he easily found an agent who would be responsible for selling his product. Businesses were already established in Cape Town. His real challenge was to work his way up the coast, first to Durban and then on to Mombasa. After traveling to Johannesburg to visit the gold and diamond mines, he would head for Durban.

William writes, about his arrival in Cape Town and his view of the surrounding areas in a letter to his parents:

Dear Parents and Friends,
"After an uneventful ocean trip of some 3000 miles, we could see, on the morning of October 2nd, 1894, the famous Table Bluff of South Africa, and by lunchtime, we were nearing the docks at Cape Town. As I stood on the deck

of the "Moor" and took a good look at the town and the people who thronged the deck, I felt that, to use a slang expression, "my work was cut out for me."

There is no use in this letter, telling you the trials and tribulations of an explorer for business, but you can imagine the situation. A total stranger, not only in a social and business sense, but also to their manner of conducting business.

I will not discuss the hotel question as I found them, nor the means of transportation. The language that I would have to use would not be very becoming. The facilities for business need not be mentioned or the numerous holidays that make the life of a commercial man very tired.

The motto of South Africa should be the Dutch expression, "Wag-en Beetjie, pronounced Watchein Beetche, or "wait a little." They are never in a hurry, to them day after tomorrow is as good as today.

One poor unfortunate said I made him dizzy, because I wanted to do business with him the same day I saw him. When one stops to consider that Cape Colony is as old as the U.S. and no more progress has been made, they can easily grasp the spirit that has moved it. Dead I will not say, simply dormant.

The term South Africa is used to describe all that country that lies south of the Zambesia River. And it is doubtless that you can find 750,000 whites in that entire section.

Within this section named, you will find Cape Colony, Natal, Orange Free State, South African Republic, and then many other small divisions that are British protectorates, as Pondoland, Zulu-land, British Bechuanaland, Mashonaland and Matabeleland. With the exception of Free State and S. A. Republic or Transvaal, all are under British flag.

The greater part of both of these states is elevated table and, known as the Xaroc, a great sandy desert that is used for grazing purposes. To be sure, now and then, you run across a Boer farmer who had enterprise enough to sink a well or build a dam, than they can raise anything. The ostrich farms are to be found in that section, lying between the sea land and this Karoo. In making my drive over the Country, I saw some big flocks; on one farm in the Oudtshoorn district, they had over 3000.

In the Colony, you only find three towns of any size, Cape Town, Port Elizabeth and East Lenden, all the rest are trading villages. These are shipping towns, and do considerable business.

We will go north to the Transvaal, Johannesburg, being the objective point. This country occupies a peculiar position. It has no sea port, yet it dictates to the other countries. Peopled by the largest, dullest race of whites on the face of the globe, "The Boer" Republic they call it, but is more of a monarchy than anything else. Its history is one of great interest for the fact that the Boar measured arms, with the English Government and by Gladstone sanction, their efforts were successful and their independence secured.

They have enacted law, at once contrary, to advancement, in fact everything they do is a fair shadow of themselves. The click that runs the government have feathered their nest, by granting concessions to themselves. Twas the foreign element that rescued the state from poverty to affluence. They did not know that there was any gold in the ground and were too lazy to even think of such a thing.

By a system of licenses and other impositions, they have increased their treasury to such a point that it alarmed the men in power to have control of so much money, so last year they loaned vast sums to their friends without interest.

At least 80% of the money comes from the Uitlander or foreigner, and he has no say at all towards the local government. The Boer has passed laws that give them the absolute control, and I could stay here the balance of my life and then never become a citizen. The foreign element today outnumbers the Boer and some of the days they will take things into their own hands, or I miss my guess.

The president, Paul Kruger, is a coffee drinking Dutchman who has been identified with the country ever since its first occupation. His salary is $40,000 with a coffee allowance of $2,500 more. He does not speak English, and they say he can only sign his name, so illiterate is he, but I will give him credit for being a good "ward politician". While the best avenues of business have been blocked by the vile laws and exclusive franchise, still without a doubt, the town of Johannesburg is a wonder. And it is after one has been all over the place, seen high buildings of iron and wood and glass, knowing that these same structures were erected before the advent of the railroad, at an enormous expense, for often the transportation cost more than the material, that this impression is confirmed. Nearly all of the town was hauled by bullocks wagons, hundreds of miles.

I doubt if there is a place in the world, where the money spending power is so great, and where it is more expensive to live. As a place to make money it is all one could desire, but as to saving it, that is another question. As a place to live in it is far from being agreeable. One of the objections being the sand and dust storms that occur with too frequent regularity. Sometime in turning a corner, you get a dash of dust in the face as heavy as if someone had thrown a pan full. Aside from the buildings on the main street, nearly all the houses are constructed of corrugated iron, roof and sides. There is no question but that they are warm enough in summer.

Everything is expensive (even the town is high, 5,700 feet above sea level). Street car fare is from 12 to 25 cents. Soda water is 25 cents. Hotels are poor but they charge from $2 to $5 per day. Cigars are from 35 cents. For a man who does not drink it is an ideal place, for he might dislike to pay 40 cents for a glass of beer. When it comes to amusements, a show that one would not attend at home costs $2 per seat. A decent seat at the circus cost the same, and on it goes at the same rate. No one objects, they are all making money, and must have a chance to spend it.

As will be found in all places where money is made rapidly, gambling cuts quite a figure, and it does not make much difference on what they place their money. Mining stocks of course, is the main article, but horse racing cuts quite a figure. On Christmas they had a race where the first prize was $150,000.

The town has lots of snap and go, but I missed that element that made our western mining towns so famous. Now I was two weeks in Johannesburg, and never saw a man shot, or even saw a fight. I missed the music from the dance house, and it made me sad not to see any cow boys charging up and down the street on their horses.

It is estimated that they have nearly 60,000 natives working in various mines. All the bosses are whites, and a large proportion is from the U.S. The output last year was very nearly to 2 million ounces of gold. The month of December sending about 185,000 alone.

Leaving Johannesburg, with all her gold and dust, we will drop into what is today the second place of attraction in Africa. For years it was the first, but the luster of her diamond has been dimmed by the brilliancy of so much gold. Kimberly in Cape Colony is noted for the past, that it has been the diamond headquarters for the world. The diamond is controlled by the DeBeers Co.

which is an amalgamation of the many small concerns that use and operate here.

This amalgamation was planned and executed by Hon. C. J. Rhodes, whose history reads like a page from romance. He is the ambitious man of Africa. This company was organized with the capital of $4,000,000. Today that stock is nearly $100,000,000. On their pay roll you will find between 9 and 10,000 blacks, and nearly 2,000 whites.

Their entire plant and grounds, save farms and village, is guarded day and night, and it is only an iron clad pass, that one can gain admission. The manager, Mr. Gardner Williams, had the good luck to be born an American, so all that was necessary to receive a favor, was my card.

It was very interesting to trace the blue ground or rock in its flight, 800 to 1000 feet below the surface to the time the sparklers appeared in the hands of the sorters. The rock as it comes from the ground is very hard, so they spread it over a large field, called floors, to let the elements help to decompose it. When it is in the proper shape it goes through washing machines that take away all the soil and large rocks. Then in the pulsator where there are sieves of different sized meshes that sort the stuff, and then it is taken by bucketfuls to the sorters, scattered on a slate table and the man commences to pick out the diamond, and it is good to see the diamond among all the little pebbles, sometimes the mass seems alive with them. The stuff is gone over several times, but the last picking is very small. I saw them find a 64 carat stone, and it was a beauty, though it was yellow.

While it only takes a short time to write the above, still I was nearly a half day going over the place and had to have a hack and carry from place to place. Saw their vast machine shops and shafts, but aside from the actual sight of diamonds at the pulsator, the most interesting sight was the compound. They have several but I only visited one.

A compound is where they keep their native labor, and it is a regular barracks. When a native agrees to work, he signs a contract for a certain time and he never leaves the place until his time is up. It is a large hollow square, housed on four sides, and open in the center save for a fine wire netting that covers the entire square; this puts a stop to natives throwing any diamonds out. There are stores of all kinds in there, and a very decent hospital. A few days before the native's time is up, he is given very careful attention to see that he *does not smuggle any stones away. He has to wear a pair of heavy gloves so that he could not pick at anything small.*

The company owns a nursery and have an ideal village for the white labor (Kenilworth). Have stock farms and nearly everything else that man needs on earth.

The people of Kimberley say, that the De Beer Co. have ruined the town, for they don't allow the natives to run around, and trade where they want to. That it is a big monopoly and so on. But a close inquiry will show that this amalgamation was the saving of the place. It was all right when they had surface digging, then the small operator was a good as any, but the moment they had to go to great depths, then the little concerns commenced to lose money. It takes ponderous and expensive machinery to cope with water at deep levels, and careful management to even make this company pay dividends. I was invited to come down to the strong rooms, and see some diamonds, and never again do I expect to see such a sight. It was a lot ready for the markets, and was worth two million. They were sorted, and I could see anything from the finest white to the ordinary mechanical stuff; all sizes were there. I cannot say that my mouth watered for some, but I can confess that when I was letting hands full run through my fingers, that the palms itched just a little. But several years hard labor would not pay very well even if diamonds put you behind the bar.

Africa has a great future ahead of her, but before great progress takes place, some new blood must be imported.

Your loving son, William

(History of Johannesburg—Aside 2)

William was in Johannesburg in 1894, barely 8 years after George Harrison had stumbled on the gold-bearing reef. William was amazed at its fast development.

The British had set up the British East Africa Company in competition to the German's. Pressure was put on the Sultan of Zanzibar to hand over control of his remaining East African lands to this British Company under William MacKinnon. A temporary agreement with the Germans to respect each others' spheres of influence was ratified in 1886. A more comprehensive agreement was signed in 1890 which basically gave Britain primacy over Zanzibar and a line stretching from the island of Pemba to Lake Victoria and then the Nile watershed whilst Germany was free to create its colony of Tanganyika between Lakes Victoria and Tanganyika.

The British East Africa Company was eager to bring in outsiders to help establish white colonies, especially those from the US. William was eager to work with the British East Africa Company, and later the British Government. William was there during a transitional period for that part of Africa, but it was a great opportunity for him.

It took William 4 days to travel the 200 miles to Durban, catching a ride on make-shift wagons, causing much discomfort while traveling. The party camped out along the way and sometimes stayed in inns that were very rustic, quickly set up to accommodate the new influx of British getting ready for the railroad that would be going up the coast. William was amazed at the primitiveness of the Africans in Durban, especially in their dress, or lack thereof. He had a photograph taken of himself and several of the natives and sent it back home to his family. It was a picture of William standing amongst 8 scantily clad African women. He commented on how uninhibited the natives were, often suggesting when he wrote to his family that maybe that wasn't such a bad thing.

He wrote about the Durban area:

"We will not find anything that will attract one's attention 'til we reach Natal—Durban being the port of entry. Natures beauty spot in South Africa is Natal, and it is a wonder that it does not show a great white population. History tells us that on Christmas, 1407, a Portuguese sailor, Vasco de Gama, discovered this place while in route to India.

The location may have something to do with this backwardness, for it is somewhat out of the beaten track. While its climate is almost tropical, still it is considered very healthy. The vegetation along the low lands that skirt the Indian Ocean is most beautiful to the eye. The wild flowers are especially bright.

All through this section you find immense fields of sugar cane and rice, while fruits like the banana, pineapple, loquats, guava, are in their element and most luscious to the partaker.

The most interesting subject of study is the natives here, and the finest specimens are to be seen, for Natal is bordered on one side by Zululand, on another by Pondoland, and Basutoland, all of which are noted for the fine forms of their inhabitants. I never saw as fine specimens in the Natal as I saw in their native homes. The Zulu in the first instance is all that one could want in way of a truthful, sober and moral race. In fact he would be a shining example to many of us today. True it is that he may have numerous wives (the English Government allow him that favor) still they are all his own, no one else's.

They say that since the missionary element came among them, they have retrograded, still I don't agree with them on that point, but think that it is the natives contact with civilization that has contaminated them. Around the town they are always the worst, but while they may have skipped down a peg or two in the scale, still the Zulu can claim morality as a high standard.

It is at first rather shocking to our idea of the "proper" to see them as they run around at home. And one uses the term "see them" advisedly, for they are as they came into the world, save a small loin cloth. But after the first shock you do not pay any more attention to them, than were they dressed in a Worth or Poole outfit. And it is after you leave this State, that you appreciate their manner of dressing, for in most other sections, they are the filthiest, raggedist looking lot of mortals that I ever behold. They will put on a dress or pair of pants and wear them until it falls off, and it is when they commence to dress in this fashion that they die off rapidly. When a small boy I used to contribute my mite towards clothing the poor savages, now I would rather send money to unclothe them. I do not suppose there is on the face of the earth as fine specimens of men and women as you find among these natives, taking them as a race. Splendid figures of animated bronze skins of velvety softness. The women are very straight and have the walk of a queen. Their carriage is owing to the fact that they carry everything on their head. Twas, very amusing to see a luna come into a country store, make some purchase, and be it either a package of tea, a plow shear, or a bottle of oil, on the head it goes, and out she sails, as graceful as one wants to see.

The laws in the Natal are good for the natives, even having a superior court to appeal to, if their difficulties cannot be settled by a chief. They are great talkers and to see a part at it, you would imagine that some great event was about to take place.

A Zulu's importance in a tribe, his social status as it were, is all determined by the number of wives he possesses. All buy them, 10 cows per girl being the price at this writing and market steady. Sometimes it takes a man several year's hard work to get the required number of cattle together before he can claim his wife. But he had made arrangements for her long before and they always live up to their contracts. The ambition of each man is to secure cattle, buy wives, follow the injunction of the scriptures, sell their girls for cattle, buy more wives, and so on. Where a man has a dozen or so of wives he is fixed for life, no more work, he flits like the bee from Kraal to Kraal. The wives do all the work, and they would consider themselves disgraced did they allow him to do a single thing. I could not help contrasting all this with the States where it was all a man could do to make a living for one woman.

They have some very curious laws among themselves. A man must never look in the face of a mother-in-law; if he sees her coming he must either lie down or should he have a shield, he will simply cover his face until she passes. Now when a man has a dozen of them he has to keep his wits about him. I did not have time to inquire whether the mother-in-law ever visits her daughter or not. It would be rather awkward. A woman must never speak her husband's name, as it is too sacred. Should there be any word in their vocabulary that is the same or even resembles a chief's name, it must be omitted.

The men here (as you have already grasped the situation) are Lords of Creation, and could you see some of the young dudes, you would see something most wonderful to behold. The girls take great delight in decorating their sweethearts and after a fellow has a few bead ornaments they all swamp him with them. Tis the same the world over, :you are either in it or you ain't.

I will try to describe these dudes to you. Starting with his head you will find they have strung different colored beads on to his hair, making most beautiful bangs to their eyes. Around his head there will be a beaded band. In his ears are immense holes from which are earrings. His neck is encompassed with a bead collar and from this is suspended both front and back, a short ribbon 1 ½ inches wide. Around his waist is another band to *which is attached his loin cloth. Around his arms and ankles are bead bracelets. In one hand he carries a small shield, in the other a walking stick. The colors of the beaded ornaments make a pretty contrast with his bronze skin. When thus attired he is ready for a "Josh" which means he is out for a walk or call.*

On the banks of a small stream I saw a picnic party of natives and ever since I have imagined that it will take more than a spectacular show to interest me again.

When returning from Zululand, we passed a crowd of Zulu Belles. Noticing that one had some very pretty beads on, I told my boy to tell the girl I would give her a shilling for her wardrobe. I have her costume, and as I drove away she stood there ala nature, a most charming smile, and the silver in her hand.

Anyone would find Natal interesting, for besides the climate, vegetation and natives, you will find quite a cosmopolitan crowd. The Coolie from India is especially prominent. It is the costume of their women that would make a rainbow blush, so brilliant do they dress. Then again you see quite a few Malay and even Japan is represented by its Jimricksha."

From Durban, William took a make-do ship up the coast to Mombasa, a city long known to Europeans. The Portuguese had used it as a trading base for many years. The Sultan of Zanzibar extended his rule over the East African mainland throughout the nineteenth century, and the African tribes in East Africa resented this Arab rule but could do little to resist it. The Arab control was tied up with the ivory and slave trades; this attachment to slavery brought the area to the attention of the British public. David Livingstone, an explorer, used Zanzibar as a starting point for his explorations of the interior, and he was eventually joined by explorers interested in discovering the source of the Nile, found to be Lake Victoria. They would send reports back to Britain publicizing the evils of the East Africa slave trade, encouraging powerful lobbies back in Britain to put pressure on the Sultan of Zanzibar to banish slavery in his lands, which he reluctantly agreed to in 1873. So the British had already put their influence in motion before William arrived in 1894.

Chapter 4
2014
Traveling to a Changed Africa

My curiosity for Africa had peaked during the presidential campaign of 2008. Since then I have wanted to visit Africa, but never felt I should spend the money. Because expenses, such as airfare, hotel accommodations, etc. had unduly increased, I shouldn't have waited quite so long to do my traveling. No one had predicted that the dollar would fall like it did. Since 2009, at the beginning of the economic downturn, the spending that took place to stimulate the economy did nothing but cause higher inflation. More money into the market has a consequence. Another impact of the downturn was the absence of investments with good return. Many people who had wanted to invest again were starting to put their money in gold coins. The stock market wasn't the source of investment it once was.

Also our relationship with the rest of the world, particularly European countries, hadn't improved and terrorist attacks on Americans traveling abroad had almost tripled. However, Americans traveling to Kenya in 2014 had found it to be one of the safest places to travel outside the United States. The increase of pirate attacks on ships bringing aid and imports to that part of the country had increased to over 125 incidents in just three months in 2009. Hostages and cargo were being held until a large ransom was paid by the shippers. But now the attacks were almost nil. In late 2010, the senate and the congress passed the first of the President's Kenyan Aid bill, which granted Four Hundred Billion dollars to help farmers produce their own products with irrigation and genetic seed implementation and helping to finance new business start ups, under the conditions that Kenya would undertake a better health care and educational system for its citizens. The President even encouraged American businesses to move into Kenya; however, he had conditions attached to that encouragement. The management and employment must come from Kenyan natives. Money would be channeled directly to the Kenyans and not through the Kenyan government coffers. The government would then tax the Kenyans in order to run the government. He established a Kenyan Czar who would be in charge of these monies. This Czar had come from his father's village in Kenya This bill was attached to the Mainland Security Bill, and as often is the case, it's impact was not fully realized by the members of congress and the senate. It was touted as a bill that would help curtail the attacks on ships bringing imports to Kenya.

After the fact, many Americans were upset that their taxes were being used to promote business inside Africa, when their own government was stifling the growth of businesses within their own country.

Evidently, the President didn't listen to his citizenry, but he did hear the voices from Africa. Early in his presidency on his trip home from the G8 summit in 2009, he stopped in Uganda and gave a speech on Africa's need to help themselves

He seemed to be echoing what Mr. Muluka, an editor and media consultant for Myule Africa Publishers, had written on PoliticalArticles.net on January 31, 2009. The title of his paper was "The American Presidency and Kenya."

"No, President of America, you owe us nothing. You must not worry yourself over our cargo cult mentality. Prof Achebe taught us how to say 'Yes we can' even before you were born. And he was only 22. But we love free things. We therefore do nothing for ourselves. Don't let us bother you. It is up to Africans to liberate themselves from greed and laziness and from the thieves and dictators they call leaders. It is up to them to fix their

countries. Meanwhile here is wishing you well. God bless you. God bless Africa."

Mr. Muluka was referring to Prof. Chinue Achebe who had written his world famous novel, **Things Fall Apart**, in 1950—a story about a young man who became self-made by becoming a wrestler and who was intolerant of those who did nothing to further themselves. It showed how little value was placed on life and the senselessness of letting mysticism control one's life. Some 2,000 copies were published in 1958. **Things Fall Apart** has since been translated into close to 50 languages. The English edition alone has sold millions of copies worldwide. It is the most read book of modern African literature.

The pirate attacks carrying cargo ships up the eastern coast toward Kenya became less and less after Kenya had become a partner with the West, protecting the seas against attacks.

Until now the Industrialized nations had been agonizing over Africa's poverty and sending "cargo ships" full of aid, but by late 2009, "the Chinese had already realized the potential of Africa's commodities: forests, oil fields and the mining of copper and cobalt. In exchange the Chinese agreed to create a new infrastructure for Africa, building roads, railways, hospitals and schools across the continent. They were in Africa for their profit, not just to do good. Setting out to do business is less demeaning, then sending aid." (Time, March 23, 2009) America wasn't going to be outdone, especially in Kenya. This was the President's rallying call when he had to explain it all to the American people.

The controls in the United States being placed on big business drove many to a more business-friendly Kenya, a sort of a business-corps developed, as opposed to peace-corps. Jobs became abundant; the African youth found purpose and self respect and the streets became safe and people friendly. It seemed like the decline of the U.S economy was a blessing for Kenya.

I began my adventure to Africa in the fall of 2014. Since I wanted to visit one of my children in Kansas, I decided to leave from the Kansas City International Airport. I would need to connect in New York and then would fly to London and on to Cape Town, South Africa.

I had done my research on East Africa in the 19th century by reading "Travels of South-East Africa" by Frederick Selous*. After reading Selous's book, I thought that he might be the famous hunter that was on the ship with my grandfather.

(Selous—Aside 3)

I wanted to start out at Cape Town and then take the railroad up the coast to Nairobi, stopping in Durban and Mombasa on the way, assuming this was the a trip my grandfather took . The modern rail system available to me would, of course, made my trip much easier and more comfortable then the buggy ride my grandfather took. I also had the opportunity to hook up with a caravan, which stopped at night in little huts along the way; however, this seemed likely to appeal to the young, not to someone who was retired. It was soon after my grandfather had been in East Africa that the British government would finance a railway—the purpose being to open up the highlands to white settlement. The highlands combined a pleasant climate with fertile and tillable land. It was thought that the area would be suitable for a variety of cash crops. The railway was completed by 1906. The city of Nairobi was established for setting up camps to build the railroad. Now it is the capital, moving it from Mombasa, and is the largest city in Kenya.

The plane from Kansas City to New York was full. I suspected there were few on the plane who were going to Cape Town this time of year.

I arrived in Cape Town about 2:00 p.m., which was actually 8:00 a.m. New York time. Having plenty of time to find a place to settle for the rest of the day, I found in my travel guide this quaint little hotel just a few blocks from the train station. When I called, there was no problem in getting a room, so on my way, I stopped to get my ticket to Nairobi, with stops in Durban and Mombasa.

When I got to the station, I noticed an African American woman. She had boarded the plane in Kansas City and was on the same plane from

New York that I took to London and then Cape Town. She seemed to notice me at the same time. She smiled, but quickly looked away. I bought my rail ticket and headed to the Britehouse Hotel. Having no trouble getting a room, I decided on eating an early supper. My train left for Nairobi at 8:00 a.m., and since my biological clock was off, getting to bed early seemed like the best plan.

The restaurant was small and very busy. I had to wait in line for a table. As I was waiting, I noticed the same African American woman entering the restaurant and signing in to be seated. This was too coincidental, so I approached her and said that since we keep running into each other we might as well introduce ourselves. Her name was Bella Porthouse . She seemed quite shy, but very pleasant. I asked her to join me since my name was being called to be seated.

She was a very nice looking woman with light brown skin, and dressed very stylishly, but appeared to lack self-confidence, always talking to me with her head down and with minimal eye contact.

We sat down perusing the menu and both of us kept flipping through the pages, hoping there was something we could recognize. I settled for the: Jerusalem Artichoke and Kalahari Truffle Soup, Dill cured Franschhoek Salmon Trout, Summer Mushroom Risotto, Salad of Tempura Goats Feta and Marinated Asparagus, and Sautéed Frogs legs, watercress and parsley purée. My dining partner only had a salad.

Bella was quite talkative for just meeting me, and I could tell she felt uncomfortable if there was a lull in the conversation. She seemed anxious to talk about her life. I am not sure if it was because she wanted to talk about her life or she wanted to fill the air space. She spoke quickly and seemed to ramble. She barely took a breath between sentences. The first thing she told me was that her mother had died not very long ago and had left a void in her life.

What I got out of the conversation was that at age 13 Bella's mother was sent to Hawaii to live with a friend of her grandmother's, because Hawaii didn't seem to be prejudiced against blacks. Her mother became pregnant with Bella when she was quite young, and they stayed in Hawaii until Bella was two. After returning to the states, they lived in the same house as her grandmother.

I did have a little trouble following Bella's story, but I thought I should at least make some comment. I told Bella that I wasn't aware of Hawaii's early tolerance for diversity, and that it must have been a hard thing for her grandmother to send her 13 year old daughter so far away to live. She mumbled something that I didn't understand. She seemed a little distraught talking about her mother and grandmother. She immediately excused herself, saying she wasn't feeling well. I was surprised at her abrupt departure, but suggested we meet early for breakfast before leaving for the train station. She agreed and was off.

Chapter 5

Grandmother's Story

That night I began thinking about my grandfather and my grandmother, very interesting and extraordinary people. I had brought along a folder with all of my grandfather's letters that had been written from Africa and a few other letters and also the autobiography that my grandmother had written when she was alive. I must have accidentally stashed it between the letters of my grandfather's. I was glad I had brought it along. It reminded me that my grandmother was also very confident, hardworking, adventurous, spiritual and very loving.

Catherine, my grandmother, was born in England in 1872 at Great Barton in Suffolk, England. Her father was a farmer and miller. There were 10 children in their family. While my grandmother was a small child, her father had business reverses and he decided to uproot his family and go to Australia, which was offering many opportunities for young people. Two years prior to their leaving England, my grandmother's brother Frederick, who was only 18 at the time, had gone to New Zealand and Sydney, New South Wales, Australia to scout it out. The letter he wrote back home to his brother tells a lot about my grandmother's family. He writes this letter to his brother George.

December 9, 1882
Dear George,

I received your letter of last September and was both surprised and grieved to hear you were getting on so badly. I wish you had told me the truth all along as I then should not have done so many things I have done. As it was, I thought you were getting on and I need not trouble myself.

I should have written to you before, in fact this is the second letter I have written, but I scarcely knew what to advise; you did not mention what you and Tom were earning or what you would get in a Year's time. At first I decided to come home and see all about it, but then I thought that the money I should spend coming home and what I should lose through not working (as I am at present getting 10 per day) would be better spent providing a home for you to come to, if you should decide to come; so I shall stay here, save what I can and wait for a letter from you to let me know whether you are coming or not, and if you do come it will be by a sailing vessel, you writing by the mail boats would give me plenty of time to prepare for you.

In this letter I will do my best to tell you what we should be able to earn here and also what our necessary expenses would be, of course I cannot guarantee anything and if when you come you should be disappointed (which I do not think likely) do not blame me as I shall give you as correct an account as I can. If you think you would be better off in England then I will come home and do the best I can with the rest of you. If you were any of you tradesmen you could not do wrong coming here, as 10 to 14 a day is what they are getting, clerks and drapers assistants are not quite so much in demand, still I do not think you would have difficulty in getting two pounds at first. I have known fellows getting over three, still that is not the average.

As far as I can understand, the screw varies with a man's ability and trustworthiness and if Tom or Spencer would be willing to turn their hands to anything that seemed most suitable, they would both be able to earn more than enough to keep them. Allie could easily earn more than she would want and I could promise between two and three pounds per week into the general fund without any difficulty.

I believe we could make over five pounds per week and all live together at home. By Allie going out she could earn more but I do not think we should find that necessary.

I have underestimated the amount we should be able to earn, but you will see it would be quite sufficient to keep a comfortable home over Mother's and our sister's heads. And I believe there are dozens of chances to start a business here for like the one at home and with your knowledge in one line and mine in others, I think we might do so after a bit.

There are, however, three things necessary to success, viz. perseverance, steadiness and sticking one to the other. Not having the first two, nine out of ten that do not get on have to thank for their want of success, and if people would only stick to business out here as they have to at home, they could not help getting on.

Our chief expenses would be house rent which is high, grub is about the same as at home. There would be ten of us. I am speaking without Father and from five to six shillings per head a week, we could easily live on. Say six as it is well not to underestimate. That would be three pounds. Rent would be one poun. This makes four pounds per week for current expenses which would be ample. Of course it depends on how we live. There would then be one pound per week left over, out of five which is certainly a low estimate after we had been here a month or two.

As to what you should bring with you. I may say as a general guide, anything you have that is worth anything. If you would have to look about for a place to take them to, then too many traps could most likely be more trouble than they were worth. You would be able to bring them straight to the house and so avoid all bother as to storage and shifting etc. I should say, blankets, sheets, in fact many as you can. I would have bed stands and mattresses etc. ready.

On the other hand if you are able to get on comfortably at home or would be with what I could do and mother does not care about leaving England and her friends, which no doubt would be a great trial for her. Even supposing we should be better off here, she and you would miss their sympathy and influence.

As I need scarcely tell you that here it is not what you have been but what you are that is looked at. Mother would, I am sure, and our sisters too, feel very keenly the loss of the society and pleasure they receive from being connected with Uncle etc. Here we should have to be all in all to each other until we could make friends. And from my own experience, I know that at first they would strike you as being rather rough. I do not notice it at all now but remember doing so when I first came out, another thing I may tell you pride is a nuisance out here and you had better one and all if you have any leave it behand.

In short you need have no fear about our being able to make a living here and a good one too. More I would not promise as it depends entirely on ourselves. Money is as easily spent here as earned. If you think the same can be done at home and mother would prefer to remain there then write and say so and I will come home, and by Mother shifting to London and our living at home we should be able to knock along.

By same mail as this is a copy of the regulations for the Management of Immigration. You will see by it that you could all come out here and come together which a great boon for thirty two pounds that is if Mother could pass for under thirty five years old. If not it will be ten pounds more. I would have nominated you had I been sure you would come. Still that does not matter much as it costs less. I believe by applying at home than it does if you are nominated here. You will be better treated, coming out that way than by taking a steerage passage as the Government is very strick. The Agent General for New South Wales is the man to apply to in London and from him you can get any particulars about the colony. There is no question that at present New South Wales is the leading Australian colony.

I should not advise you to come out alone as it would do no good and would deprive the rest of the benefit you can be looking after things for them.

I do not know if there is anything else of importance to tell you. In answer to this, write decisively one way or the other, and I will either prepare for your coming or go home. In my last letter when I said I could not stay at home, I meant as far as inclination went. We never know what can we can do till we try, and even supposing the worst that I could do nothing at home, I could always join the Cape mounted Police or something of that sort where there would be regular income that Mother could draw on and for which my colonial life here would fit me.

I have sent a copy of this letter to you by another mail in case one should go astray and you had better do the same in return.

You can tell them all that Sydney is a beautiful a city as they could wish to live in, a fine climate and one of the grandest harbors in the world. Boating, fishing, cricketing and plenty of holidays. The colonials are terrors for pleasure.

If you asked me straight whether I advise you all to come out or note, I should say if you are not better off than when I left home. Yes, Yes, Yes.

Below are a few hints for the passage and now, good bye, with love to all and

Believe me to remain, Your loving brother, Frederick

1. All things not wanted for use on voyage pack in cheap strong cases and put down hold.

2. Pack things for use into as small a box as possible, have as few as you can do with and let them be old.

3. Keep boys and girls things separate as you will not be together.

4. Take tins of preserved milk, jam or any other little luxury you can get for the girls.

5. Pick fore and aft bunks if possible and get near a port hole.

6. If you have any money get a draft or a colonial bank payable in Sydney.

7. Make friends with the cook.

And keep a good heart for you will be coming to sunny New South Wales.

An aged old truth was found buried in this one letter sent from an 18 year old boy home to his family. What wisdom was had by such a young man.

There are, however, three things necessary to success, viz. perseverance, steadiness and sticking one to the other. Not having the first two, nine out of ten that do not get on have to thank for their want of success, and if people would only stick to business out here as they have to at home, they could not help getting on.

And:

As I need scarcely tell you that here it is not what you have been but what you are that is looked at. Mother would, I am sure, and our sisters too, feel very keenly the loss of the society and pleasure they receive from being connected with Uncle etc. Here we should have to be all in all to each other until we could make friends. And from my own experience, I know that at first they would strike you as being rather rough. I do not notice it at all now but remember doing so when I first came out, another thing I may tell you pride is a nuisance out here and you had better one and all if you have any leave it behind.

The family left in 1883 from Plymouth by sailing vessel via the Cape of Good Hope. My grandmother was ten. She was educated in the public schools in England and Australia. She taught in one of the Australian schools for four years as a pupil teacher which meant she was given instruction herself before school hours in addition to a small salary. After completion of these four years, she entered the nursing profession having two years of training in the Sydney Children's Hospital then located at Glebe Point, a suburb of Sydney, and received a diploma from there.

Her father managed a farm; Frederick William had established himself in New South Wales in business as a painter, decorator including the importing of glass; George Alfred started out as an accountant and later established wholesale ladies and children's ready-to-wear; Althea Louisa became a governess; Thomas Shipp became an accountant in a department store; Spencer helped his brother Frederick; Gertrude was a nurse, but died when a young woman; Martha Grimwade had instruction in dressmaking, but later took up nursing; Priscilla Gertrude also became a nurse.

Catherine did private nursing and in 1898, at the age of 26, she took a patient to Rotorua in the North Island of New Zealand, near Auckland, the capital of the island. This patient's doctor had recommended that she take a course of these noted medicinal baths in that town. After remaining there seven weeks, they joined the American passenger steamship, Mariposa from San Francisco, at the Auckland harbor to return home to Sydney. An American, Mr. William A. Peairs, who was a passenger from San Francisco, upon reading over the passenger list, recognized that the name of my grandmother's patient was familiar to him. He discovered that he had traveled with her brother on a trip to Africa. They became casually acquainted during the three day trip, but before leaving the ship Mr. Peairs asked my grandmother if he might call on her at her home, which was then in Glebe Point, Australia. She agreed and it was the beginning of a relationship that lead to their marriage in 1901.

They had a nine month honeymoon in the United States of America going to Zanesville, Ohio, to meet his parents and friends. It was on this trip that they visited the White house in Washington, D.C.

and she had the pleasure of meeting the President, Theodore Roosevelt.

The following notation was at the bottom of this autobiography:

It was a letter written by her eldest son October 15, 1972 on her 100th birthday.

> *Catherine Mary Peairs, nee Catherine Mary Gissing, and known to many as "Kitty," celebrates her 100th birthday today. We know you join us in the love and regard we have for Mother and in our wishes for the very best on this important day.*
>
> *It seems to us that she has handled each phase of her life in a unique and beautiful way. Just a few days ago her nephew from Australia visited her with his wife. He told us that his father, Uncle George, thought his sister, Kitty, was almost perfect. Later her husband, William Allen, reflected her love in his love and never was there any discord between them in our home—at least to our knowledge. As our Mother, we just can't put into words how we feel—suffice to say we are richly blessed. Then as a grandmother and a great grandmother, she somehow continues to bestow upon these young ones the impression of a great and good woman and, above all, a Christian. And now this same aura surrounds her in the hospital and she is loved there, too. She is a happy and uncomplaining patient who contributes something intangible to those who serve her so willingly."*

I began reminiscing about my visit to my grandmother's when I was fifteen. I think it may have been the last time I really got to spend some alone time with her. My friend and I hopped on a train, with our parent's approval, and traveled from Nebraska to California. She visited her grandmother and I visited mine. At that time Grandma Catherine was living with my uncle, who had built a two room apartment connected to his home.

I remember that I didn't have much to do at her apartment because all of my cousins lived in other cities, and we only got together on the weekends. I spent my time reading a few books that my grandmother had sitting around, eating nectarines, which I remember quite well because that was the first time I had eaten one, and munching on chocolate chip cookies, alternating each bite—a wonderful combination. One book that I began reading was a book by George Gissing entitled *The Odd Woman*, a book about the situation of emancipated women in a male-dominated society. At that time I only skimmed through it, but later when I was in my 40's and the woman's movement had surfaced, I remembered that book and bought a copy. I read it from cover to cover, amazed at the insight of this man concerning women and their plight in the 19th century. I was even more amazed that he took the time to develop a story around that plight. I always wondered if George Gissing was related to me. I never asked my grandmother and only looked into it a little bit on the Internet. I do know that his father was born in Suffolk, England, the same as my Grandmother's father, and that his occupation was a chemist. His father was a shoemaker. I thought to myself. Maybe that will be my next big project.

Grandma Catherine lived there until she had to be put in a nursing home at 94; her eyesight had failed her; however, because she wasn't well taken care of, my uncle moved her to a hospital, where she lived for 7 years until she died at 105, in 1977. I couldn't imagine that ever happening today.

In spite of her blindness, she continued to knit, making afghans for all of her grandchildren and great grandchildren. Mine lies on my sofa back home. I am lucky to be her name sake.

In this biography, my grandmother had mentioned that William had traveled with this woman's brother. Could the woman on the ship be the sister of P.J. O'Mera or the hunter, and would my grandmother and grandfather be visiting the President for a little tit-a-tit or did my grandfather have business. I did know that in the earlier days of the presidency, the white house was open to the public and if someone wanted to say hello to the president, they could by just walking in the front door. If he was available, he would stop by and give them his greetings. That sure isn't the way it is today. There are now barricades around the white house.

I was beginning to see the broader picture of two people, not just a grandmother and grandfather.

I woke up in the morning with my grandmother's autobiography in my lap. I had to hurry just in time to get dressed, pack and to meet Bella for a quick breakfast. We had decided we would travel together and find a place to stay in Nairobi.

We stopped in Durban just for the night, only because I wanted to see what the city was like today. It was a city full of tourists, but a safe city with a bustling coastline with ships bringing in cargo to sell from all over the world and sending out cargo to all parts of the world. This is one place that had really changed since the time my grandfather sent his picture postcard home to his family. We splurged and stayed in the Hilton Hotel. Bella had said that if it weren't for the trust fund that her grandmother Jemeya had left her and her mother, she wouldn't be on this trip with me. But she also reiterated that she couldn't be staying in first class hotels too often.

We left the next morning and Bella agreed to stop with me in Mombasa for the night. I had done some research on hotels in Mombasa and found one that had been around since 1851, had been remodeled, and had some of the same décor as the 19th century. We found our way to the Chelsea Hotel, with its brocade drapes, elaborate chandeliers, dark pecan furniture with wicker backs, reminiscent of African furniture in the Colonial era; it was exactly as I had pictured it, slightly Victorian, but with an African feel. They even had the guest registries going back to 1851.

We went to our room immediately because Bella wasn't feeling very well. I couldn't help but think to myself that this girl has funny eating habits. She hadn't eaten much the night before and now at breakfast she also had very little. No wonder she has to rest so often. She suggested that I go down to the lobby and look through the registry. I had mentioned to her on the way into the hotel the night before that I might find my father's name in the registry, although, it would probably be a long shot. I went to the lobby to look through the registry. My grandfather had visited this city in 1894 and there weren't that many hotels at that time that catered to foreigners. The registries were lined up on a shelf by years, so I selected 1894 and went directly to October. I didn't find his name, but there was a P.J. O'Mera from the United States and Frederick Selous from Great Britain. That was exciting, but no William Peairs. I went to the 20th, 21st and the 22nd and there he was, arriving on the 22nd of October. I couldn't believe it. It appeared that he stayed until October 25th, as did Mr. O'Mera and Mr. Selous. I surmised they all got to know each other very well.

I immediately went back to my room to tell Bella what I had found. Seeing my grandfather's name and that of Frederick Selous, whose book I had already read by planning my trip, only made me more excited about my adventurous journey into the highlands of Eastern Africa.

Chapter 6
1894
William Hooks Up with P.J.

It took William 2 days to reach Mombasa by boat. He was glad to reach Mombasa by nightfall on the 22nd. Upon entering the small lobby of the Chelsea hotel, he spotted P.J. O'Mera sitting at a table with another gentleman, who was obviously dressed as if he were going on a safari. O'Mera signaled for William to come over and he introduced him to Mr. Frederick Selous and an employee of Mr. Selous by the name of Thomas Primrose. William recognized Mr. Selous as the famous hunter on the ship from London to Cape Town.

The three of them were talking about the backwardness of the African people and their reluctance to move forward and how hesitant they were to have the white man intruding in their lives. It seemed that Mr. Selous admired the African people and was quite disturbed about the earlier slave trade carried out in East Africa. He was glad the British had taken a stand against this practice, and had pressured the Sultan of Zanzibar to ban the Arabs from the practice of slavery. Even though he was born into a business family, he always had an emotional tug of war between colonizing the tribal regions of Africa and leaving their clans intact.

Selous was obviously in Mombasa for the service of P.J. O'Mera. He was there to keep the American safe, but also to keep him in line, not allowing his arrogance and wealth to off set any of the good that the British had achieved.

P.J. O'Mera, Frederick Selous and William Peairs spent the rest of the evening drinking and talking. P.J. O'Mera was impressed with William's resume, his wide travels and his humble demeanor. Selous felt that William would do well among the Africans, even though he was white. He was very soft spoken and offered no negative comments when referring to the African people. Selous couldn't say the same for P.J. O'Mera. P.J. liked his booze and became loud and obnoxious showing little respect for anyone around him. And he did like his women.

They also had many heated discussions about the Gold standard and Silver standard. William, of course, in favor of the monometallic standard and P.J. in favor of the bimetallic standard because of the free coinage of silver with a ratio of 16 ounces of silver to one ounce of gold. Those in favor of the Gold standard were quite nervous by the deflation this situation would cause. However, William had heard that two Scottish chemists had developed a cyanide process of extracting gold from low-grade ore. This would bring down the price of gold because there would be a larger supply. This was a blow to those advocating the bimetallic standard. The process was going to be used around Johannesburg, South Africa, where William had just visited. P.J. had also been in Johannesburg and blew off the importance of the cyanide discovery. William was surprised that he hadn't run into P.J., but P.J. said he didn't really tour the area; his time was taken up with some business he had to do. P.J. also didn't visit the diamond mines. William couldn't believe that P.J. wouldn't take the opportunity to learn as much about the gold mining process as he could, or be interested in visiting the diamond mines, but then that may have been one of the many differences between the two men. William was always eager to learn as much as he could about the area he was visiting. P.J. always was interested in his agendas, moving from one personal agenda to the next.

(What is the gold standard? (Aside 3a)

They all had agreed that they would travel together. Selous had made arrangements for O'Mera and himself to stay in a plantation not far from Lake Victoria, near the highlands. The British were carving out these plantations for people moving into Africa to set up businesses or those who were experienced in farming the needed crops. Selous told William that he would have good prospects for his business if he were to travel up into that area and that he was free to travel with them. William agreed to continue on up the coast, traveling inland and staying at the plantation Selous had recommended. It was common for people moving into the area for business or work to stay with those who were already established.

They would meet in the morning and continue by buggy up the interior toward the highlands.

When they met that morning Mr. Selous had come down with a fever, and it was assumed he had the "sleeping sickness" caused by the tsetse fly**, which is very prevalent in Africa. He suggested that they go on and meet later at the Plantation. He told William and P.J. that Primrose was as familiar with the area as he was and that he had also stayed at the Plantation on their previous visit to the highlands just a year earlier.

**There are 22 different species of tsetse fly, and they live only in Africa. These flies are slightly larger than a horsefly. They breed along rivers and streams. They are active during the day and feed exclusively on blood. Unlike most biting flies where only the female feeds on blood, both male and female tsetse flies are blood suckers.

Chapter 7
2014
Research in Nairobi

It ended up being a 10 day trip traveling from Cape Town to Nairobi because of our stops in Durban and Mombasa. Bella and I got to know each other very well. Or more to the point, I got to know a lot about Bella. I was surprised at how open she had been when we first met, but her abrupt exit had made me feel that maybe she had divulged too much. But again, she seemed eager to share her life with me. She always spoke so quickly; I had trouble following her story. The more she told me and the more she talked, I realized that this young woman had been socially sheltered most of her life. She had trouble carrying on a two-way conversation. I remembered from our earlier conversation that her mother had passed away quite suddenly and this had left quite a void in her life. She needed a friend.

Bella was going to Kenya to find out more about her family. She had no living relatives left in the United States of which she was aware. She felt that her relatives in Kenya would be easy to find. Her grandmother Nora had come to the United States in 1917 as a baby with a white family that had been living on a plantation in the highlands around Nairobi. Nora's grandmother Sudra had served as a housekeeper with this wealthy family on a coffee plantation. Because of World War I and the conflict between the British and German territories, the Porthouse family with Nora in tow left the plantation deciding to move to the US to be near her husband's parents in Kansas.

Bella had heard that the family Sudra had worked for were very caring people and always took good care of the entire clan, so when they left the plantation in a hurry, they left the small plantation to Nora's clan which was comprised of cousins, aunts, uncles, grandparents etc. When Nora came to the US, she took the last name of the family that brought her to the United States—Porthouse

Bella's objective was to go to the Porthouse Plantation where she thought her African kin may still reside. She just wanted some knowledge of her roots and a sense of some family. However, there seemed to be a vagueness in Bella's story.

When we arrived in Nairobi, Bella and I found a hotel near the train station because both of us were going to travel outside Nairobi. I had planned on going up around Kendu Bay; she was planning on traveling by taxi after she found out where the Porthouse Plantation was. She was going to the Nairobi library to research the Plantation. It had been almost 100 years since her great grandmother had lived at this Plantation, and she was a baby when she left. A lot had happened in the last 100 years, much of which was within the last 5 years.

I decided to go to the Kenyan History Museum while Bella visited the library. The museum was very modern and explained the history of Kenya, dating back to the 1st century.

Arab traders began frequenting the Kenya coast around the 1st century AD. Kenya's proximity to the Arabian Peninsula invited colonization, and Arab and Persian settlements sprouted along the coast by the 8th century. During the first millennium AD, Nilotic and Bantu peoples moved into the region, and the latter now comprise three-quarters of Kenya's population.

Swahili, a Bantu language with many Arabic loan words, developed as a *lingua franca* for trade between the different peoples. Arab dominance on the coast was eclipsed in the 16th century by the arrival of the Portuguese, whose domination gave way in turn in 1698 to that of Oman, an Arab country in southwest Asia on the southeast coast of the Arabian Peninsula.

The United Kingdom established its influence in the 19th century. A means of establishing this influence was through the missionaries beginning with the Church Missionary Society of England in1846 and later French Catholic Missionaries.

The 19th century exhibit wasn't very flattering to the Colonization by the British. In fact the British were blamed for the deterioration of the culture and family life of the African tribes. Because of the need for labor for businesses in the newly formed cities, the male often left the home to work in the cities. So even though the British brought education into the villages to educate these laborers, they also changed the whole dynamics of the family.

Prior tribal communities were made up of homesteads, comprised of mothers, fathers, sons and their wives and families, aunts, uncles etc. The women were basically in charge of running the home, the finances, the teaching of the children; they were also in charge of organizing the chores around the house and the fields and they were especially important in attending to the health of the tribal members. The men were in charge of the homestead, which included all of the separate quarters of the women and children, the field, and farm buildings; they were the directors, the women were the players. It was a very paternal society, men often having several wives.

Having children was very important in this society, boys to work in the field and carry on the lineage and girls to bring more cattle or goats to the homestead. A woman's main purpose was to have children. It was not her choice to find another husband if her husband should die. She was property of the clan in which she had entered with her first husband. For instance, if a woman, who was still reproductive and became a widow, her husband's brother or other male member of the family would become this woman's surrogate husband, and any children they reproduced would be the children of the woman's dead husband. Women were the glue that kept the home together, and the men maintained and protected the homestead and carried on the lineage. First the men went into the cities to work and then the women. The dimension of the families were certainly changing.

Because tribal culture is based on communal sharing, capitalism was not easily understood by the Africans. They had no concept of ownership, so were exploited by those who did. Those were also different times, especially between 1876 and 1945. Darwin had written his "Origin of Species" in 1864, and after reading Darwin's book, philosopher Herbert Spencer coined the phrase "survival of the fittest" replacing Darwin's term "natural selection." But it was interpreted by many as the "preservation of a favored race in the struggle for life." This was taken up as a hypothesis for those justifying their oppression. The British introduced many progressive ideas to East Africa, of which many have helped Africa to develop to where it is today, but their attitude of superiority did not allow that country to prosper by its own people. I thought to myself that American cargo ships of aid, as benevolent as it seemed, was just a continuation of that same philosophy.

The exhibit for the era from 1945 to 1964 was entitled "Our fight for Independence"

They were adding a new exhibit called "The New Kenya—a look forward."

I had hoped to view these exhibits on our return to Nairobi, because my time was running out and I wanted to see the small display devoted to the advancement of medicine in Kenya.

Right there were glass jars with the name of my grandfather's Pharmaceutical company with labels such as "cough remedy," "Pain Balm," "Colic, Cholera and Diarrhea remedy" or "hair vigor." I had this same type of jar with the name of his company embedded in the glass, framed in a shadow box which had been passed down to me by my mother.

In the brief display it mentioned that the representative of this medicine company had first visited the Luo tribes because they were the best educated and most friendly toward the white settlers. The Luo tribes were divided up into many different clans: Jo-Gem, Jo-Seme, Jo-Kasgunda, Jo-Alego. "Jo" meaning "people of."

The Jo-Alego was notorious for witchcraft and the area was nicknamed "Alego tat yien" (Alego the root of medicine"-literal interpretation). This name was given to Alego because of their wide knowledge of traditional medicine. Today Alego people, especially in the village of Kogelo, are well educated and often hold key positions in Kenyan politics.

It went on to show the advancement of medicine in Kenya. The advancement of medical technology in Kenya was partially due to the influx of Americans and Europeans who were now seeking medical measures that were not always available in their own countries.

My grandfather had been there; this display was some indication that he may have helped pave the way for others.

When Bella returned she had her arms full of reading material; she had found out where the Plantation was. It was located in an area that was rather isolated because white settlers were not welcome in the early part of the 1890's. This area was heavily protected by hills and trees. The British government on July 1, 1895 established direct rule through the East African Protectorate, subsequently opening the fertile highlands to white settlers in 1902. Because the plantation was so protected and out of view of the plantations sprouting up after World War I, it was allowed to stay in the hands of the Luo tribe. This tribe seemed to be the most accepting of the British colonization.

Since it was one of the Plantations still standing, much had been written about it. Because it had been occupied by a few of the Luo tribe, during the Mau Mau Uprising in 1959, it had been spared. The Luo tribe was not part of this uprising. They were not dispossessed of their land by the British, avoiding the fate that befell the pastoral tribes inhabiting the Kenyan White Highlands. This plantation was now used as a tourist attraction several miles outside Nairobi. It was almost the same as it was when her great grandmother's family lived there after the Porthouse couple left for the states. She found out that all of her relatives had gone back to the area north of Lake Victoria, in the district of Siaya. In the African culture, clans live in tribes and Nora's relatives gradually gravitated back to the home from where they originally came.

Bella was rather certain what part of Kenya her kin had returned to because she glanced through a book that described the cultural landscape of Siaya which was where her ancestors had originally come from. She read that women who were pregnant always returned to the home of their husbands to have their children.

When it was time, an elderly woman who is experienced in midwifery attends to the birth. The umbilical cord is disinfected by a charcoal paste made with the mother's saliva and is rubbed onto the cord, which is then tied with four knots for a boy and three for a girl—the larger number showing the importance of the boy. The mother then brings her baby out into the light after four days for the boy and 3 days for the girl. After covering the placenta with salt it is put in a jar and buried under a tree "that corresponds to the symbol of the Asian year of the child's birth" A boy is buried on the right side of his mother's house and a girl on the left. "...the left side relates to impermanency and vulnerability, whilst the right signifies permanency and authority." (*Post-birth Rituals; Ethics and the Law*, Knapp van Bogaert D.

> *"Home is where the placenta is...People in Siaya say that the weak and awkward are those whose placentas were buried outside their respective homesteads and, worse still, those whose placentas were buried away from the lands of familiar people. They refer to these individuals as* jooko, *the 'outsiders'. Indeed, those who are thought of as weak and Clumsy may be referred to as* biero *(placenta), as in the remark 'Nene oyik dhano to owe biero'('we buried the human being and left alive the placenta'). In contrast, those whose placentas are: buried within their respective homesteads are seen to belong, to be upright, to be secure.*

Importantly, the value of the homestead is articulated in each discussion of *biero*. Tension is introduced into the thinking of young people considering moving elsewhere to seek work or new lands to settle. They are exposed to the likelihood that they will be received as *jooko* elsewhere; and they are pressed to discover and secure the support of known relations in the new setting.

Intimate concerns and discussions in the homestead feed into the construction of enduring social and ethnic boundaries, in Siaya and elsewhere. The discussion of *biero* also places pressure on young women to return to their country homes to give birth. And the *biero* discourse is part of the pressure placed on young men from Siaya to return to the countryside to enhance the *simba* (the 'bachelor's house') and to make investments in the countryside. While composing an ideology reaffirming the country homestead, concepts such as *jooko* and *biero* are joined to other issues and interests." (*Landscape of Siaya:*David William Cohen, E. S. Atieno Odhiambo. Publisher: James Currey; Place of Publication: London; Publication Year:1989,*)*

With this information and the letter that Anah had left for Bella, she knew that Sudra and Tera, Sudra's daughter, had been born into the Luo tribe which were mostly located in the Siaya district. She learned that by 1900, the Luo ruoth Odera of the Jo Gem tribe was providing 1,500 porters for a British expedition against the Nandi, which was a pastoral tribe in the Kenyan highlands. A Nandi tribesman had killed a British trader and forced the British to retaliate. Until that killing, both the Nandi and the foreigners had ignored each other. There has been an interest in the Nandi tribe, which was often mentioned in the bible. Folklore has it that Cain was of the Nandi tribe. When he married, he moved to the Jo-Alego homestead.

By 1915 the Colonial Government sent Odera to Kampala, Uganda. He was impressed by the British settlement there and upon his return home he initiated a forced process of adopting western styles of "schooling, dress and hygiene." This also resulted in the rapid education of the Luo in the English language and English ways.

Because early in the 19th century, British missions were set up in areas around Lake Victoria, the tribes had some experience with the British. It was no accident that some tribes were more easily swayed toward Colonial rule then others. The British knew that educating Africans would allow them to be more fruitful and create a desire to move beyond the rural areas toward the cities to work and earn wages. By the time my grandfather got to the area of the Luo tribe, they were friendly to the white man and knew a little English.

It looked like Bella and I might be headed in the same direction—to the villages around Lake Victoria.

Chapter 8
1894
On Their Way to the Plantation

William, P.J. and Primrose boarded their stagecoach and began the long journey on the very rutted dusty roads to the Plantation. P.J. O'Mera went right to sleep. He had had several nights of drinking and had disappeared most evenings, appearing in the mornings quite disheveled and exhausted. Both William, who always respected everyone, no matter their circumstance and Primrose, who had been a close friend of Selous and a gentlemen in his own right, knew what P.J. was up to and were quite disgusted by his shameful behavior. William thought that Primrose will have his hands full taking care of P. J. O'Mera. It was obvious by now that P.J. was through with his business and was now free to hunt and do whatever he liked doing, which was not always in his best interest.

It took four long days to get to the Plantation. When they arrived they were greeted by Mr. and Mrs. Jonathon Porthouse, who had no children. William learned that Jonathon had moved to the United States from Britain when he was a young boy. His parents still lived in the state of Kansas.

Jonathon's father was originally from a city outside London and had always worked the fields and had not become a member of the Anglican Church and felt like it was time to leave England. He had learned that if a person settled in the Midwest part of the United States, he would be given several acres of land to farm. If he stayed there 5 years this land would become his.

Jonathon's father arrived in Kansas around 1875, about 11 years after Kansas became a state. Jonathon was 10 at the time. The first few years were difficult for the Porthouses, but it continued to get better as more people moved into Kansas. However, about 1887, when Jonathon was 22 and the farming wasn't as productive as it had been because of a two-year run of bad drought, Jonathon's father thought his son, who was unmarried, should explore the possibility of going to Africa. He had learned that the British East Africa Company was eager to help young men set up farms or businesses in East Africa so that the British could have a stronghold in that part of Africa. Jonathon had moved there alone when he was 22. He met his wife, Beth, whose family had moved to Kenya from London in 1885 when Beth was 9. Beth's father farmed this land that was very fertile and where the rainfall was great for growing crops. These crops were sold to the newcomers who were coming into Kenya to work on the roads and later railroad.

Beth's parents were given the land, and built the house in which they eventually lived. When Jonathon arrived into the area, he was offered a place to stay at their home in exchange for working on the farm. . Unfortunately, Beth's parents died within a month of each other in 1892 from sleeping sickness, leaving Beth the Plantation. She was only 16 when they died. Jonathon stayed on at the plantation and they were married in 1893. Beth was 17 and Jonathon was 28.

When William, P.J. and Primrose got to the Plantation, the Porthouse's had just begun planting their first coffee bean crop.

Chapter 9
2014
Leaving Nairobi

Bella wanted to visit the Porthouse Plantation before trying to find members of her family who were of the Alego tribe. She wasn't visiting for any particular reason other than to see what the plantation was like. She said there is something about putting your feet on the soil on which your ancestors toiled. She wanted to see the bedroom where Sudra would sneak to every night to meet her lover and where she learned so much about love and life through the books and poems that her lover read to her. Beth had told Jemeya the story of Sudra's love affair, and Jemeya had passed the tale down to Anah and Bella. I thought that Bella was getting very sentimental; it didn't seem like the same person I had met earlier.

We hired a driver to take us on our travels outside Nairobi. This was a common practice for tourists. It gave tourists a chance to see the countryside and the driver could be an interpreter when needed. However, almost everyone spoke English. It was just in the far outer villages where one could still hear the Bantu tongue. Because Americans aren't used to bartering, we often get taken advantage, so the driver could do the dealing.

We couldn't wait to get out of Nairobi. The city was very congested with cars going every direction. One thing they hadn't learned from Westerners was the art of driving in an orderly fashion. There was a lot of construction going on, not only making new streets but building homes for the influx of new immigrants. Bella and I were impressed with the attention to building green. All of these new homes had solar voltaic panels catching enough daily sun to supply the home with much of the electricity they needed. Part of the electrical energy they produce is used to turn water into hydrogen for power when the sun isn't shining. The hydrogen is also burned in kitchen appliances and used for heating when necessary. It is more efficient and burns cleanly and diffuses rapidly, instead of building up to catch fire like natural gas. It is also not poisonous to breathe. We also noticed that quite a few cars were using hydrogen and there were hydrogen-filling stations being built to accommodate these cars.

Because many of the older Kenyan natives could speak English and had been educated, they were a rising class in Kenya. The president of the US had stipulated that businesses could move to Kenya as long as the Kenyans were put in positions of management. The businesses were taxed if the American companies did not follow this rule. Kenya welcomed the new immigrants. The Westerners who had moved there were in no way prejudice toward the African. It took a while for the indigenous to trust them, but we could tell by their intermingling that the process was moving quickly and smoothly.

When Nairobi was established in 1890 as a means to open up that part of Africa to the railroad, which was to travel from Mombasa to Uganda, there wasn't a need for wide streets . In the early 1900's no one had anticipated that cars would be such a needed commodity. Today in Nairobi, everyone has a car or two. Many live outside the city and need to drive into town to conduct business. It has become the central banking and business system of all of Africa.

We left for the Plantation in the morning, which was about an hour's drive from Nairobi. As we began driving out of the city the roads were wonderful, but as we drove further west they were less tended, but you could tell that in a few years the road system would be very efficient. They were also developing a tremendous train system which traveled in different directions outside the city to the outer villages. Businesses in the big city needed workers. The businesses were now operated and often owned by native Kenyans; an affluent class began to develop and they tended to build homes outside the city.

Many of these homes could be seen from a distance along side the terraced tea plantations. The fertile soils and sunny but cool climate and misty rainfall made Kenya the perfect environment for the cultivation of high quality teas. The majestic hills swirling across the landscape was breathtaking. Often you would see a man hanging from the terraced hill with a bag on his shoulder and a scissor-shovel like tool in his hand, clipping the leaves and throwing them into the bag with one swooping motion. He moved quickly. He seemed like a single dot in the landscape, for the terraced hills went on for miles. It was hard to believe that it was still done by hand. Because of the high quality of tea grown in the Kenyan highlands, the leaves had been most often used in blending with other leaves of less quality in order to create a more satisfying flavor and aroma. But now Kenya was coming into its own market. Because people are willing to pay for a more sophisticated tea, they have started packaging their own gourmet-leaves, offering a unique flavor for a perfect cup of tea.

Bella had thought that the Porthouse Plantation had grown coffee beans. Finally as we neared the city of Kiumbu, dotting the landscape were tiny plots of land, averaging half an acre—nothing like the large span of the tea fields. All one could really see was a mass of red berries and white flowers. I had once owned a coffee shop specializing in espresso and using the Kenya AA coffee bean. Seeing the plantations up close was a beautiful sight to see. It was hard to imagine those beautiful berries turning into a black cup of coffee. Our driver told us that as late as 2004, children, often carrying siblings on their backs, were working in the toxic coffee bean fields, picking and sorting coffee beans. As the plantations got larger and trees were cut down, pesticides were used to kill the bugs harming the coffee bean plant. These pesticides burned the hands and faces of these young children who were picking the cherry.

Now more plantations are returning to the smaller plantations, specializing in organic growing, which required the cessation of all chemical use. The coffee plant had traditionally been grown in the company of shade trees and other food and cash crops. This approach made for healthier soil and prevented water contamination. Later the loss of the shade trees had a direct impact on migratory song birds. While an obvious connection may not immediately come to mind, the relationship has actually been symbiotic. These birds used the shade trees as their habitat as they migrated, and as a result they provided a natural defense against many of the bugs and pests that could ruin a coffee crop. Without them, pesticides had to be used to do the job. Now unlike the earlier large, commercial coffee plantations, organic coffees are returning to the small farms with plenty of shade cover. There are plenty of migratory birds to control insects, and pesticides are unnecessary. Kenya now requires that organic coffees be grown on shaded land and be completely chemical free for three consecutive years. Coffee drinkers are now willing to pay more for their coffee if it is organic; they have discovered the richer taste of the organic coffee bean. Fields are starting to recover from the overuse of pesticides. Children are no longer working in the fields but attending schools. Schooling is now required for all children in Kenya.

When Bella and I got to the plantation, there were two rooms decorated as it had been when the Porthouses were there, but the remainder of the house was the same as the Luo tribe had left it when they moved back to their people. The untouched two rooms were located upstairs, where the furniture may have been stored when the Porthouses left so quickly. The clan had built smaller buildings around the larger house for the women and children. The men were the ones who stayed in the main house as was the custom of the Luo tribe. Bella looked disappointed. It just didn't look like she had pictured it.

The main part of the house was now devoted to the history of Kenya's coffee plantations. Coffee is the second largest commodity market after oil. "It was introduced to this area around 1893 by the French Fathers of the Holy Spirit, who brought young trees from Reunion Island. Initially, the Catholic mission farms were the nucleus around which Kenyan coffee growing developed. The Arabica beans thrive in the rich, loamy, red volcanic soil of the broad, gentle ridges, which slope down into great valleys, full of swift, perennial streams. There is good drainage here and the weather is mild with rainfall throughout the year, for totals of 40 to 50 inches. The coffee grown at these altitudes of 4500 feet to 6000 feet is some of the best in the world. There are special varieties of Arabica coffees unique to East Africa.

In the far west portion of Kenya, coffee is grown on the slopes of Mt. Elgon, near the Uganda border, including the Kenya Blue Mountain variety, which came from Jamaica. Experts say the best Kenya beans come from the gentle slopes of the Aberdare Mountains, north of Nairobi and the south facing slopes of Mt. Kenya." (*Keen on Kenya coffee*, Jerry M. Stein)

(Life of a coffee bean—Aside 4)

We were disappointed in not finding out more about how the people lived on the plantation, but it did give Bella a chance to see where her great, great, great grandmother Sudra had been introduced to love and respect in 1894, even if wasn't what she had envisioned.

Our driver took us to a small Inn, near the town of Kisumu. He was going to drive us up to the village of Kogelo in the morning.

Chapter 10
1894
Arriving at the Plantation

It was difficult finding the Plantation because it was set way back from any road, nestled between many trees and all the fields were in back of the house. They were met by the Porthouse couple and a male and female Kenyan, who were signaled to carry their luggage into the house. Always having to be the center of attention, P.J. managed to use his sarcastic demeanor by mimicking the waddle of the slightly plump female who could hardly lift his suitcase. But he didn't offer to carry it either. He found such pleasure in watching her struggle. Both of the servants were rather elderly. William and Primrose didn't hesitate to carry their own luggage. They were led to their rooms. Primrose had suggested he stay with P.J., so William took the room down the hall.

They all met for an early dinner, being served by a very lovely young woman named Sudra, who was obviously the granddaughter of the elderly lady. Sudra did speak some English that she had learned from the Porthouse couple. After dinner, everyone, except Beth Porthouse and the servants, retired to the central room to have a glass of port. Jonathon was curious why the three had come all this way into the upper highlands. William told him that he had been invited by the British East African Company to open up a pharmaceutical distributorship so that when the British started moving into the area, they would have the opportunity to get modern medicine. He was aware of the interest in medicine of the Jo Alego clan of the Luo Tribe. He wanted to introduce some of his elixirs to the tribe. P.J, who could never be very serious, said he wanted to shoot a few elephants, drink a little port and look for a good woman to enjoy in his spare time. Jonathon said the later may be hard to come by. P.J. said things were looking pretty good already, probably referring to Sudra. Primrose said he was here at the disposal of P.J. O'Mera.

William had learned that the elderly servant couple and their granddaughter Sudra were from the village of Kisumu, of the Jo-Gem clan, and that they stayed at the Plantation from Saturday through Tuesday. Then they go back to the village and another couple from the clan comes from Wednesday through Friday. This was Tuesday evening, so the family they had first met would be going back to their village early the next morning. P.J. was sorry to hear that.

Heading up to their rooms after their evening chat, P.J., seeming a bit intoxicated, suggested that maybe he should have the single room and William and Primrose could share. It made no difference to William or Primrose, so Primrose moved to William's room. Before entering his room, P.J hollered downstairs and asked to have another glass of Port be brought to his room and he suggested that Sudra might bring it to him. That was the beginning of P.J.'s relationship with Sudra.

Early the next morning Sudra and her grandparents left for Kisumu. P.J. and Primrose left on a 2 day hunt for elephants. William did not go. His interest was not in hunting. In fact, he had heard that because of the ivory trade and people coming into Africa to hunt, the numbers of elephants had diminished considerably. He just didn't see the purpose. He stayed back to visit with Jonathon and Beth.

Chapter 11
1894
William Meets Turko

Often, while Primrose and P.J. went on their hunting trips, William used one of the buggies from the Plantation and traveled to several villages, introducing his elixirs to the witchdoctors. He was turned down one by one until he got to Kojello village and met the routh of the Alego clan, Turko Kendo. Turko had met and took an interest in the Anglican Church Missionary Society which had arrived in his village around 1877 and then in 1879, the first French Catholic missionaries came. By the time William arrived in 1894, Turko had learned a little English.

Turko had 3 girls and so disparately wanted a boy. He half-jokingly asked William if he had anything that would help his wife in producing a son. William said he didn't have anything specific, but that he did have something that would help his wife with the terrible cough she had. William had heard her coughing when he was approaching Turko's home. William found out that Turko's wife had this cough for at least 3 weeks. Turko agreed to give his wife William's elixir and within an hour she had stopped coughing. William instructed Turko's wife to take the cough medicine three times a day until her cough disappeared.

Turko was very curious about this man from America who came with medicines that cured many different ailments. The Alego clan had gotten its name because of their knowledge of medicine, using specific herbs to treat certain health conditions. In fact each time William came to visit Turko, he left there with some herbs that he did not know. Each herb was used to treat different ailments. He was excited to be able to pass this information on to his company's laboratory. A friendship developed between William and Turko. The last time William saw Turko, his wife thought she was pregnant. Turko kidded William about the elixir that he had given his wife.

When William returned to Glebe, Australia, in late 1895, there was a letter waiting for him from Turko. His wife had given birth to a son. He named the boy Hussein Kendo.

William continued to travel to different parts of the United States, often returning to Des Moines, Iowa, where his company's headquarters was located. It gave him time to rest before resuming his travels around the US, revisiting areas he had already been to make sure that his agents were promoting his products and to introduce them to new products.

Chapter 12
1896
Two Men Meet in Chicago

By the summer of 1896, William had worked his way to Chicago, which was also the city where the Democrats were having their presidential convention. William had made this trip at this time because he and P.J. had continued their friendship and agreed to meet at the convention. P.J. was always trying to change William's affiliation and William knew this time would be no different.

P.J. was selected to second the nomination of William Jennings Bryan at the convention. William Jennings Bryan was a staunch bimetallic and gave his famous "Cross of Gold" speech. However, the speech given by Bryan, no matter how powerful was lost to deaf ears. The newly developed technique of using cyanide to extract gold from inferior ore brought down the price of the gold mined in South Africa. Thus the Silver Democrats lost the most valuable plank in their platform.

William and P.J. met up for lunch on the last day of the convention. P.J. was all hyped up about the Democratic platform and brought along a summary, again trying to gain Williams Support:

The Democrats opposed the gold standard, wanted free and unlimited coinage, opposed the issue of bonds; wanted an income tax so that the burdens of taxations may be equally and impartially laid, to the end that wealth may bear its due portion of the expenses of Government. The Democrats also felt the most efficient way of protecting American labor is to prevent the importation of foreign pauper labor to compete with it in the home market; extended our sympathy to the people of Cuba in their heroic struggle for liberty and independence; wanted no man be eligible for a third term of the Presidential office; denounced the issuance of notes intended to circulate as money by national banks as in derogation of the Constitution, and demanded that all paper which is made a legal tender for public and private debts, or which is receivable for dues to the United States, shall be issued by the Government of the United States, and shall be redeemable in coin.

William listened and he and P.J. were able to discuss the pros and cons. William was sure he wanted his Republican party to win the election, he liked their position on the gold standard, especially now that it could be mined less expensively, and to have free and unlimited coinage would cause considerable inflation. It is true that the high price of gold would encourage deflation, but now that its price was reduced there didn't seem to be that concern anymore.

He was also in favor of the Republican's expansionist platform which would allow businesses larger raw resources and a broader market for their own products. Most democrats were not in favor of expansionism; they liked to refer to it as Imperialism instead of expansionism; that was a more negative meaning. William, after all, had found Africa and other parts of the world a wonderful opportunity for his company and for his country, as well. William would never accept the fact that entering a country in order to do trade was a form of Imperialism. He said there was no purpose in expanding into other countries other than for trade. America had everything else it needed.

P.J. told William about Sudra and the money he left with her. After he met Sudra and realized her enthusiasm for Western ways and how she relished in the books that he read her, he understood the need to educate the African children because they would be the ones that could lead Africa out of poverty. He wanted to set up some educational funds in Kenya that could be used for children, starting with those in the village where Sudra was born. Thus he anonymously set up a fund out of the US which would give money to a Catholic Mission school near Sudra's village. He said that he was setting up funds in his will that would go to helping educate the children in Sudra's homeland and that he hoped that his family in years to come would also keep this fund going, directing it to be used in the best way possible.

After the democratic convention, there appeared in the Chicago Independent a small article about an American Citizen from the United States bribing the Beloit Gold mining company in Johannesburg, South Africa in 1894. They mentioned no name. It said this citizen offered Beloit $20,000 to postpone the use of cyanide until after the US elections. William believed that the citizen was P.J. O'Mera. William felt that it was the old O'Mera that had bribed the mining company, not the new O'Mera that left the Plantation in the early part of 1895. He was going to let the matter drop.

Chapter 13
1899
Catherine

By late 1899, the depression was over and the economy had bounced back. William had continued his travels around the country introducing new medicines that his laboratories had developed. Some using the herbs he brought back from Africa. He was now headed to Australia.

He boarded the ship "Mariposa" in San Francisco. The ship made a stop at the Auckland harbor on its way to Sydney, Australia. A young nurse who had taken a patient to Rotora in the North Island of New Zealand near Auckland, to partake in the medicinal baths in that town boarded the ship with her patient. Upon reading the passenger list, William recognized the last name "Selous" and found out that the woman patient was his sister. Thus William met Catherine and they became acquainted on the three day trip to Sydney. William's oversea's headquarters was located in Sydney, Australia. While waiting for his next assignment, he continued to court Catherine.

After 3 months of courting Catherine, William wrote a letter on March 15, 1899 to his mother:

My dear Mamma,
  By the last mail I forwarded you a photo of mine. By the mail I am sending you another for inspection. Catherine Mary Gissing, age 26—but 30

*in disposition, fair looking, but no beauty. Sweet disposition, but has enough
spunk to hold her own. Domestic English birth—been out here 16 years,
member of Church of England, Family has no great means. Been educated for
a teacher but a few years ago took up the profession of nursing and they say
she is a good one. At least they keep her on the go all the time. She is about
130 to 140 pounds in weight. Is very quiet, modest and lady like and a girl
no man need to be ashamed of to introduce to his mother as his wife. Has not
much experience as a housekeeper.*

*I may add that her mother is not very much stuck on me and that nothing
is certain.*

Give me your opinion and advice, best as you can at that distance.

I do not care to have any of this go outside our home.

Your affectionate son, William

Then on March 21, 1899, after receiving a letter from his mother, he
wrote to her again. William was definitely having a hard time dealing with
his relationship with Catherine.

My darling Mamma,

*I was real pleased to receive your letter and appreciate it knowing what
an effort it is for you to write.*

*When you read this other letter don't think I am going to do anything
rash. I fully realize what kind of a life I have had and am living and at best
feel that I ought to become settled, but despite this desire, I am nearly afraid
to make the attempt. As you know, I am nervous and rather reluctant and
this causes a question in my mind whether or not I can make any one happy.
The spirit of this 18 years (nearly) of intense travel and strain has made its
mark and I feel at times as tho I did not know myself and fear that the mere
act of quitting same would cause depression. Remember I have passed the
romantic spirit of boyhood and capable of letting my emotions lay dormant
while thoroughly looking into the future. Sometimes I have thought that He
had caused this "Kitty" to cross my path, but when these terrible forebodings,
misgivings cross my mind, I feel as tho I was unequipped to the task of deciding
what was for the best. I have asked for Guidance and have resolved to let the
future work out my movements. I know you will be surprised to receive such*

a letter from me, but when a man feels as I do there is only one on Earth who can advise or console.

Then on May 6, 1899, William wrote his mother,

Dear Mamma,

 Aunt Mame wrote "we are most anxious to hear more about that girl." I take this opportunity to tell you that so far as I am concerned it will be some time before you will have any daughter-in-law. While there are many things in favor of this girl there are some very vital points to be taken into consideration and after careful consideration, I have decided to never be but a good friend to her.

 In a letter received recently from my "Co.," I see there is not much chance of my being located for several years, and when I consider that we are just on the eve of leaving a big business one that cannot help making me fairly wealthy if I stay with them, I do not think it good policy to throw up my situation and prospects for any girl. There would be no satisfaction in being married and having to be away from home all the time and until I see a show of settling down, I do not propose to offer any encouragement to anyone.

 Kitty is a fine girl and will make someone a good wife, but I think she will make a better wife to one of her nationality then to me.

 We have been raised entirely different. Our home customs are varied, and another strong thing was, all of her people are out here, mine in the U.S. and when I settle down, I don't want any of Australia in mine.

 Her mother is one of the stiffest dames I ever saw and as I said has no use for Americans, and me in particular.

 About a month ago, I received through Kitty a letter written to her by her father and when I had perused the contents, I made up my mind that while I might be willing to take the girl, I did not care to have her parents, so chucked the whole thing.

 So looking at everything from a matter of fact stand, I think I am right to do the way I have done. My course has been most honorable all the times and while I never asked her or her parents, still they saw nothing in earnest. Perhaps I may regret it later on in life, but I argued that if I was not willing to sacrifice my position for this girl, that perhaps I did not have the true spirit

necessary to make a happy union. In some ways, I am sorry I wrote to you about this affair, but I was very much perplexed at the time. I sincerely believe that I have had Divine Guidance in this matter with love.
    Your son, William

William wrote P.J. about his new acquaintance and said that he was getting tired of traveling and wanted to settle down. He also didn't want to give up his position in a company that could make him wealthy. P.J. too was settling in as a father to his son J.P, who was now 10. He wrote back to William that J.P was not going to have to work as hard as he did to make a living and that he believed that education was the sure ticket to a good life. His son would go to the best schools. William never knew much about P.J.'s wife; he never wrote or talked about her. His life revolved around his son.

P.J. had done well in the liquor business and had also invested in the stock market and owned a major share of a bank, which was doing quite well, especially since the gold standard was enacted. He admitted to William that he was glad that the scheme to postpone the mining of raw ore had not come to be. He didn't admit that he was the citizen that bribed the mining company. Times had become good again.

Chapter 14

Circumspection

By the fall of 1899, William was sent to India. While in India William writes to his family from Madras, India, which was the Military Headquarters for the British, usually housing 10,000 to 15,000 troops, but "just now many of the regiments are in Africa." Mounting tensions between the Dutch, or Boer, settlers and new British arrivals seeking to capitalize on South Africa's rich gold resources led to the outbreak of the Second South Africa, or Boer War in October 1899. The Boers quickly mounted attacks on British controlled areas in the country using guerrilla tactics and laying siege to the towns of Mafeking and Kimberley on the borders of the gold-rich Transvaal area. They also attacked and besieged the heavily defended British town of Ladysmith. William wrote:

> *"Of course you people are following the events there same as all the world, but I am especially interested in knowing each of the locations as well. To be sure business so far as our company is concerned is at a stand still, but when all is settled look out. We will be right there."*

William seemed to find something he liked about every place he went. He continues in his letter from Madras, India:

"The more I am in this country the more I like it, and as I gradually put new men into the various countries that I have visited. I propose retaining hold of the last."

Because William was so enthralled with India, he wanted to make sure to return as often as he could, so he had decided that he would service India himself.

By the end of this letter, he had almost decided that it was time to settle down. The rest of his letter from Madras was quite a reflection on his life. Meeting Kitty had certainly changed him. His letters became more circumspect. She obviously had aroused feelings in him that would not go away no matter how hard he tried to convince himself otherwise. He always addressed his mother when he needed advice. None of the letters were ever addressed to his father. If they weren't to his mother, they were addressed to "dear ones at home."

William continues in his letter:

"Many times people ask me, "Am I not tired of traveling." In ways I am, but in many other ways I enjoy it. Could I have you all with me, to see what I see, to be able to talk about this or that. I would not feel as tho I was not completely alone then. I could spend many more years in my work.

I take pride in seeing how my work grows and to overcome the obstacles of one year, but success the next makes it most rewarding. And I like my business, for we are bound to be one of the biggest houses in the near future.

I realize that I ought to be settled down and have a wife. And have been more impressed with this idea during the last year than ever, but when I take into consideration what an active life I have and I know that it would take time to domesticate me. I naturally shrink and hesitate till my fear chills any regards I might have for any. Perhaps if I was married and after giving my wife, a couple years of globe-trotting, that this companionship would gradually withdraw me into domesticity. I do know that my nature is hungry for companionship for I mix very little with people abroad. Do not care for the clubs; for if you don't drink or gamble, they think you are a monstrosity, so those I avoid. And I have lived as long alone and stifled all desires that there is no wonder, I am at times impatient and cranky. We all like to feel as tho we were appreciated and a little demonstration does not go amiss.

I know that I have been very impatient over many things and actually hasty to say or to act, but if I have sinned I feel as tho I had suffered in return. I can consciously say today that I am in many respects a different man than I was one year ago. And tho you may think actions recently do not bear out the assertion, still I know how I feel toward things in general.

It has been a hard year on me so far as worry, but I can assure you today that I am in better condition physically than I was when I left home.

I realized that for me to be at peace of mind, there must be Divine Love, and while I cannot say that all affairs are clear to me, still I am not discouraged and just by act and deed to realize all that makes life livable. Tho I do not see why we should reflect to be very happy here on Earth—for surely Christ was most miserable while here, so far as immediate surroundings were concerned.

There have been many times that I felt a desire to have good talks with Mamma on this and other subjects, but I did dislike the thought of having my mind and heart handed from one member of the family to another. Not that I am ashamed, but rather over sensitive.

And the same thing regarding Kitty.

No doubt my letters were misleading and they were intended to be to a certain extent. The fact that I was able to give her a house cut no figure. For I know the girl cared for me before she knew anything about my personal affairs. And I believe the only reason she is not here today is simply because her mother was so bitterly opposed—and I am sorry to say that I did not do very much toward smoothing her out.

All of this opposition and what was the worst part, was not being given any reasons, has nearly made me lose all confidence in myself so far as Kitty is concerned, fearing that it was willed to be otherwise. I know that I am a coward so far as matrimony is concerned. If I were engaged today, I know I would quit what I was doing.

And instead of being happy as some men profess to be, I would be very miserable til all was adjusted and I was convinced in my own mind that I had done the correct thing. As for treating a woman right, I know that I cannot do otherwise. Perhaps all of this comes from living so long alone and within ones self—that it has created a sort of a worse dilemma, and has made one suspicious of everything and everybody.

I feel as tho I wanted to commence making some preparations for a comfortable home somewhere and trust that the next few months will, so far as my company is concerned, allow me to.

I know I have worried you nearly sick and you may imagine I have not been very happy myself, but I am trying to be reconciled about things as they come daily, and not worry too much about this or that. To try to do my duty—live correctly and put my trust in Providence that all must be for the good.

I will not apologize for this letter for these are times one feels as tho they must talk to someone and there is no one on Earth more sympathetic than our mothers."

With love to you all at home, I am your affectionate son, William

1900

- **1889-1893** Ben Harrison, president
- **1890** AFL founded
- **1890** Sherman Antitrust Act The purpose of the act was to oppose the combination of entities that could potentially harm competition, such as monopolies or cartels.
- **1893-1896** Grover Cleveland President
- **1896** Supreme Court rules separate but equal legal
- **1897-1901** William McKinley President
- **1901-1909** Theodore Roosevelt President
- **1902** Roosevelt begins conservation of forests ********(Aside 6)**
- **1909** Roosevelt retires and goes on safari with Selous ********(Aside 6)**

William and Kitty didn't marry until 1901. William was 39 and Catherine was 29.

1910's

- **1909-1913** William Howard Taft is President
- **1909** NAACP is founded
- **1910**, April 21 Author Samuel Langhorne Clemens (a.k.a. Mark Twain) dies
- **1911, March 25** Fire kills 146 workers at the Triangle Shirtwaist Factory
- **1912, April 14** HMS Titanic strikes an iceberg on April 14, 1912.
- **1913** Willa Cather publishes *O Pioneers!*.
- **1913** The 16th amendment made graduated income tax a permanent fixture in the U.S. tax system.
- **1913-1921** Woodrow Wilson President
- **1914**, August 15 The Panama Canal opens to shipping
- **1917** George M. Cohen writes the popular World War I song *Over There*
- **1917** Military conscription
- **1918** "Standard Time Act" establishes daylight saving time in the United States during World War I.
- **1918 and 1919,** a deadly Influenza strain kills 20 to 40 million people.

FACTS about this decade.

Population: 92,407,000

Life Expectancy: Male 48.4 Female: 51.8

Average Salary $750 / year

The Ziegfeld girls earned $75/week.

Unemployed 2,150,000

National Debt: $1.15 billion

Union Membership: 2.1 million Strikes 1,204

Attendance: Movies 30 million per week

Lynchings: 76

Divorce: 1/1000

Vacation: 12 day cruise $60

Whiskey $3.50 / gallon, Milk $.32 / gallon

Speeds make automobile safety an issue

25,000 performers tour 4,000 U.S. theaters

Chapter 15

Home Sweet Home

William had moved to Des Moines, Iowa from Sydney, Australia in 1909. He had stopped traveling and became manager and vice president of the Pharmaceutical Company. He had already sired 4 children since his marriage in 1901 and before moving to Iowa. Eva was born several months after leaving Australia, Tom and Chuck followed, and his youngest child Celia was born in 1915. Celia was named after his mother.

Because of his large family and because of his age, William did not volunteer nor was conscripted into the military when the US declared war against Germany in 1917.

(WWI—Aside7)

Some of the first clashes of the war involved British, French and German colonial forces in Africa. On August 7, 1914, French and British troops invaded the German protectorate of Togoland. On August 10, German forces in South-West Africa attacked South Africa; sporadic and fierce fighting continued for the remainder of the war. Most of the African men who fought in the war were used as carriers or "porters."

Because of the expansive area in Eastern, Western and Northern Africa and there were not many railroads yet; carrying supplies was one of the biggest problems of the war. The British recruited over a million laborers for the campaign. One such person was Odera from the Luo tribe, father of Sudra. He himself was a porter for the British before the war and provided the British with over 1000 more carriers from his village.

Chapter 16

The Story of Tera
~daughter of Sudra

Tera laughed easily and was never unhappy. She never wondered why her skin was light brown not the rich ebony of her mother and the other members of her family. Like five year olds every where, she was only aware of the pleasures of the world seen through the innocent eyes of youth. She could hardly remember her assumed father who had left her mother Sudra. It was said he left to find work in the south. It seemed like a very long time ago to Tera. Two years is a very long time when you are five.

She never walked anywhere. She had two speeds fast and stop. She could not delay getting to the next moment of her life which she was sure would be full of adventure and discovery; just as the previous one was.

She lived with her mother and her mother's parents, and was loved unconditionally by them. Her mother had spent many hours reading books to her in a language called English. This was the same strange tongue used by the Porthouses who treated Tera as a member of their family.

She had no siblings, but never felt lonely. Her family was the whole village. Every member knew the little reddish girl who always smiled, and was comfortable in every situation. No door was closed to her.

Her mother often took her to the farm of the Porthouse's. The visits had become less frequent in the past year, but her mother would go there to work when she was needed. Sudra always admonished her to be on her best behavior while at the farm and to stay out of the way. These words would have been better spent on Beth Porthouse. Beth had remained childless and lived for the days Tera would visit and she doted on this perfect child as if she were her own.

These were happy days which quickly became years. Youth is very short lived and even shorter in a culture where girls are expected to marry with the onset of womanhood.

Because Tera and her mother Sudra lived with Sudra's parents, she did not experience the rejection and critical treatment that she would have received if her mother and father had been living with her father's family. Her paternal grandparents had died before she was born.

Sudra did not remarry, and spent her time taking care of Tera and improving the lives of her family. Her mission was teaching the women of the village English and showing them the importance of their lives. Sudra made sure that Tera knew English and communicated to Tera what she had learned about love from P.J. She told her how wonderful it was to truly be in love and be loved in return. In the social structure of the tribe where marriages were arranged, normally to increase the wealth of the bride's parents, love was not a part of the mix.

In 1907, Tera was 12. The time had come for Tera to be thinking about getting married. Her grandfather told Sudra that he wanted Tera to marry into the Jo Alego clan because they had been more accepting to the ways of the new settlers. The ways he was convinced would lead to prosperity and opportunity. In fact Turko, the rueth (leader) of Jo Alego, had made an edict to introduce Western dress and manners into their culture back in the early 1900's. By this time the British had a significant impact in the area. Their numbers were steadily growing in the highlands due largely to the completion of the railroad from Mombasa.

When Sudra worked at the Plantation, she had often heard William, her lover's American traveling companion, talk favorably about Turko. William had often visited Turko's village introducing his elixirs. The fact that William liked Turko made Sudra a little more reassured about Tera becoming his wife.

Sudra reminisced with herself about the one evening when she was serving dinner at the Plantation, she overheard William tell everyone that Turko seemed so interested in the Western ways but he continued wearing that single loin cloth around his hips. William said he had tried several times to convince Turko to try Western clothes. She remembered this conversation, because P.J. winked at her and had said that it might be something that he might like to wear and wondered where he might get one. No one seemed to think he was very funny, but Sudra knew what he meant. She remembers blushing. William couldn't convince him to wear Western garb, but he could convince him to use some of his Western elixirs. Sudra chuckled to herself.

Sudra had higher hopes for her daughter. She had hidden a large sum of money that P.J. had given her and was hoping that she could get her daughter to England to be educated and have a better life—a life that she had read about in P.J.'s books. But this was a life for a Western child, not that of an African native and there was a lot of strife now between the British and many of the tribes of Africa, trying to resist the colonization of East Africa. .

Tera was wed in 1908 into the Alego tribe to Turko Kendo, the routh that was befriended by William in 1894. She was his second wife. Many Luo men were allowed as many wives as they wanted. This caused great disappointment to the missionaries as they had tried to get those who became Christians to have only one wife. A man's status was largely based on the number of wives and cattle he had, so the concept of one wife was something that would take time. For the sake of increasing their influence, the missionaries looked the other way and said little about marriage.

In 1909 Tera became pregnant and gave birth to a daughter. She named her Sebrinko. Turko was not pleased. Having a son was a sign of masculinity and only baby boys were celebrated. His only son by his first marriage had left when he was quite young. Tera was living with Turko's family and saw little of her mother, Sudra. It was as if she left her heart with her mother and her family. She existed and the constant smile was replaced by an emptiness of expression. Turko took no notice as she was just a woman. Tera was lonely and missed going to the Porthouse Plantation. She would often go into the village when the missionaries were there. She would ask them about the Plantation and the happenings there. The missionaries became her conduit of communication. They gladly took her notes of greeting and inquiry to Beth and her mother. She had learned to write English from her mother. Thus began a line of letters that went back and forth from Tera to Beth and then Beth to Tera. Beth, was thrilled to be in a part of Tera's life. She felt a fondness for Sudra and could almost see herself as Tera's grandmother.

Being mother to Sebrinko was about the only thing besides her corresponding that brought any happiness to Tera. The rest of her life was marked with loneliness and a sense of something being missing. The years would pass quickly and soon Sebrinko would be wed and leave to live with her husband's clan.

Her husband Turko paid little attention to her. The reason for him marrying her was to produce sons, which was not happening. He had three daughters and their only worth was a few goats or cows. He did have a son, but he left the village when he was very young and Turko no longer considered him a son. A son would carry on his lineage. He needed a son. There would be no males at his homestead if he should die.

Turko died suddenly in 1916. Tera was 21 years old and still held dreams. She had always remembered what her mother had taught her about loving the man you married. That hadn't been the case with Turko. Tera thought she would never get to experience this blissful state of which her mother spoke so often and with such feeling.

Sebrinko had been betrothed in 1914, at the age of five, to Odanto of the JoSeme tribe. He was the same age as Tera. Sometimes a child is married at a young age, before maturity, to a male from another tribe in order to seal a deal between male members of a tribe, usually heads of families. Odanto was a routh of the Jo-Seme clan, and it was his advantage to wed to a daughter of the Jo-Alego.

Tera was still of the reproductive age, and Turko did not have any brothers or sons. He had disowned his only son. It was suggested that Sebrinko's husband impregnate Tera. This was a common practice among the Luo tribe. When a husband dies, his brother or some other male relative, not directly related to the woman, and who lives with the clan impregnate that woman and the children would then become the dead husband's children, taking on the dead husband's name. This continued the lineage of that family if the child was a boy.

Thus Tera became pregnant by Odanto and bore a child. She named her Nora, thus becoming Nora Kendo, taking the last name of Tera's deceased husband.

It was about this time that the British and Germans were skirmishing in East Africa and it was not safe for the British or many of the Africans who were sympathetic to the British. Tera was obviously very sympathetic to the British and the letters going back and forth from the Plantation were proof. Beth's last letter to Tera, told her that they were fleeing the Plantation and moving to America. They would be leaving the Plantation to Sudra's family. Tera wrote one last letter to Beth and she also wrote a letter to her mother, Sudra, by way of the missionaries. Tera met the missionaries when Nora was one month old. She would never see her daughter again, but she hoped that she would be safe in her new home.

Tera told her family that she had given her daughter away to a family that couldn't produce any children. Some families that couldn't produce any children would often take in a girl in order to marry her off to a young man in order to get 8 to 10 goats or cows for the family. No one questioned Tera's decision.

Chapter 17
1917
Ida the Calf

William loved living in Des Moines, Iowa, and relishing in his life of a father and husband He was so glad Kitty had not given up on him so many years ago. He took fatherhood very seriously. Because the U.S. had now entered the war, much of the country rallied around the President, trying to offer support in some way, either buying liberty bonds, volunteering to serve or becoming involved in the Red Cross. In 1917, when Maurice, his 10 year old son, came up with a scheme to sell his pet calf, William encouraged him to write a letter to the Chicago Tribune. So Maurice sent the following letter to the Chicago Tribune.

"Red Cross Man, The Chicago Tribune: The other day my Dad gave me a little calf. I call her Ida. Dad says it is a fine calf, her mother being a Holstein and her dad a Jersey. If I was a little bigger, I would go over and knock a lot of Germans loose of their shoes, but I am too small even to get a job anywheres except at home digging dandelions and there ain't much money in that. I want to do something for the Red Cross on my own hook. So I will sell Ida, my little calf, to the man that will give The Tribune the most money for her and you turn the money over to the Red Cross man. I will have my dad send the calf by express to the man that buys her. Dad has some fine cows and the other day he sold a girl calf for $50. Another time he sold a gentleman calf

for a big lot of money, but that one got on the railroad track and got all mussed up. My calf is quite big one which was born May 15, and dad says it will be a fine cow. I want to sell Ida for enough to give a membership in the Red Cross to me and two of my little sisters and three brothers. The rest can hustle for themselves. I asked dad if I could do this and he said sure thing, maybe somebody will come across. He said there was lot of loose money among The Tribune readers, and something about war babies and Chicago bulls and bears, and I didn't understand it. Please put this in the paper right away."
Maurice Peairs.

That turned out to be quite an experience for the calf of young Maurice. As was written in the Chicago Tribune in 1917:

"William, Maurice's father, had the calf sent to Chicago in a special Pullman crate, draped as befitting the journey of its tenant, in star-spangled bunting, with a sign on one end reading "Buy a Liberty Bond." A delegation of boy scouts met the calf sent by Maurice Peairs. It was Troop 516 of Englewood, commanded by Scoutmaster John A Jacobs. They gave Ida a military reception. A triumphal procession is planned for Ida today. Cy De Bry has asked to have Ida as a guest at his country home in Lincoln park, and unless her business engagements interfere, she will probably spend the week end at the De Brys. A complimentary luncheon of milk was given Ida by The Tribune on her arrival. She had three quarts of it, served by little Miss Mildred Pilbrit. In an automobile, preceded by a regimental band, followed by an escort of boys scouts, Ida will tour the loop, the Michigan boulevard, athletic clubs, and will wind up at the board of trade around recess time, when Ring W. Landner, the eminent authority on calves will auction Ida off."
Auctioning went on for a week with the highest bidder for $750 going to a man from Davenport Iowa. "Ida is an Iowa calf, she ought to come back home to the farm," said the highest bidder.

The calf finally brought in $1350. Maurice bought a Red Cross membership for all the children in his class.

Chapter 18

Two Men

William continued working during the day and returning to his family at night, traveling infrequently. He seemed to have been domesticated quite easily. He now had the opportunity to do things he had put off doing because of his traveling—one of those things he learned to love was gardening. He planted fruit trees and many different varieties of flowers on his property of several acres. However, his love for gardening took a turn when his son, Tom, fell out of the apple tree he had planted many years before. Tom hadn't climbed up very far in the tree, but as he leaned out to get a few branches which he was going to use to make a bird house for a scouting project, he slipped and fell on his head. He developed meningitis and died several weeks later. It took a toll on William and it was several years before he would again find pleasure in his gardening.

He had kept in contact with the Porthouse couple and had received a letter from them stating that they were leaving the Plantation because of the war and that they didn't feel safe staying there. They said they were giving the Plantation to Sudra's family. Beth wrote in great length about what had transpired since he and P.J. had left. William had already heard from P.J. that he thought Sudra might be carrying his child, and William didn't think that P.J. knew that he had a daughter and now a granddaughter. The Porthouses would be moving to Kansas to be near

Jonathon's parents. The most shocking news was that they would be taking Tera's baby, called Nora, with them and raise her as their own. She said if he ever traveled their way, she would love to see him.

William immediately sent off a letter to P.J. because he was sure he would want to know that his granddaughter would be living in the United States. This did not appear to be the case. P.J. said that this was not a good time for him to become involved in his granddaughter's life, especially since she was black. His main concern was getting his son established because he thought he would have a great career in politics.

P.J. had sent his only son, J.P., to the prestigious Latin high school in Boston where he didn't get very good grades but was very popular with his fellow classmates, becoming president of the class. His son went on to college at Harvard and graduated in 1912.

In 1913 P.J. used his influence to get his son J.P. a job as a state bank examiner. Here, his son had access to useful information about the confidential affairs of companies and individuals who had credit lines with major Boston banks. J.P. found out which companies were in trouble and which had extra cash, who was planning new products or acquisitions and who was about to be liquidated.

J.P's strategy was to obtain inside information about troubled companies from banks, then drive their stock down so he could buy them more cheaply. While still on the state payroll as a bank examiner, he made an acquisition that was aided by inside information. He bought a Boston investment company called Realty Associates Inc. and turned the company from an old-line investment firm into one that made money on the misery of others.

Under his direction, the company specialized in taking over defaulted home mortgages. He would then paint the houses, and resell them at far higher prices. By the time the company was dissolved, his $1000 investment had grown to $75,000.

With his job as state bank examiner, he learned the ins and outs of running a bank and borrowed enough money to purchase his father's bank which was in trouble. In 1913 he became President of that bank, being the youngest president of any bank in the nation.

Now it would seem strange that P.J. would need to find another job, but his father-in-law got him a job as manager in a steel company that made transport and war equipment for the war. P.J was too old to serve in World War I, and his son, J.P., who was now 29, avoided the draft in this war because of his job at the steel company. This was despite the fact he knew nothing about steel manufacturing. Men who were working for companies that supplied equipment for the war were exempt from fighting in the war, therefore, because of J.P.'s job with the steel company he was not drafted.

P.J. wrote William that he was a little worried about his son because he was quite ambitious just as he himself had been before he went to Africa. He saw a lot of himself in his son and felt that his son didn't care who he might hurt along the way as long as his ambitious plans were accomplished. But he also felt that if he could keep his eye on his son and steer him away from these destructive tendencies; he could use his personal popularity to better use. He also told William that J.P. had just given him a new grandson, named J.F. O'Mera. It seemed a coincidence that he had a new grandchild the same year that Nora, his granddaughter, was born. William just shook his head.

William thought to himself that P.J. seemed to be hurting his son more than helping. After all P.J. was the one that used his influence to get his son the positions that seemed to be self destructive. There was certainly a dichotomy about P.J. O'Mera.

Chapter 19

The Story of Nora
~daughter of Tera
~granddaughter of Sudra

It was 1917, when Tera had the Christian missionaries take her one month old daughter, Nora, to the Plantation. Sudra, Tera's mother had the same missionaries take to Beth a book and an envelope containing money that could be given to Nora when she was older. The Porthouse couple were packing up the belongings they would be taking with them to America. It would be a long trip by train from Nairobi to Mombasa and then on to Cape Town where they would catch a ship to America. When they reached America, they would have to find a train that could take them to Kansas. It had been over 25 years since Jonathon had been in America and the first time for Beth. She was nervous about taking a young baby on such a long trip. She had never had a baby and wasn't even sure what they needed. Luckily, one of the servants who knew of Sudra's and Tera's plan had gathered up all the things that Beth would need for Nora on this long journey.

Nora was a darling little baby, with jet black hair, light brown skin and dark black eyes, features similar to Beth's, who was part Italian. Jonathon did have brown hair and brown eyes. Neither Beth nor Jonathon had a broad nose like Nora's. However, they stood firm in their decision to call

Nora their own child, and planned to tell no one of her true identity, not even Jonathon's parents.

It was a long journey from Nairobi to Cape Town. They had decided to stay in a hotel in Cape Town before taking the even longer journey by ship to America. Beth and Jonathon were amazed at the architecture found around Cape Town. It seemed like another part of the world compared to the highlands of Kenya.

The trip by ship wasn't quite as bad as Beth thought it would be. They had enough money so that they could stay in the best quarters on the ship away from those who were fleeing Africa back to London because of the difficult life they encountered in South Africa. Most of them were sleeping below in the galleys at night and working on deck or in the kitchens all day.

When they arrived in New York, they were met by a young couple that Jonathon's parents had known from Kansas. This couple had come to Kansas, but could not put up with the hardships of working a farm. They had passed through New York when they first came to America from England and felt the prospects of a job in New York would be a better life for them. They gave their land to Jonathon's parents. Jonathon and Beth had to check in at Ellis Island where all new comers had to pass through. This was the first time they became apprehensive about Nora passing as their child. They listed themselves as Jonathon, Beth and Nora Porthouse. There were no questions asked. After clearing the necessary procedures at Ellis Island, they spent the night with the couple that met them and then left the next morning on a train to Omaha and then on to Wichita, KS. Jonathon's parents owned a farm close to a small town near Wichita.

Beth and Jonathon arrived in Wichita and were met at the train station by Jonathon's parents who were very surprised to see that they had brought a baby with them. They didn't know that Beth had even been pregnant. Nora was a baby and baby's sometimes have features that they soon out grow, so Jonathon's parents said nothing about Nora's looks. They were just excited to see the couple and their new grandchild.

Jonathon's parents were having a good year farming and since they also had acquired the land from their neighbors who had moved to New

York, it was becoming even more profitable. They had started building a house on the extra land for Jonathon and Beth. They were going to have to add another room for the baby.

Nora had a very happy disposition, smiling and giggling all of the time, until she started school. She began to realize that her broad nose and curly hair made her look different from the other children.

There were several black families that lived in their town, but they did not go to Nora's school. Nora's looks caused her a lot of ridicule and she did not understand why. She wasn't a little black girl like the children said. Her mother and father were white. Beth and Jonathon ached inside for Nora. Nora was more black than white, but if they told Nora, how would that help. She still would not have a place where she would fit in. They chose not to tell her.

Beth had put the money, along with the book Sudra had given her for Nora, in a safety deposit box in the bank. Included with the book and money, was a note explaining how Nora's biological mother had brought her to them so that she could have a better life in America. Beth and Jonathon had decided to tell everyone that Nora was their child. Beth included the note in the box just in case something happened to her and Jonathon. No one else knew and they felt that someday Nora had the right to know her true African heritage.

1918

A hero is born

On July 9, 1918 a young man from Iowa was born who would have a great influence on William's daughter Celia.

1920

- **1920** 18th Amendment prohibits alcohol
- **1921-1923** William Harding President
- **1920** 19th Amendment gives Women right to vote
- **1921, November 2** KDKA in Pittsburgh, PA, becomes the first radio station to offer regular broadcasts
- **1922** Lila Bell and DeWitt Wallace begin publishing *Reader's Digest*
- **1925** F. Scott Fitzgerald publishes *The Great Gatsby*
- **1925,** July Tennessee school teacher John T. Scopes' trial for teaching Darwin's "Theory of Evolution" begins.
- **1926, March 16** Robert Goddard fires his first liquid-fueled rocket.
- **1927, May 21** Charles Lindbergh lands "Spirit of St. Louis" in Paris successfully completing the first trans-Atlantic flight.
- **1927** Audiences see the first motion picture with sound *The Jazz Singer*
- **1929** William Faulkner publishes *The Sound and the Fury.*

FACTS about this decade.

106,521,537 people in the United States
2,132,000 unemployed, Unemployment 5.2%
Life expectancy: Male 53.6, Female 54.6
343.000 in military (down from 1,172,601 in 1919)
Average annual earnings $1236; Teacher's salary $970
Dow Jones High 100 Low 67
Illiteracy rate reached a new low of 6% of the population.
Gangland crime included murder, swindles, racketeering
It took 13 days to reach California from New York .There were 387,000 miles of paved roads.

Chapter 20

Different Paths

The Prohibition Act was enacted as the 18th Amendment to the U.S. Constitution. It prohibited the sale and manufacture of alcohol. It went into effect on January 16, 1920. P. J. and his son benefited greatly from the amendment. There were several loopholes for people to legally drink during Prohibition. For instance, the 18th Amendment did not mention the actual drinking of liquor. Since Prohibition went into effect a full year after the 18th Amendment's ratification, it gave P.J. and his son an opportunity to stockpile a large inventory of good liquor and sell it at high prices after the Amendment went into effect. The Volstead Act allowed alcohol consumption if it was prescribed by a doctor. Needless to say, large numbers of new prescriptions were written for alcohol and P.J.'s son cashed in on those deals and stock piled a larger inventory, with the help of AL Capone from Chicago, so that they would be ready when Prohibition ended.

The 1920's had a boom just as the 1880's. The first television system was invented in 1925, and in 1928 the first color television was demonstrated. The first movie with a soundtrack was shown in 1926 and the first all-talking movie in 1928 and the first all-color all-talking movie in 1929.

J.P. O'Mera, was an investor in the movie-making business, producing several movies and becoming a Hollywood fixture. Rumor had it that he had an affair with a Hollywood starlet. It is estimated that J.P made millions from his investments in Hollywood.

While P.J. and his son were putting their energy into stockpiling liquor and investing in Hollywood, William was an ambassador of sorts for the United States.

William's extensive travels to many parts of the world gave him knowledge and understanding of many diverse cultures. These experiences along with his calm and accepting demeanor made him the perfect person to advance and promote the new discoveries and enhancements to the everyday life, both civilian and military. He was a perfect ambassador for American business, ready to enter world-wide markets.

The New York Times wrote in February 1920, that when William Peairs went to Mexico City for the first American-Mexican trade conference he proposed:

> "a plan for the interchange of Mexican and American students under the auspices of the American Chamber of Commerce in Mexico. As Peairs said "Imagine what the result would be to have several hundred young men returning to their native country after remaining in our universities two or more years. Would it not soon become a powerful factor in creating an ideal condition socially and financially for both countries? Under no circumstances should the selections be made by political preferences, but by competitive examinations, where not only mental ability but also character and ambition would be taken into consideration. Every section in the entire Republic should be represented."

The Times stated that more than 30 colleges had already shown an interest in Peairs's plan such as John Hopkins, Oberlin, Brown's University, Minnesota and Iowa State."

With so many new endeavors in the US, William and other businessmen knew that the US needed to go outside their borders and compete with other countries. In the article, William said

> "...Americans in Mexico can't even speak the language well, and it is the bad habit of Americans there to flock together and hold the native at arms

length. There must be a change if Americans are to compete successfully with their trade rivals, particularly the Germans, French and Spaniard, who select their representatives for efficiency and gainful social qualities."

New products for trade developed out of many innovative endeavors, such as the Charles Lindbergh's solo flight across the Atlantic Ocean in 1927, of the Cathode Ray Tube (CRT) in 1922, record companies' electrical recording process to phonograph records in 1925 and the first flight of a liquid-fueled rocket in 1926 created hot markets for Initial Public Offerings. The "Roaring Twenties" were exciting times with very speculative trends.

Stock market bubbles frequently produce hot markets in Initial Public Offerings, since investment bankers and their clients see opportunities to float new stock issues at inflated prices. These hot IPO markets allocate investment funds to areas dictated by speculative trends, such as new airplanes, new record companies and Hollywood production companies, rather than to enterprises generating longstanding economic value record of sustained growth.

There continued to be large investments in all of these new endeavors, and it appeared that the markets were over speculated again, but also stock market players had learned to manipulate the market with selling and buying, thus over inflating the stock market. One such individual was J.P. O'Mera.

The bubble came to an abrupt stop; 1929 was the year of the great stock market crash and luckily J.P and his father had pulled out considerable sums from the market. J.P. had been involved in many stock market schemes, including insider trading, that were controlling the flexibility of the market and he knew when it was time to withdraw. They pulled out of the market just before the crash, leaving thousands of investors losing their life's savings. One of those investors was William. Luckily, he still had his job and a chance to recover some of what he had lost. It didn't look like William would be retiring soon. He had a family to support.

The same year as the crash, P.J. summoned William to his house. P.J. was dying and he had a favor to ask of William. He would write William a check for $250,000 which he in turn would cash and then give a second check for the same amount to Beth for raising Nora and sending her to private schools and to college. She would be 12 by now. He did not want any trace of this money to come back to him. That would ruin his son's political career.

By the end of that year, P.J. had passed away leaving his son a considerable amount of money. In his will P.J. specified that a certain amount be given to an educational fund in a small village in Kenya. Included was also a personal note addressed to J.P. explaining his reason for the money being sent to Kenya.

The Stock Market Crash in 1929 was the beginning of the Great Depression.

That same year, William went to Chanute, Kansas, on a business trip. He also went to Arkansas, Kansas, a small town near Wichita, to visit the Porthouses. To his dismay he found Nora pregnant and she was only 12 years old.

Chapter 21

The Story of Nora II
~*daughter of Tera*
~*granddaughter of Sudra*

Nora did not have any friends in school except a little white boy whose parents were so poor that he often came to school smelly and hungry. When he came to school with clothes that looked like he had worn every day, the children would taunt him, telling him he smelled like a skunk. Nora often shared her lunch with him, and Beth would bring him home some times after school and clean him up and give him a new set of clothes. Beth was always surprised that the little boy's parents hadn't noticed what she had done. She later found out that the little boy's parents would often disappear for several days, leaving the little boy home all alone. Those were the days he came to school with no lunch.

Beth was concerned that Nora was spending too much time with the boy, so she thought if Nora could get a little job, it might give her a new direction as well as take up some of her idle time.

Beth had gotten to know a black lady from her church. It seemed odd because this was the only black person in their church. Mrs. Podery was in the same situation as Nora, light skinned but had many characteristics that often come with being black. Mrs. Podery said she would be willing to hire Nora to help her once a week. Actually, Beth gave Mrs. Podery the money that she would use to pay Nora.

Beth hoped that this would be a place where Nora would feel more comfortable and give her something to look forward to each week. Mrs. Podery had a daughter, Jennifer Davidson and her son Fred, who also lived with her. The grandson was seldom there. He was 24 and had attended Friend's College in Wichita for one year and then began attending K-State Agricultural college majoring in Industrial Journalism in 1924, several years before Nora started going to Mrs. Podery's house. He was one of 20 blacks enrolled in this college. He left to go to Chicago before he finished college, but did return in the fall of 1928 to get his degree, before moving back to Chicago for good. Nora met him the day he returned from Chicago.

Beth remembers the first time Nora met him. She was so excited. He was such a friendly young man and she was so impressed with his college degree and he was even black. He wrote poetry and Nora loved listening to him recite it, even though the topics of his poetry went way over her head. She loved the sing-song of his lyrics.

One day, Nora came home from school and was sad because her friend hadn't been to school for over a week. She was afraid he wouldn't be coming back. She said that she felt bad because she and her friend had gotten into a little spat about her having a job at the black lady's house. The boy's parents didn't like him being with Nora because she had black friends. Her friend never returned to school. Nora began going to Mrs. Podery's house more than once a week and Nora seemed to be much happier.

Then one day, Beth noticed that Nora wasn't doing much school work and she ignored Beth whenever she would try to speak with her to find out what was wrong. Then Beth found out that Nora hadn't been to school for the last two weeks, about the time that her friend had quit coming to school. She asked Nora where she went when she wasn't in school and she just said that she liked visiting Mrs. Podrey. Nora was complaining about not feeling well. Beth thought that maybe she had begun her period. She was about the right age, and she had heard that African girls tended to mature earlier than American girls. This was one area that Beth had not talked about with Nora. And she wasn't sure how to approach the subject with her, and Nora had said nothing about seeing blood on her clothes. She would wait for her to bring it up.

Beth had decided that Nora would not finish out the school year. There were just a few weeks left, and she had already missed several weeks for not feeling well. It looked like she would have to repeat the 8th grade. Beth decided to take Nora to the doctor to find out if she was depressed because she had lost her friend at school or because there might be something else wrong with her.

The doctor reported to Beth, that Nora had a kidney infection and that her pregnancy had complicated the situation. Beth was stunned. She didn't even know that Nora had ever had a period, much less was able to get pregnant. The doctor said that they would need to deal with her kidney infection and that because Nora was around 4 months pregnant it was too late to do anything about it. And Nora had no idea that she was pregnant.

Beth and Jonathon discussed what to do with Nora's pregnancy. It was 1929 and the country was in a turmoil with everyone pulling their money out of the stock market and the banks. Beth remembered the money that was put into the safety deposit box. Was this the time to use the money and send Nora away to have the baby. The stigma that this would bring to Beth and Jonathon was something they would have a hard time handling, but it just wasn't in their nature to abandon Nora now. They loved her and wanted to see her through with this pregnancy and they would deal with the consequences later. They could always give the baby up for adoption. Abortion wasn't even in the picture even if it was legal.

When Nora was about 81/2 months pregnant and looking like she could deliver any time, William appeared at the Porthouse home. He had written a letter to them to tell them he would be coming, but it hadn't arrived yet, so they were very surprised when he appeared, but very pleased. They had always liked William and felt that he was a very wise man.

They hadn't seen him since he left the Plantation in 1895, but he had kept in touch by mail at least once a year. William brought with him a $250,000 check. He specified that the money should be used by the Porthouses to take care of Nora and that they were to be sure she had a good education . After seeing Nora and realizing her condition, he told Beth and Jonathon to put some of the money in a trust so that after Nora had the baby, they could arrange for the baby to be taken care of while Nora continued her education. They then could arrange for her and the baby to have their own home in a black community, maybe away from the small town, like in a larger city such as Wichita. Jonathon and Beth had already decided not to give the baby up for adoption. William asked who was the father of Nora's baby and Beth did not know, but assumed it was her little white friend who had left town abruptly.

Nora went into labor the day after William left. The doctor said that there might be complications because they had not been able to cure Nora's kidney infection during her pregnancy. The doctors thought that she might have a disease that they called polycystic kidney disease, but that it is something that is difficult to diagnose. In older people it sometimes causes renal failure if it has progressed too far. It can also affect the liver and cause high blood pressure.

August 2, 1929, Nora had a baby girl after a very long labor. Nora had lost a lot of blood and her blood pressure had shot up to a dangerous level and along with that her kidneys were not functioning. The next few days would be important. If her kidneys did not begin to work, they would need to put her on a dialysis. However, Nora went into a coma and even though they did attach her to the dialysis, she died two days later.

Beth and Jonathon named Nora's baby Jemeya, after Sudra's grandmother, who had worked for Jonathon and Beth when they were on the Plantation.

1930's

- **1930, January 13** The Mickey Mouse comic strip debuts in the January 13, 1930, edition of the *New York Mirror*.
- **1932,** Shirley Temple makes her film debut in *Kid's Last Stand*.
- *1933, January 31 The Lone Ranger* premiers on radio station WXYZ, Detroit, MI.
- **1935** The Wagner Act gives workers the right to unionize.
- **1936** Jesse Owens wins four gold medals during the Summer Olympics.
- **1937, May 6** The German airship Hindenburg is destroyed while attempting to land at the Lakehurst Naval Air Station.
- **1937, July 2** American aviation pioneer Amelia Earhart disappears over the Pacific Ocean while attempting to circumnavigate the globe.
- **1939** Ted Williams makes his Major League Baseball debut with the Boston Red Sox.

FACTS about this decade.
Population: 123,188,000 in 48 states
Life Expectancy: Male, 58.1; Female, 61.6
Average salary: $1,368
Unemployment rises to 25%
Huey Long proposes a guaranteed annual income of $2,500
Car Sales: 2,787,400
Food Prices: Milk, 14 cents a qt.; Bread, 9 cents a loaf; Round Steak, 42 cents a pound
Lynchings: 21
The world's largest building with 3,000,000 square feet of floor space was built in Illinois.
Presidents Herbert Hoover; Franklin Roosevelt

Chapter 22

The Depression

William was nearing 70 and was still working since he had lost much of his savings in the stock market crash of 1929. The depression was not over yet. William had been around in the 1893 depression and he noticed the same signs after the stock market crash. He often said he should have noticed the stock market crash coming, but because of the ups and downs of the market, controlled by a few investors, he wasn't sure when to pull out. William saw the same over indebtedness and deflation that he saw in the 1890's. William saw the availability of credit that fueled speculation and asset bubbles in the 20's just as he did in the 1890's.

He was hoping that this depression would not last as long as the last one. But all the signs were there: people and businesses were liquidating their debt, a reduction in output, trade and employment, hoarding of money, lowering of interest rates, a rise in deflation and worse than anything lack of confidence in the government and the market. Banks began to fail as debtors defaulted on debt and depositors attempted to withdraw their deposits en masse, triggering multiple bank runs. Government guarantees and Federal Reserve banking regulations to prevent such panics were ineffective or not used. Bank failures led to the loss of billions of dollars in assets Outstanding debts became heavier, because prices and incomes fell by 20-50% but the debts remained at the same dollar amount.

The stock market crash and the state of the economy started changing people's opinion about how to solve the consequences of the crash. People needed jobs. The government needed money. Making alcohol legal again would open up many new jobs for citizens and additional tax reserves to the government.

1932 brought good news for J.P. O'Mera. He was ready to open his liquor stores as soon as the 18th amendment was repealed. With his stock pile of liquor he would be the first to have his stores well supplied.

It was also a good year for J.P. personally, his youngest son Theodore O'Mera was born.

By the end of that year, William had a stroke and died. Catherine, his wife, felt the stress of the stock market crash and the depression that followed took quite a toll on him.

He never got to hear the stories of his oldest son's bravery fighting in World War II in Okinawa; he never read about his middle son's part in the development of a soft water conglomerate and his numerous inventions. This was the same son who auctioned off his pet calf, Ida, in 1917. He never got to campaign for Celia's, his youngest daughter, political aspirations, being the first woman in her district to be seated as Council Woman. He never got to see the success of his two daughters who never married, one becoming a librarian and another an author. He never got to attend Eva's wedding for he died that same year. He never got to know Willy and her two sons or her two daughters.

His obituary explained it all.

"William was a successful business man who loved his family and country. He traveled the lengths of the globe several times over, spreading good will wherever he would go and shared his letters that offered insight to those who were less fortunate to go to all the places he was able to travel. The scholarship funds that he started up in some of the countries that he traveled are still in use today, thanks to his generosity. His entrepreneurship, citizenship and love of family and country shine through his wife and his 8 of 9 children that survive him."

Chapter 23

New Deal

The New Deal Roosevelt promised the American people began to take shape immediately after his inauguration in March 1933. Based on the assumption that the power of the federal government was needed to get the country out of the depression, the first days of Roosevelt's administration saw the passage of banking reform laws, emergency relief programs, work relief programs, and agricultural programs. These programs helped the lives of those in desperate need except it did not create jobs. Unemployment remained high.

Roosevelt was in favor of ratifying the 21st Amendment, which repealed the 18th Amendment, making alcohol once again legal. This was the first and only time in U.S. history that an Amendment has been repealed. He felt that repealing this amendment would create more jobs and bring more tax revenue to the Federal government. J.P. saw his liquor business expand because on December 5, 1933, the 21st Amendment to the U.S. Constitution was ratified. With his stockpile he was ready for business.

One Roosevelt supporter named Wendell Willkie, a Democrat, came forward in direct opposition to some portions of the New Deal. He was against Roosevelt's proposed legislation allowing government agencies to compete with private corporations. His argument was that if the government competed with private corporations it had an unfair advantage because the government didn't have to make a profit and could then run private corporations out of business.

In 1933, he convinced the House of Representatives that it would be unconstitutional for the government to enter the utility business and they voted to limit the TVA's ability to enter the utility business and curtailed the building of transmission lines in competition with C&S; however, President Roosevelt persuaded the Senate to remove those restrictions and the resulting law gave the TVA extremely broad power. Because the government-run TVA could borrow unlimited funds at low interest rates, Willkie's Commonwealth & Southern was unable to compete, and Willkie was forced to sell C & S properties in the Tennessee River Valley to the government agency, TVA.

Willkie formally switched political parties in 1939 and began making speeches in opposition to the New Deal. Willkie did not condemn all New Deal programs, and he supported those programs that he felt could not be run better by private enterprise. His objection was that the government had unfair advantages over private businesses, and thus should avoid competing directly against them. In 1939 Willkie made a highly-publicized appearance on the popular "Town Hall" nationwide radio program, where he debated the merits of the private-enterprise system with President Roosevelt's Solicitor General and a possible candidate for the 1940 Democratic presidential nomination. Most observers felt that Willkie won the debate, and many liberal Republicans began—for the first time—to view him as a dark horse presidential candidate. (Parmet, Herbert S.; Hecht, Marie B. (1968). *Never Again: A President Runs for a Third Term.* New York: Macmillan.Parmet, 122)

Chapter 24

The Story of Jemeya
~daughter of Nora,
~granddaughter of Tera
~great, granddaughter of Sudra

Jemeya was born August 2, 1929. Her mother's cause of death was listed as child birth even though her kidney disease was actually the cause. It was just easier to put "child birth." It would be difficult for Beth and Jonathon to be raising a young baby. Beth was now 54 and Jonathon was 65. They did have the money that William had given them and decided to keep Jemeya with them They would hire a housekeeper/nanny to help. The times were difficult because America was entering a severe depression and farm land was parched and producing very few crops due to the draught. Life was miserable because of the terrible dust storms. The Porthouses had a number of very good ladies to pick from to work for them. They decided on hiring Jennifer Davidson, the daughter of Mrs. Podrey, the black woman who had befriended Nora.

Jemeya would not pass as a white child. Beth and Jonathon were surprised that Jemeya wasn't even as fair skinned as Nora because they felt strongly that the father was her little white friend. Beth thought that she had read somewhere that a baby couldn't be any darker then her darkest parent. This was obviously not the case with Jemeya, so what she heard was probably false or the father was not Nora's white friend. Beth and Jonathon thought that Jemeya would probably do better if she had a black nanny.

Chapter 25

The Story of Tera II
~daughter of Sudra

In 1935, eighteen years after Tera gave Nora to the Porthouses, she married Turko Kendo's son by his first wife (Sophie), Hussein Kendo. He was born in 1895—the same year as Tera. As a child Hussein was not educated except for what he learned from his father—how to herd, throw spears and a little about the magic of herbs. Hussein had been estranged from his father Turko, since he left home as a teenager.

Hussein had heard many stories about the white man who had come to a village not far from his home. His curiosity took him to this village and when he returned home he was wearing trousers, shirt and shoes. He had discarded the clothes of the village which was only a goatskin around his waist. Even though his father had befriended the white American pharmaceutical representative in 1894, by the time his son had grown up, he had become very distrustful toward the white invaders. They had displaced so many of the tribes in the fertile Highlands.

Hussein had admired what the "white invaders" were able to do with the land and how they could read and write. His whole family ignored him when he returned a different man, so he left the village and went back to Kisumu and worked for a white man who encouraged him to attend school. The white foreigners had opened up a school to educate those in the village. They needed workers in the city of Nairobi, which was developing rapidly since the inception of the 600 mile-long-railway from Mombasa to Lake Victoria.

Hussein stayed in the village of Kisumu for several years and then found his way to Nairobi, where he worked as a house servant for a well known English military advisor. He learned how the white man cooked, his manners and how they ran their homes. Eventually he returned to Kisumu, where he had grown up, but not where he was born. He always felt like he didn't belong there. His father and mother had passed away. He married a woman upon his return, but she failed to produce any children. Because of her inability to have children, he often beat her as was the custom of the Luo men if they felt their wives misbehaved. She ran away to work in Nairobi. It was after his wife ran away that Tera gave him the time of day. Tera was not going to marry a man who had another wife. She had remembered what her mother Sudra had told her about love.

Hussein had become quite westernized and admired Tera for her Western ways. There were few African women who could read and speak English as well as she did or dressed as stylishly. He fell in love with her. She responded to him in the same way, remembering everything her mother had told her about love and tenderness. In 1936, even though she was 41, she gave birth to a son, Otango Kendo . However, in childbirth, she died. Hussein was heartbroken.

Hussein was thankful that he and Tera had produced a child, especially a son. He would keep her close to his heart. Hussein buried Otango's placenta outside their homestead in Kisumu . Later they moved back to Kogelo where most of their relatives lived.

He had great things planned for his son. Hussein had always respected the American culture. He often heard his father, Turko, brag about his friend, William, from America, and how his famous elixir helped his wife produce a son, which was Hussein. So when Tera told him about her American father, he thought it might be William. But Tera always told him it was the other American, but Hussein always hoped it was William. She also told him about Nora, her child that was sent to America. Tera told Hussein that no one knew this story except her, her mother Sudra's lover, the couple who owned the Plantation and maybe William, the other American who traveled to the Plantation with Sudra's lover. When the time was right he would tell his son that he had an American grandfather.

1940

- Radio and club patrons dance to popular singers and musicians, including Rosemary Clooney, Count Basie, Artie Shaw, Bing Crosby, and Cab Calloway.
- **1941**, March Marvel Comics introduces superhero Captain America.
- **1942** Gas rationing limits personal consumption to three gallons per week.
- **1943** Walt Disney wins a Academy Award for his animated short film *Der Fuehrer's Face*.
- **1944**, December 15 Band leader Alton Glenn Miller disappears while enroute to Paris, France.
- **1946** Department stores begin selling Tupperware®.
- **1947** Thirteen stations begin broadcasting commercial television.
- **1948** NASCAR® holds its first modified stock car race in Daytona Beach, FL.

Population 132,122,000
Unemployed in 1940—8,120,000
National Debt $43 Billion
Average Salary $1,299. Teacher's salary $1,441
Minimum Wage $.43 per hour
55% of U.S. homes have indoor plumbing
Antarctica is discovered to be a continent
Life expectancy 68.2 female, 60.8 male
Auto deaths 34,500
Supreme Court decides blacks do have a right to vote
World War II changed the order of world power; the United States and the USSR become super powers
Cold War begins.
Korea was divided—North by USSR, South by US
President Fredlin Roosevelt

Chapter 26

American Hero Perishes

Willkie was a dark horse Republican nominee against Roosevelt who was seeking a third term. In 1940, a young man from Iowa who had won the Heisman Trophy in 1939 introduced Willkie to a group of young Republicans. The young man said,

"When the members of any nation have come to regard their country as nothing more than the plot of ground on which they reside, and their government as a mere organization for providing police or contracting treaties; when they have ceased to entertain any warmer feelings for one another than those which interest or personal friendship or a mere general philanthropy may produce, the moral dissolution of that nation is at hand." *(Iowa Marion Sentinel)*

This young man's impressive credentials and early accomplishments had already gained wide recognition. The Iowa *Marion Sentinel* proposed in an article to endorse a presidential run for this young man in 1956, the first year in which he would be eligible. This young man would also be a good contender for the rising star in the Kennedy family.

He wrote in a letter to a friend: "...someday I would like to meet you as a fellow senator or representative in Washington D.C. Whether this can ever be my lot none can say now."(Hero Perished, Paul Baender)

At that same gathering of the Young Republicans in Iowa Falls, the young man met Celia Peairs, Williams youngest daughter. They became very good friends communicating until his death in 1943. In fact she received the last letter he wrote, arriving just a few days after his fatal plane crash. The politics she followed and all the community work that she did throughout her life were very much aligned with his beliefs. It was as if she was continuing his aspirations. She had moved to Dallas, Texas to be a social worker for the Red Cross a few months after she said goodbye to him on his last furlough before going back to duty.

His life was brief, dying at the age of 24, but he touched everyone in which he came in contact. He became an American Hero. Every year around July 4, the Hawkeye Nation likes to report an article that was in the Sports Illustrated in 1987 entitled: With the Wartime Death of the '39 Heisman Winner, America Lost a Leader. It outlines the character and football accomplishments of a determined young man who was only 5'8" and weighed 170 pounds. His letters and diaries have been chronicled in a book by Paul Biender entitled *A Hero Perished*. And it is his image that is on the coin that is tossed at every All Big Ten games. Each of the players receives one of these coins.

"He was named to every major All-America team. He won the Heisman Trophy, the Maxwell Award and the Walter Camp Trophy. He also won the Chicago Tribune Silver Football Award, given to the Big Ten's Most Valuable Player, by the largest margin to that date. An Associated Press poll picked him as the nation's top male athlete the same year he won the Heisman Trophy. He finished ahead of Joe DiMaggio, who merely hit .381 that year, and Jo Louis, who had KO'd all four challengers for his heavyweight championship…He was first in the balloting for college player in the 1940 College All-Star Game against the Green Bay Packers, and he was on the cover of the game program. In the game itself, on August 29, 1940, he passed for two touchdowns and drop-kicked four extra points in the All-Stars' 45-28 loss to the NFL champions. And with that, his football career came to a sudden end. He never played again."" (Sports Illustrated, 1987) He had important things to accomplish and new challenges to conquer.

His letters reflected his sensitivities and social concerns. It was these concerns that brought Celia and this young man close. She was from Iowa, but had attended Vassar for her BA and the University in Chicago for her MA. She was attending the University at the same time that Saul Alinsky was writing his *Rules for Radicals*. He was working on the continuation of his Chicago experiment of organizing the have-nots of society against the haves, through community organizations. She encountered the same social insight from the professors at the University as Alinsky. She said that "her Chicago training in social service proves invaluable in recognizing problems and needs"; although she did not walk away from that school with the same enthusiasm for radical reform as did Alinsky.

In 1940 Alinsky established the Industrial Areas Foundation (IAF), through which he and his staff helped "organize" communities not only in Chicago but throughout the United States. IAF's national headquarters are located in Chicago, and it has affiliates in the District of Columbia, twenty-one separate states, and three foreign countries (Canada, Germany, and the United Kingdom).

Celia and the young man became Alinsky's nemesis. The social concerns of all three were the same. They lamented the situation of the poor, especially the blacks, but believed that the solution wasn't paternal, but rather self motivation with an emphasis on education, job training and the promotion of the work ethic. Using anger and resentment wasn't in their vocabulary. His many visits to Chicago to see Celia were often used campaigning against those powerful forces in Chicago.

Sadly, it all ended when he joined the military and later died when his plane crashed into the Atlantic Ocean. Years later many questioned whether the plane crash was an accident or planned. Nothing came of those allegations. Many thought he would have been a great contender in the 1960's election. He and John F. Kennedy arose to great prominence at the same time.

Celia moved to Dallas, TX, and began working for the Red Cross a few months after he died. Their future political plans together came to a halt.

Celia continued being an influence in politics, becoming the first Council woman in her area and joining many community organizations.

She was the Executive Director of the Northeastern Indiana Mental Health and Retardation Planning commission and active in the Indiana Council on Crime and Delinquency. She spent summers at the Chautauqua Institute attending the lecture series given by some of America's most prominent scholars. She was truly a "social worker," not only through her education but how she lived her life.

Chapter 27

Willy Arrives at His New Home

Celia's sister Eva and her husband had taken Willy into their home when he was close to a year old. Eva and her husband were just moving to the small town where her husband had been offered a job when they took in Willy. When they moved there, everyone assumed Willy was their son. Adoption wasn't talked about much in those days. In fact many couples who chose to adopt often did not tell their children that they were adopted. Willy's parents, who were Eva's niece and nephew, had come from Sydney, Australia, and were on their way to visit Eva and her husband; however, they were in an automobile accident in route to their house. Willy was in the back seat in his basket and was not injured. The police found Eva's address in the mother's purse and contacted her. The police told them that Willy's parents were killed in that car accident. She knew that both sets of grandparents had already passed away, so Eva contacted her Aunt who lived in Sydney. All of Eva's relatives on her mother's side had continued living in Australia. Catherine, Eva's mother, was the only one who had moved to the United States. She was told by Willy's aunt that Willy's mother had been estranged from the rest of the relatives in Sydney for quite some time, in fact, no one had seen or spoken to her since they disappeared several years ago. She had heard that Willy's family was in the process of moving to the United States. Unfortunately,

Eva had no idea where they might have settled or where their belongings might be stored if they hadn't settled anywhere. The aunt suggested that Eva keep Willy with her until she got back to her. The aunt said she would discuss the situation with the rest of the family.

Nothing seemed to get resolved on the Australian end and time just passed by. Eva and her husband hadn't adopted Willy because of the limbo they were put in by the inaction of the Australian relatives. But by this time they considered Willy their own.

Willy had been a sickly child and had not developed as quickly as the other children his age, so he was kept back and he started school when he was 6 ½. This is when Willy's parents first realized the troubles that would follow Willy if he didn't have a birth certificate or adoption papers. Willy needed his birth certificate. They told the school that they couldn't find it and would have to get back to them after they found it or got a new one. In the mean time they contacted the relatives in Australia to see if they could locate a birth record there. The school never asked them again for his birth certificate.

By the time Willy did enter school, his class mates seemed a little intimidated, possibly because he towered over them, and maybe because he wasn't shy about showing off his ability to read "chapter books," a sure sign of one's intelligence. Willy's mother had spent many hours reading to Willy because he loved it. Soon he began reading to her.

He became the leader of the pack and continued being so for the rest of his life. He wasn't a bully just had a lot of self-confidence. Since Willy lived in a small town in Nebraska with no private schools, he attended a public school, which housed grades K through 12. Most of the students he attended school with were with him through all the grades. Willy was a good student but also full of spunk. His father made sure he was kept engaged in as many sports as he could. Willy and his two younger brothers were always on the same teams and competition between them could at times be rather noisy and rough. Often their father just stuck them in the basement with boxing gloves and told them to work it out. As they got older this rough and tumble relationship turned into great friendship. Willy even looked like the two other boys. Eva always thought that Willy was just like his great uncle George, the young man who had ventured into Australia all alone when he was just 18. Both were curious and adventuresome. Willy never knew any other mother or father.

Willy's father did not have to go to war, but some of his friend's fathers enlisted in the military. He was envious of his friends whose father's had enlisted, especially when they came home and were honored by the town. His Uncle Bill had served in the army fighting in Okinawa and when he returned from the war in 1945 and visited Willy's family, he would sit for hours listening to Uncle Bill's war stories. Uncle Bill always stressed that he had fought for the freedoms that Willy would appreciate as he got older. Those talks with his Uncle Bill had a profound effect on him.

(WWII—Aside 7)

Chapter 28

A Plot Hatched

When the US entered World War II, employment surged and new manufacturing for war materials was very intense. Parents sacrificed their sons. Children sacrificed their fathers. Everyone sacrificed something, family vacations were unheard of, private autos couldn't be updated, even used tires were unavailable as was the gasoline to operate them. And, there were no candy bars on store shelves. Ladies gave up hosiery. Hand me downs were the norm. Shoes were unavailable. Meat, Sugar and oils were strictly rationed and even church bells were turned in at metal drives. Life was a matter of accepted sacrifice and it was all accepted in the name of patriotism.

However, Roosevelt's entering the war did not sit well with many of his followers who were isolationists. J.P was one of these politicians. He was against the U.S. aiding the British. A resentment towards the British followed the O'Mera family. The Irish ties were deeply embedded. It became known that J.P. had gone to Germany to speak with Hitler without State Department approval, to bring about a better understanding between the United States and Germany.

This was the beginning of the end for J.P's political career. He began concentrating on enlarging his wealth, so that his own children could attain the political stature that he was not able to attain.

Because of the wealth J.P. accumulated by his liquor endeavors and money made by pulling out of the stock market before the crash, J.P O'Mera was able to purchase the building in Chicago that at one time was considered the building with the largest number of square feet in the world. This building would provide income for the O'Mera family for many years to come. It wasn't a surprise that J.P. wanted to put down a few roots in Chicago. J.P., as did his father P.J, always had strong ties to the Irish in Chicago. The Irish have consistently held high offices in Chicago politics and they always seemed to be influential in national politics as well. Chicago was the center of American politics. The war had caused a new wave of agitation and differing groups had gathered up momentum with their new ideas. These ideas often surfaced within the higher education system, especially at colleges in Chicago and California and some prestigious colleges. Harvard was also a hotbed of controversial political thought.

Saul Alinsky who had been attending a University in Chicago, had quit during the height of the war because he thought this was a great time to become more involved with his new movement for social justice; his motto was "to think globally, but act locally." He began putting his thoughts into a book called *Thoughts for Radicals*, rules for community activists. Alinsky believed that change needed to "come from outside the government and enter the government like a mole."

During the 1940's, Chicago was also at the center of a national black movement, when African Americans across the country started to see themselves as part of a single culture. There was a rise of black music and a culture that developed around it, and the development of the Associated Negro Press, which allowed the voices of well-known black artists to be heard. One such writer and poet was Fred Davidson, from a small town around Wichita, KS. When he moved to Hawaii in 1948, he was greatly missed. But before he moved he became involved with Saul Alinsky and his community activism. When J.P. lived there the summer of 1945 while purchasing the sky scraper, he went to several of Alinsky's workshops and was very impressed. It was at one of these workshops that J.P met Fred Davidson.

The three, Alinsky, J. P and Fred Davidson, became very good friends, meeting outside the workshops for dinner and drinks. Alinsky talked about his Russian roots and community organizing, Davidson talked about his blackness, and J.P. jokingly told them about his father's love for an African woman and how he fathered a baby girl who had lived in a small village in Kenya. The last he heard she had died in 1936 giving birth to a boy, which would be his father's grandson. He asked both men to honor this secret. But J.P. was most interested in bragging about his son who he hoped would become a prominent politician some day. He asked them if he could have their support. They said "for sure." But they wanted to hear more about his grandfather's indiscretion. This meeting began the "Great American Experiment." Fred Davidson was in charge of making it happen.

It was around that same time, maybe 1946, when a young man defected from his home country of Hungry and ended up in London supporting himself as a porter and waiter while attending the London School of Economics, the same school attended by several of J.P.'s children. He graduated from there in 1952. His name was George Soros. A man whose name everyone would soon come to know.

Chapter 29

No Roots

J.P. was himself out of politics because of his secret visit to Germany, but he worked behind the scenes, just as his father had done when J.P. was first getting into politics. The wealth that both men had created allowed the men in the families to go to the best schools and to become public servants without the need to ever work outside the political world. J.P.'s influence got several of his sons enrolled in the London School of Economics, where they worked with Harold Laski, a leading Jewish intellectual and prominent Socialist. J.P., just like his father, was a socialist democrat, maybe because of their feelings of disenfranchisement because they were Irish. But neither they nor many of the Irish that they grew up with were disenfranchised any longer. Most who were in politics were well-heeled, many becoming so through less than honorable ways. Government aid to the poor often make the givers of aid feel virtuous and self-righteous.

Both men used their wealth and connections to build a national network of supporters that became the base for their sons' political careers—first for J.P, and then for J.P.'s sons. Both concentrated on the Irish American community in large cities, particularly Boston, New York, Chicago, Pittsburgh and several New Jersey cities.

If there was one thing that stood out about J.P. it was his devotion to his family. Where he went, they went; consequently, his youngest son

Theodore frequently was uprooted as a child as his family moved among, Illinois, New York, Massachusetts, Florida and often London; Theodore attended ten different schools by the age of eleven. He spent his intermediate school years at one Preparatory School and spent his four high school years at another; he graduated in 1950. Were there ever any American roots put down? Did he have any friends to play hopscotch or backyard ball? Did he go to camp, singing songs around a campfire, like many other American boys? Had he ever made a smore around that same campfire?

Chapter 30

The Story of Jemeya, II
~daughter of Nora
~granddaughter of Tera
~great granddaughter of Sudra

By the time Jemeya entered school, there were numerous black families in their little town. The black population near and around Wichita was about 15%. The area had grown and since Nora had such a hard time in public school, they decided to send Jemeya to a church boarding school for blacks. Jemeya's nanny, Jennifer Davidson, took her to school on Mondays and picked her up on Friday evening, no one knew that her grandparents were white.

Jennifer had written to her son, Fred, about the sad misfortune of the little girl named Nora that often came to their house every week to work for his grandmother. She mentioned that the young girl had gotten pregnant by some poor white trash who left town, leaving her by herself. But her kind parents helped her through this difficult time only to have their daughter die in child birth. Jennifer said that she had been hired to nanny the child. She had mentioned to her son that she didn't think that the father was white because Jemeya looked like a black baby. But it wasn't any of her business, so she didn't bring it up to the Porthouses. However, they would have to deal with it as Jemeya got older.

In 1940, when Jemeya was going on ten, she had many questions for Beth and Jonathon, one of which was why was her skin so much darker then her mothers. She had seen pictures of her mother who appeared to have light colored skin. Beth and Jonathon told Jemeya something they didn't think was true, but believable. Her mother was raped by a black man one night when she was walking home from a friend's house. From that day forward, Jemeya would consider herself black.

Jemeya accepted Beth and Jonathon's suggestion that she should also go to a private girl's Jr. High boarding school in Wichita. Because of segregation, many blacks did prosper quite well in Wichita. Since blacks couldn't frequent white establishments, black grocery stores flourished; hair salons and clothing stores were established in black neighborhoods, making many blacks very prosperous. There became a wealthy black class. Private schools for black children were established which would cater to these black families. Beth used some of the money that William brought to be used for Jemeya's education.

Jennifer Davidson continued to work for Beth. Her son, Fred, often inquired about Jemeya and how she was doing. He would visit the Porthouses when he was in town. He had been working in Chicago as an associate editor of a Negro newspaper, was involved with the Civil liberties group, and his interest in music intrigued all those who knew him. Jemeya loved to hear him play the piano and sing.

However, in 1948, because his friend had recommended it, Fred went to Hawaii for a vacation and he was received so well, he decided to stay. Because he had become a well-known black writer of books and poetry, he was immediately offered a job at a Hawaiian newspaper. He accepted the offer and contacted his wife telling her how the culture in Hawaii is so different than that of the main land. No one thought twice about mixed marriages. He told his white wife to pack up their things for they were putting down roots in Hawaii. When writing his mother, he always continued to inquire about Jemeya.

Jemeya went on to attend a private black high school. After graduating from high school, Fred got her a job cleaning houses for a white couple who were friends of his from his college days in Wichita. She worked there for a few years, but then decided to go to college. Her contact with

Beth and Jonathon became less and less as she entered the world of her black community. She did come back for Jonathon's funeral in 1949, but she hadn't seen Beth since then.

Jemeya knew that she would need money for college and so she contacted Beth. Beth sent her enough money for 4 years of college. She entered a private black college, majoring in journalism. She had a knack for writing and loved poetry, which she dabbled in occasionally. She was known to frequent black hangouts where she would join others in reading poetry.

Chapter 31

22nd Amendment

Roosevelt ran again for a fourth term in 1944, but died within a year, catapulting Harry Truman into the presidency. This was the first time any president had run for more than two terms. Before it was an unwritten premise that it would be in the best interest of the country that a president served no more than 2 terms and this was evidence that the Founders saw a two-term limit as convention and a bulwark against a monarchy.

So in 1947, the 22nd Amendment was added to the Constitution: "no person shall be elected to the office of the President more than twice, and no person who has held the office of President, or acted as President, for more than two years of a term to which some other person was elected President shall be elected to the office of the President more than once. But this article shall not apply to any person holding the office of President when this article was proposed by the Congress or any person who did not act as President in the term preceding a given election, and shall not prevent any person who may be holding the office of President, or acting as President, during the term within which this article becomes operative from holding the office of President or acting as President during the remainder of such term."

1950's

- **1952, June 25** RCA broadcasts the first color television program.
- **1953,** C.A. Swanson & Sons introduces the "TV dinner."
- **1954** Ernest Hemingway's *The Old Man and the Sea* receives a 1953 Pulitzer Prize. The author is awarded the Nobel Prize in Literature.
- **1954, January 21** The USS Nautilus, the first nuclear submarine, launches.
- **1955, December 1** Rosa Parks refuses to vacate her seat aboard a Montgomery, AL, bus.
- **1957, October 4** CBS debuts *Leave It to Beaver.*
- **1958** Susan Hayward wins the Best Actress Academy Award for the movie, "I Want to Live."
- **1959** Alaska and Hawaii become the 49th and 50th states, respectively, in 1959.

Facts about this decade
Population: 151,684,000 (U.S. Dept. of Commerce, Bureau of the Census)*
Unemployed: 3,288,000
Life expectancy: Women 71.1, men 65.6
Car Sales: 6,665,800
Average Salary: $2,992
Labor Force male/female: 5/2
Cost of a loaf of bread: $0.14
Korean War 1951-1953
Bomb shelter plans, like the government pamphlet *You Can Survive*, become widely available
Truman: 1945-1953, Eisenhower: 1953-1961

Chapter 32

Junior Achievement

After the veterans returned home and women left the work place, after carrying the workload while their men were off to war, employment improved. Families were happy to have their husbands, brothers and sons back home. The business climate was positive, with new businesses starting all of the time. There was a sense of patriotism in communities, schools and business. American Capitalism was at its zenith. An example of this renewal was *Junior Achievement*. This was an organization created to promote the beliefs in:

> *the boundless potential of young people, commitment to the principles of market-based economics and entrepreneurship. passion for what we do and honesty, integrity, and excellence in how we do it, respect for the talents, creativity, perspectives, and backgrounds of all individuals, belief in the power of partnership and collaboration, and conviction in the educational and motivational impact of relevant, hands-on learning. (Junior Achievment.com)*

Its purpose was expressed so well by Theodore Vail, president of AT&T and co founder of Junior Achievement in 1918

"The future of our country depends upon making every individual fully realize the obligations and responsibilities belonging to citizenship. Habits are formed in youth…what we need in this country now…is to teach the growing generations to realize that thrift and economy, coupled with industry, are necessary now as they were in past generations."

Those ideas were just as important in 1946 as they were in 1918 after World War I. When Willy was 15, he joined this organization and was in it all through High School. The tenets of this organization seemed to be a basis of his social and political thought when he entered college in 1953.

On the exact date when Willy turned 15 ½, Willy went down to the license bureau to acquire a learner's permit so that he would be able to get behind the wheel and learn to drive if an adult was in the car with him. However, he had forgotten to bring his birth certificate with him. He called home to see if his mother would bring it to him. After she heard that question, her heart sank. He did not have a birth certificate. They were never able to adopt Willy when they were looking into it when he started kindergarten because the situation hadn't been resolved in Australia. When Willy's mother failed to bring the certificate to school, no one ever asked again. They forgot about it and never inquired. They had also neglected to tell Willy the story or to tell him he was not their biological parents.

When Eva and her husband moved to the town where Willy grew up, Willy was already part of the family. Everyone in town just assumed Willy was their child.

Willy was not able to get his driver's license that day and it was that day that Eva began what turned out to be a very tedious project of getting Willy a birth certificate. There were no records in Australia of his birth. The Nebraska Bureau of statistics gave him a "no record of birth" birth certificate which he could use to acquire a passport and a driver's license. Willy was just happy to get his license. The rest just rolled off his shoulders. However, Eva was now growing suspicious concerning the inaction from the Australian government and the estranged family members of Willy's parents. She was going to pursue this problem and get it settled so that they could get this all behind them so Willy wouldn't have trouble as he got older.

Eva, author's mother

William Allen Peairs

William and native women

Medicine jar

Catherine

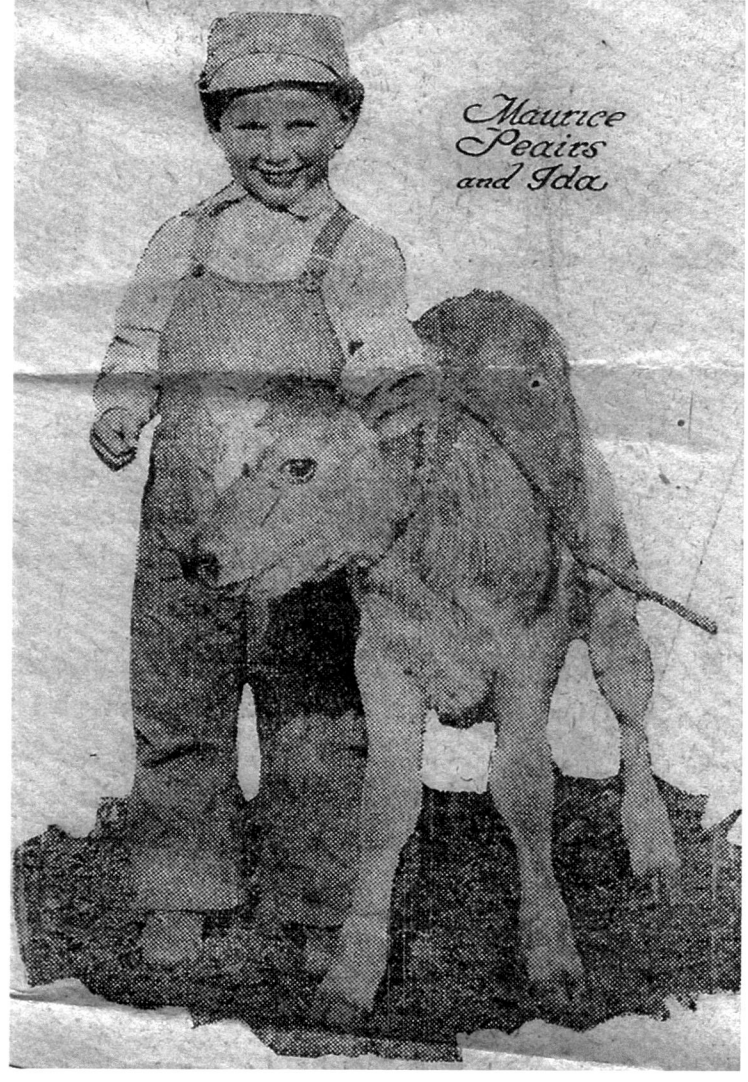

WHAT 'M I OFFERED?

Give Us a Bid — the Bigger the Better — Help Boy Help His Country.

Maurice Peairs and Ida

Maurice and Red Cross calf

Chapter 33

Korean War

Even though World War II had ended, there were still disputes as to how to divide parts of the world, like Korea. Both the US and the USSR wanted to keep their influence in that part of the world. The US wanted the citizens of Korea to vote on the type of rule that would best suit them, but the USSR would have nothing to do with that; consequently, Korea was divided along the 38th parallel, dividing Korea into North and South. In 1950, North Korea invaded South Korea, beginning the Korean War, in which the US participated, ending it quickly with an armistice in 1953, leaving Korea divided as it was before the invasion. There were approximately 36,000 US troops killed and 92,000 wounded. The end of the wars also created a sense of civic duty and responsibility.

In the little town where Willy lived, the adults of the community opened a canteen where young people could hang out with adult supervision, but they also built a small look-out station outside the canteen which students took turns manning. During the 50's, cities and small towns often had black-outs, which were to help prepare citizens for any attacks that might come. Willy got his first dose of "civic duty" helping man these look-out stations.

Willy continued being an excellent student in high school, playing first string football and basketball and often allowing his popularity to misdirect his activities. Luckily these dalliances were minor so that they could be learning experiences and not life threatening. Once in 1953, his father taught him a lesson in humility. When Willy was a senior, he and a few buddies had been out drinking which was against the law as well as against the rules for athletes. When Willy arrived home drunk, his father met him at the door. His father said nothing but sent Willy to bed. The next morning his father met him at breakfast and told Willy that he would go to the coach and tell him what he had done the night before and that Willy would have to deal with the consequences. His father knew that his coach would find out and thought that it would be a better lesson if Willy had to confront the coach alone, without his father or the support of his peers. The consequence was that Willy could not play in the homecoming game and he would not be able to run for Homecoming king. The night of the game, his father made him sit in the front row bleachers. Willy sat through the whole game with his head slightly lowered. He never forgot that night and the lesson he learned from his father—he was responsible for his own actions, and there are consequences for them especially if they are not actions within the law. More importantly, Willy's father would not be rescuing him from any shenanigans.

Willy graduated from high school in 1953 and entered undergraduate school, where he was very active in school politics. He was the leader of the Young Republicans and helped with Eisenhower's campaign. He entered Nebraska University law school after graduating from undergraduate college in Kansas, where he earned a social science degree. Willy had always thought he would join the military after finishing law school, but he got married right out of law school and the Korean War was over. The only war America was in was the Cold War.

After law school, Willy joined a law firm in a small farming community. He became involved in Rotary, his children's sports and was always on the school board. The type of school he attended and his high school math teacher had a great influence on his views about education. He also never forgot the tenets he learned when he was in Junior Achievement.

When fighting for his beliefs, Willy often referred to the school he attended in his small town. There were 25 students per class, the school was a single building housing students from K through twelfth grade, and teachers were usually wives of business owners or wives of government employees. School rooms were not elaborately painted and the books had been used over and over for many years, probably not as up to date as those in the big city, and the inside cover had names of one's brother or sister from years before. At his school there were many dedicated teachers and coaches. One teacher in particular stood out. She was the math teacher for all the students at his high school. It was her goal to make every student that she taught reach his or her potential. Every night you would see her sitting out on her porch with a student, helping them with their math if they were having trouble. Some came with the excuse that they needed help with their math, but were really coming because they wanted to get away from what might be happening in their own home. This teacher made all students feel welcome in her home. Many students at Willy's school often scored in the 90th percentile or above on the math portion of the state required exams. These scores were all the result of a teacher who cared. Where money should be allocated was always a constant argument between members of the school board. Willy always said it should be spent on the teachers; some thought structure; others thought text books and some thought sports. Willy always remembered this teacher, using her as an example as to what really matters in education.

In this same decade, Theodore O'Mera entered Harvard, and played football; however, because he hired someone to take his Spanish language exam, he was expelled. Theodore's father could not come to his son's rescue this time, but Harvard would allow him readmission after two years of proof of constructive behavior. Because Theodore didn't want to get drafted and because he had no working skills, in June of 1951, Theodore enlisted in the Army Intelligence division. However, he was dropped with no explanation. He was then assigned to the honor guard in Paris and with his father's connections he avoided any duty in Korea during the War. Theodore reentered Harvard and graduated in 1956 with a BA in history. Theodore graduated in 1959 with a degree in law from an eastern law school.

In 1957 George Soros immigrated to the United States to use his investment strategies in the American market. He became the arbitrage king of "hedge funds."

Chapter 34

The Story of Tera's Son
~grandson of Sudra

Hussein moved to Kogelo from the village where he and Tera had settled. But she was gone now and he wanted his son to have the best opportunities. When Otango was 12, his father received a considerable sum of money that was to be used for his son's education. It was from an anonymous donor. He assumed it was from Tera's grandfather. Her father would be dead by now.

He was hesitant about moving to Kogelo because he was afraid his son would be thought of as a *jooko* as he got older because of the Luo custom of living where you are most welcome—that being the place you were born. Kogelo seemed more friendly to Western ways and the good missionary schools were established near there.

When he was to enter high school he went to an exclusive Christian boarding school. After Otango finished secondary school, Hussein contacted Tom Minoya, an older classmate of his son's. He told Minoya to let him know if there was ever an opportunity for his son to go to the U.S. to study.

Minoya was born in 1930 and had been educated in the schools of the missionaries as was Otango. And even though Minoya was six years older than Otango, they crossed paths regularly, Hussein made sure of that. Hussein had seen the way Minoya grasped all that was Western. Minoya was of the Luo tribe also. He was from a poor family, but in 1946 he went to the Holy Ghost College where he passed well enough to proceed to do his Cambridge School Certificate. In 1948 Minoya joined the Royal Sanitary Institute's Medical Training School for Sanitary Inspectors at Nairobi, qualifying as an inspector in 1950. In 1955 he received a scholarship from Britain's Trades Union Congress to attend Ruskin College, Oxford, where he studied industrial management. Upon his graduation in 1956, when he was just 26, he returned to Kenya and joined politics at a time when the British government was gaining control over the Mau Mau uprising.

Even though most of the Luo tribe did not participate in the Mau Mau uprising, Hussein had spoken out against the British in this uprising. He was imprisoned for a few months and had always had stories about how he was tortured; however, because of Hussein's proclivity for embellishing almost everything, he was not taken seriously by those in his village. After he returned home, he contacted Minoya again about the possibility of his son going to America.

By 1957 Minoya developed a close relationship with Kwame Nkrumah of Ghana who, like Minoya, was a Pan-Africanist.

Because of his involvement with the movement, Minoya had come to the United States many times. In 1959 he was enthusiastically welcomed at the Civil Rights Movement Rally in Washington DC with Martin Luther King and Baynard Rustin. He was there to get funds for his student airlift program for students from Kenya to attend college in the US.

Chapter 35

Tom Minoya

In 1959, Tom Minoya, Minister of Economic Planning and Development in Kenya had his first airlift of students to America to attend universities. The year before the first airlift, Minoya had contacted some black Americans who might be interested in financing this airlift. Several stepped forward offering their help. The late fifties and early sixties had brought about a black consciousness, a black pride evolved and a connectedness with Black Africa. Many black Americans, such as Harry Bellefonte, Jackie Robinson, Sydney Poitier and Fred Davidson contributed to the African educational fund. Fred Davidson suggested to Minoya that he contact Hussein to see if his son might be interested in attending the University of Hawaii. Minoya was sure he would be interested because Hussein had been inquiring about this for his son.

Minoya contacted his good friend Hussein, telling him that his son was eligible to be part of the airlift. It was at this time that Hussein confided in Minoya about the connection of his son to a famous politician in America. Minoya was quite skeptical of what Hussein had said and shrugged it off as an exaggeration; Hussein was known for his tales. Minoya thus arranged for Hussein's son, Otango to fly to Hawaii and enter the university there. Minoya was hopeful that Otango would then return to Kenya and use what he had learned. He was a disappointment to Minoya. Before the young man had finished his undergraduate work, he impregnated Abigal, the daughter of Fred Davidson's friend, even though he was already married to a woman back in Kenya. He married the pregnant mother, and then divorced her before the child was even two. He married a wealthy women that he had met at Harvard, taking her back to Kenya. Minoya had great hopes for this young man, but his womanizing, drinking and need for the best material accruements kept him from becoming a respected member of Minoya's team. It didn't help either that upon his return to Kenya, the arrogant young man published a paper titled "Problems facing our Socialism," criticizing the plan that Minoya had set forth for the government of Kenya.

Chapter 36

The Story of Jemeya III
~daughter of Nora,
~granddaughter of Tera

When Jemeya was in her last year of college in 1954, she met a young man when she had gone to a Journalism forum at American University the summer before her senior year. He was an Intern for a Democratic Senator from South Carolina. He was at the forum because the topic was "How to avoid prejudices in Journalistic writing." He often was assigned the job of writing Public Relation articles for the Senator who at times was judged to be slightly biased in favor of his white constituents. Jemeya happened to sit next to the young Intern because he arrived late and the seat next to her was the only seat available. This was an open forum with four moderators, two whites and two blacks, directing the discussions. There was an equal number of black and white participants, Jemeya being one of the black participants and the Intern a white participant. Jemeya wasn't shy and often expressed her opinions with great clarity and passion. The intern was also quite passionate about what he believed.

The area that created the most tension between the two was when they were discussing the decision of the U.S. Supreme Court to desegregate public schools that was made this same year. The Intern's premise was that the decision was all well and good, but that the decision would not alter where people lived, went to school or worked and therefore, equality could not be achieved. Jemeya's premise was that it shouldn't matter where one lived, went to school or place of work. Good education could be achieved through good parenting and equal access to good books and good teachers. Success in America could be achieved by everyone by having a good education and embracing Americanism, The Intern was shocked to hear this from a black woman, but was also impressed by Jemeya's confidence in what she was saying. He also thought she was really cute, especially when she was passionate about what she thought. Jemeya didn't like the arrogance of the Intern and when he asked her out to dinner after one forum, she was hesitant to go. She thought why waste her time. But he enticed her to go by inviting her to The Village Gate Jazz Club which was frequented by famous writers from time to time. She couldn't pass up this invitation. That night began the love/hate relationship between Jemeya and the Intern.

Jemeya got pregnant before she could return to school. She did not tell the young Intern because she knew that he might suggest she get an abortion. She knew his career would keep him from marrying a black woman and even if that weren't a problem, he wasn't ready for a wife and child. Abortions were illegal. She had heard that women were getting abortions, but often the conditions were such that many became sterile from the procedure or became sick. This did deter many from getting abortions. But that wasn't Jemeya's reason. She just thought to herself. She wouldn't be here today if Nora had gotten an abortion.

Jemeya had spent all of the money that Beth had given her for college and wrote Beth asking if she might live with her until the baby was born. Beth, who was quite old now and not in good health, was anxious to see Jemeya; she needed to clear up a few things with Jemeya. Having her in the same house for a time would give them a chance to talk.

Beth died before Jemeya came home.

Jemeya came home for Beth's funeral and even though she hadn't really been with Beth since Jonathon's funeral, she felt a real loss, a feeling she didn't know she would have. Why had she left Beth out of her life? Did she feel betrayed because Beth had sent her away. What kind of life would she have had if she had stayed. After the funeral, Jemeya went back to the house which was her's now and began going through Beth's belongings, searching for something, but she didn't know what it was. While she was looking in Beth's desk rummaging through some papers, she noticed a single key attached to a string with a round notation ring. This ring gave the name of the bank and the number of a safety deposit box.

Jemeya went directly to the bank to retrieve the safety deposit box. In the box she found a note written many years ago by Beth to Nora, Jemeya's mother. There was also a book that had an inscription on the inside "Read these poems to guide you through life." Love, Your Grandmother Sudra. There was also an envelope with $125,000 certificates. Jemeya was stunned. Where had all of this money come from? Jemeya put most of the certificates back into the box, except for enough to last her until she had the baby. She would then use some of the money to go back to college.

When Jemeya got home she sat down to read Beth's note that was written to Nora, which Nora never had a chance to see.

"Dear Nora, It is painful for me to write this note to you, because it is probably something that I should have told you many years ago when you were growing up, but as time went by it became harder and harder. Soon your father and I began believing the lie because we loved you so much. As you know, you, your father and I came to America when you were one month old after living on a Plantation outside Nairobi, Kenya. In 1917, after the war started, we felt it would be safer if we left Kenya and came to America to live near your grandparents in Kansas. What we have not told you is that you were born to a woman named Tera, who was the daughter of Sudra, a young woman working for us at the plantation. She was from the Siaya district. Sudra had fallen in love with a man from America who for a short time was a house guest at the plantation. She became with child and he was the father. He was as much in love with her as she was him; however, the time and circumstances were not right for them to be together. The American and Sudra spent each night together that she was at the plantation where he read his books as she followed along. This is how she became fluid in English and learned wonderful things about Western life, especially, the love and tenderness of a man. Sudra returned to her village and raised the child, your mother, as if she were her African husband's.

Sudra named her baby Tera, who was very light skinned. When Tera was 13, her paternal grandfather told Sudra that Tera would marry into the Jo Alego clan, moving to an area several miles from her mother. Tera and I communicated through the missionaries that visited her town and our plantation. When Tera heard that we would be leaving for America, she asked us if we would take you with us. You were a light skinned baby with dark eyes, as was I since I was mainly Italian. Jonathon and I decided that we would say you were our baby born in Kenya. No one questioned this. When you entered school, the children began to taunt you, calling you a "black chilen." You didn't understand why they would call you that when you were white. We should have told you then. We didn't know what good it would do.

After you began going to Mrs. Podery's house, you seemed so much happier and so we decided not to tell you. You seemed so happy whenever Fred, Mrs. Podery's grandson visited; you loved listening to his poetry and stories.

We are sorry that we did not tell you. Your life may have turned out differently if we had. We love you like you were our own. I hope you can forgive us."

Love, Beth

This letter explained a lot that Jemeya had not understood; why her grandparents sent her to an all black school, allowing Jemeya to become part of a black community, something that Nora never had a chance to do. She was not Beth and Jonathon's biological grandchild.

Jemeya had her baby in 1955 and named her Anah. She was born with a round birthmark on the left side of her neck, the same type of mark that Jemeya had, only a little smaller. With the money that was left to her, she hired a nanny for Anah and drove everyday to Wichita to finish her journalism degree. After college she was hired as a columnist for a Wichita newspaper. She became a very successful journalist and authored one book entitled "Nora." It was a novel based on her mother's life, a black child living the life of a white child, but fictionalized it to be a life that lasted more than her 12 years and one where she did not get pregnant and die in childbirth. Jemeya wanted to envision what her mother's life would have been if she had realized that she was black, but continued living with her white adopted parents who obviously loved her very much. It was a best seller.

One day Jemeya received a letter from Hawaii from Fred Davidson, congratulating Jemeya on her novel. Fred had always taken an interest in Jemeya and seemed excited that she had found a career in writing. They continued to correspond, often discussing the multi-diversity of Hawaii and how the diverse society seemed to lack prejudices, but Fred never wrote much about his life in Hawaii.

The money Jemeya made from her novel was put in a trust for Anah to be used for her education when she went to college. Anah was put in very good black schools, but the 1960's were very tumultuous times for blacks. People were encouraging Jemeya to enroll Anah in public schools just to make a point, but Jemeya didn't want Anah to be used for that purpose.

She believed in education and she felt it was her duty to contribute money to black schools, but she always made sure that the money was used for books and reading programs for children whose parents could not read to them at home. Once black children are educated, she honestly felt the world would be open to them. Jemeya tried to keep her political views to herself. She had often been criticized for her comments about the logic behind literacy tests before one could vote. She thought that the person who was educated might vote with their heads and not for those who promised them something in order to get their votes.

1960's

- **1960, May 1** Frances Gary Power's U2 spy plane is shot down over Sverdlovsk, U.S.S.R.
- **1961** Harper Lee's book *To Kill A Mockingbird* is a bestseller.
- **1961** Peace Corps created by Pres. Kennedy
- **1962, October 1** James H. Meredith becomes the first black student to attend the University of Mississippi.
- **1963** Martin Luther King delivers his "I have a dream speech"
- **1963** Pres. John F. Kennedy is assassinated in Dallas, Texas
- **1963** Lyndon Johnson becomes President of the United States
- **1963** Sidney Poitier wins the "Best Actor" Academy Award for *Lilies of the Field.*
- **1964, February 1964** The Beatles make their U.S. debut on *The Ed Sullivan Show.*
- **1965, March** The 9th Marine Expeditionary Brigade arrive in Vietnam on.
- **1966** The National Organization for Women is founded.
- **1967, January 27** Apollo astronauts Virgil Grissom, Edward White, and Roger Chaffee die during a simulated launch exercise.
- **1969, August 1969** Woodstock Music and Art Fair draws more than 450,000 people to Bethel, NY.
- Robert Kennedy and Martin Luther King were assassinated.

FACTS about this decade.
Population 177,830,000
Unemployment 3,852,000
National Debt 286.3 Billion
Average Salary $4,743
Teacher's Salary $5,174
Minimum Wage $1.00
Life Expectancy: Males 66.6 years, Females 73.1 years
Auto deaths 21.3 per 100,000
An estimated 850,000 "war baby" freshmen enter college; emergency living quarters are set up in dorm lounges, hotels and trailer camps.

Chapter 37

Willy Makes a New Friend

Theodore was just biding his time until there was an opening in the Senate. He was overshadowed by his 2 older brothers, who were now prominent politicians. However because of their influence and help from his father, he was elected senator in 1963. J.P. was so proud. He now had 3 sons in politics. J.P. had lost contact with Davidson and Alinksy and thought of the "Great American Experiment" as only a fantasy of three drunken politicians.

By 1964, Willy had become a very successful lawyer and had found his calling. His ability to rally parents, teachers and the community had helped him create a base that would support his nomination for State senator. However, his life would be an open book. His handlers had discovered in their vetting process Willy's "no birth" birth certificate. They felt that this was going to be a problem. Willy knew that his parents had never legally adopted him. His mother had tried for several years to find out why there were no records of Willy's birth. In her search, she had found out that there was a record of his death as well as the death of his parents. Obviously, someone in Australia had notified the authorities of the car accident and death of the three. Willy's parents felt that it was a mistake and that it was just assumed that Willy had also died in the accident. Willy's parents didn't do anything about the death certificate, thinking it probably wasn't any big deal. When his parents looked into adopting Willy, they were told that it might be better if they didn't adopt him. This was the story told to them by the Australian government:

A few years before Willy was born, his parents entered the "Protection Program" and had been relocated to a small town in northern Washington state. Eva was not allowed to know the reason why his biological parents were in the this program. However, after a year in this small town, their true identity had surfaced and the U.S. government who had been aware of their relocation, felt that it would be better for Willy and his parents if they just disappeared. His parents disappeared the night they had the car accident. Willy always wondered if his biological parents were still alive or had they really died in the car accident many years ago. Some day he would look into it.

Willy's handlers never did know the story because Willy withdrew his run for State Senator. But he did become a lobbyist and took his fight against the new educational reforms that were being developed to Washington D.C.

This is where he ended up butting heads with Theodore O'Mera, a senator from Massachusetts. Willy couldn't understand why a person who had the privilege to attend private schools all of his life was so vehemently opposed to giving children of lesser means the same opportunity. Willy was not only lobbying for teacher reform, he was lobbying for a voucher system that would allow students who wanted to attend private schools the ability to do so. He lobbied for congress to pass a bill which would allow federal and state monies, which were ordinarily sent to public schools, be sent to the private school of the student's choice. Theodore campaigned against any legislation that would take monies out of the public school system. Willy understood his concerns, but the teacher union's protection of teachers using the tenure principle, made it impossible to get rid of the bad teachers. Complacency developed in the teaching field. Willy felt the voucher system was a good solution. Competition would be a good thing.

It was during those times in Washington D.C. that he met, John Dickerson, from Dallas, Texas, a young intern for a Texas senator. He shared Willy's enthusiasm for education. Willy got to know John very well. They gravitated toward each other. John was younger than Willy, born in 1943 in Dallas. Willy's wife and children had stayed at home instead of moving to Washington, and he usually went back home on weekends, often taking John with him. He had told Willy that he was adopted, had no siblings and was unmarried. John had searched for his biological mother and father, but nothing had come of his search. He just gave up looking. Willy and John were about the same height and had similar features and people often thought Willy was John's older brother. Willy's children called him Uncle John. After lobbying for education reform for a few years in Washington. D.C. and getting nowhere, Willy returned to his law practice. He continued to stay in touch with John, who had stayed on with the administration because he wanted to test the waters to see if he would fit into the life of a politician.

Chapter 38

Minoya Meets Theodore

Minoya, the Pan Africanist, who had brought several Kenyan men to America to study in 1959, came back to give a speech in Harlem on the African connection between African blacks and American blacks. However, he never got to tell the audience what he was referring to because his speech ended by hecklers throwing eggs at him. He did explain himself in an article which was written before he was assassinated. The article appeared in the *The New York Times Magazine* on July 13, 1969, a few weeks after his assassination. His article entitled "The American Negro Cannot Look To Africa For An Escape," begins by acknowledging the special relationship between Africans and black Americans and the parallels between their respective struggles for independence in Africa and for legal and political equality in the United States. But the nub of his argument points out some crucial separations between African nationalism and black nationalism in America.

"African nationalism," Minoya writes, "is, by its very nature, integrationist, in that its primary objective is to mold numerous tribes into a single political entity." Black nationalism in the United States, on the other hand, had more in common with tribalism than with African nationalism. Minoya recognized how "extraordinarily difficult" it was for a group that had been "an oppressed racial minority" to resist letting a new racial pride degenerate into "a form of racialism." But he saw such nationalism as a dangerous trap for American blacks. The task ahead was clear and should be faced with firm resolve: "Just as the African must reconcile the differences between his tribal and his national identity, so too must the black American realize to the fullest extent his potential as a black man and as an American." Minoya wrote, "American cousins"— that, if the black American can overcome racialism and "merge his blackness with his citizenship as an American…the result will be dignity and liberation."

If there was any African that was well known by many Americans it was Tom Minoya from Kenya.

When Minoya was in the U.S. he called on Theodore, the youngest son of J.P. O'Mera, to give him his condolences about his father's death earlier that year. He also wanted Theodore to look over the article he had written, hoping that it would be printed in the New York Times so that he could assuage his reputation after getting booed when he gave his speech in Harlem. Theodore told Minoya, that he was impressed with his straightforwardness; he had said what many people thought, but he disagreed with him about overcoming their racialism. Theodore thought without black racial tension, white people would become too complacent if the guilt was lifted. Racial tension is needed to stir up the movement if it was going to succeed. Minoya disagreed.

Minoya had mentioned how much good Theodore's grandfather's educational fund had done in that little town in Kenya, where he traveled in 1894. Theodore wasn't aware that his grandfather had taken a trip to Africa in 1894. His father had never told him about his grandfather's trip to Africa in 1894. But it did explain why his father made it clear in his will that the educational fund that Theodore's grandfather had started be continued. Minoya and Theodore hit it off and continued to see each other while Minoya was visiting, dining and drinking and discussing politics. Minoya told Theodore about the story that Hussein had told him. Hussein Kendo's son was the grandson of a well-known American and joked that maybe it was Theodore's grandfather that Hussein was referring to. Minoya started to explain how the Educational fund worked and how much good it had done, but Theodore seemed more interested in hearing about his grandfather's travels and indiscretions in Kenya then hearing about the Kenyan Educational Fund.

Four months after his visit to the US and his visit with Theodore O'Mera, Minoya was assassinated in Kenya, July 5, 1969; his car blew up as he started his engine, after he was seen arguing with a young man outside his car. This young man who was a friend and an associate of Minoya's testified at the inquiry that took place in the latter part of 1970; however, because of the several threats on this man's life, he left the country in 1971 on a vacation to Hawaii.

Twelve days after Minoya's death, Theodore O'Mera, felt like celebrating and decided to attend a staff party at the Hotel De Franco in New York. Unfortunately, a woman staffer, who was attending the party fell off the balcony and died. It was later learned that Theodore had been alone with this woman in the hotel room. He had left before the police arrived, but several people at the party reported that they saw him entering the woman's hotel room around the time of the incident. He was exonerated of any misdoing because of the alcohol level of the victim. But the investigation showed that he was negligent in leaving the crime. His colleagues were disappointed in him because of the incident and his lack of remorse; he thought he would have little chance of advancing his career. Theodore laid low for the next several years.

William joined his friend John Dickerson in the campaign for Nixon in 1969. John was becoming a force in the Republican party. If it hadn't been for his lenient views on immigration and a few other minor issues, he would have been elected Chairman of the Republican national Committee. The Anti-Abortion group were his best supporters. In this group were many adoptees. He had very stern words for those who supported late-term abortions.

On December 29, 1969, John Dickerson married Anna Dubary, an intern from Iowa. John continued working in Washington D.C., but now had become a speech writer for a prominent Senator from Iowa.

Chapter 39

The Story of Anah
~daughter of Jemeya
~granddaughter of Nora
~great granddaughter of Tera
~great, great granddaughter of Sudra

Anah was born August 4, 1955. She was the product of her mother's affair with a white man which occurred the summer of her third year in college. Her mother moved back to where she was born in order to have Anah; her mother had not been home since her father's death in 1949. By the time Jemeya returned home, Beth had died. She had left some money for Anah's mother which allowed her to finish her schooling and to hire a nanny for Anah when she was gone from early morning to late at night driving to Wichita every day, getting her masters and Phd. in journalism and then working at the Journal.

In 1960 Anah started kindergarten in an all black school several miles from her home. Her life was very uneventful, in fact a little boring for Anah. She just went to school every day and her nanny picked her up after school. She didn't have any friends in the neighborhood. She and her mother were still living in Beth's house.

By 1967 when Anah entered middle school, her grades had gone from getting A's to getting C's and sometimes D's. Out of defiance, she often skipped school to attend black rallies that were being encouraged by some members of their school. Anah's focus was influenced by her peers. And Jemeya was not home enough to have a major influence in her daughter's life. All Anah saw was her mother working hard and not finding enough time for her. Jemeya didn't want Anah's life to be consumed with riots and anger, she wanted her daughter to concentrate on her studies. So when Anah was 13 and was invited to go to Hawaii to live with Fred Davidson and his wife, she accepted his invitation. Jemeya wasn't able to go with her because she was going to enter the hospital to have some cysts removed from her kidney

Because of Hawaii's diverse culture, Jemeya's friend Fred Davidson, had stayed in Hawaii to live after going there on a vacation. He was one of the blacks who seemed to have prospered, he was a well-known black journalist and poet, but he was also one who believed in social justice for the blacks, and attended many socialist/communist groups while in Chicago, maybe not as a member, but working for their agenda. When he was in Chicago he had read the book *Reveille for Radicals by Saul* Alinsky, which was a book to show how community organizers set up in black neighborhoods could promote their social agendas. He had become a friend of Alinksy's. In the 40's this was a hard agenda to push in Chicago. Fred visited Hawaii in 1948, at the suggestion of an activist friend from his Chicago days. After he was hailed for his writings by the Hawaiian media, he decided to stay. He also realized that Hawaii had the perfect atmosphere for the "American Experiment." He was ready to go to the next step.

When Anah reached Hawaii in 1968, she was welcomed by Fred Davidson; however, it was obvious that his wife was not pleased with the situation.

The fall of 1968, Fred enrolled Anah into the best middle school in Hawaii. The public schools were very diverse and he knew that Anah would fit right in. Anah did well in school and often wrote home to tell her mother how much she liked it in Hawaii. She did mention to her mother that Fred and his wife were heavy drinkers and partied a lot, but that it didn't affect her. She would go to her room to get away from all the noise.

The Story of Jemeya IV
~daughter of Nora

The Civil Rights movement which had started many years ago by now was a national movement. Because Jemeya was a known figure in journalism, the movement was encouraging her to have a more active voice. Jemeya did not participate in this movement. Because her grandparents were white and because of the money left to her, she had always had the luxury of belonging to the "upper segment of black society" where blacks had prospered, going to good schools and becoming doctors, lawyers, journalists and professors. Jemeya realized this was not the majority of blacks, but she was also of the belief that in order for blacks to advance themselves they needed to take advantage of the education that was offered to them. She often thought about those in slavery who had gone behind closed doors just to learn how to read and educate themselves without the benefit of freshly painted classrooms. These were the people who eventually had set up shops in black neighborhoods and had prospered.

Jemeya's hero was Booker T. Washington, who called on black Americans to work hard to improve their educational and economic status, in order to more fully participate in the American political process. Because it was illegal for slaves to be educated before 1865, he wrote:

"I had the feeling that to get into a schoolhouse and study would be about the same as getting into paradise."

It was soon after Anah turned 13 that Fred Davidson suggested to Jemeya that the two of them move to Hawaii. Jemeya was ready for the two of them to take a trip to Hawaii to see if they might like living there, but Jemeya was hospitalized for a kidney disease that she had had for several years. She knew that she had a kidney disease and that some day, she would probably need to have dialysis and the doctors recommended that she stay in the states. Fred said that he and his wife could take care of Anah until she was through high school and then she could return to the states when the times may not be as tumultuous. Jemeya hated sending Anah to Hawaii, but knew that Anah was in need of some structure. She had worked all of Anah's life, leaving her home with a nanny and then sending her off to school. She was a teenager now and a more accepting society is maybe what she would need.

In this same letter Fred told Jemeya, in great length, about the Dunbar family that had moved to Hawaii in the early sixties. This was the same family that Jemeya had worked for before she took off for college. Fred had gotten Jemeya this job. He and Sal Dunbar had been acquaintances when he went to college in Kansas City. He now considered him a very good friend. He mentioned the Dunbar daughter named Abigale, who was attending Hawaii University, majoring in Archeology. Fred told Jemeya that she would enjoy this young women. She was a free spirit, participating in Union demonstrations, rallying for black rights and calling for legalizing abortions for women. Jemeya felt that Fred Davidson didn't know her very well. These were not necessarily the issues that she would be supporting. Fred also pointed out to Jemeya that this family would also be a contact for Anah. After reading this letter from Fred, she began to have second thoughts about sending her daughter to live with him. But which alternative would be the best for Anah, staying in America with all its bitterness and killings or going to Hawaii to live with Fred, who might have differing views then she had. It would only be a few years. She thought at least Anah would be safe there.

Jemeya continued as a columnist and advanced to become assistant editor of the Wichita Journal. She had a weekly column writing about things that pertained to both the black and white reader.

Her columns were almost poetic. Her topics were always about things that might be troubling to both blacks and whites, but she never wrote about things that would pit one race against the other. She had a knack for using analogies instead of specifics in her articles. People could then see an "ah ah" moment when reading her articles. "An unsharpened pencil is like a talent undeveloped: "Life is like a dream. We get so caught up in 'our lives,' that when the situation changes greatly, our bubble is burst." (http://teacher2b.com/non-fiction/analogies.htm)

Jemeya never took sides but always painted a picture of different points of view. Her columns became very popular and she was approached by groups on both sides of the racial issue to speak. When asked to speak, she always referred to the lack of education and parental influence as the reason for poverty and discontent. She refused to allow race to lead to a "victim" mentality.

1970's

FACTS about this decade.
Population: 204,879,000
Unemployed in 1970: 4,088,000
National Debt: $382 billion
Average salary: $7,564
Food prices: milk, 33 cents a qt.; bread, 24 cents a loaf; round steak, $1.30 a pound
Life Expectancy: Male, 67.1; Female, 74.8

IMPORTANT HISTORICAL AND CULTURAL EVENTS that set the tone for the 70's. A turning point in American culture. Many 60's radicals had entered the college system as professors.

- **22 April 1970** First "Earth Day" celebrated as environmental movement launched.
- **4 May 1970** Four students killed when National Guardsmen opened fire during anti-war demonstrations at Kent State University in Ohio.
- **28 June 1970** First Gay Pride march held in New York City commemorating the first anniversary of the Stonewall Rebellion, considered to be the beginning of the modern GLBT movement.
- **24 April 1971** Huge anti-war march in Washington, D.C.
- **1971** Daniel Ellsberg leaks the Pentagon Papers, massive collection of top-secret government documents, whose publication helps to discredit the Vietnam War policies of the Nixon administration.
- **17 May 1972** Republican agents burglarize Democratic headquarters at Watergate.
- **29 May 1972** Strategic Arms Limitation Treaty (SALT I) signed by U.S. & Soviets.
- **5,6 September 1972** Nineteen killed in terrorist siege at Munich Olympic Games
- **1973** Arab oil embargo causes severe shortage and energy prices skyrocket

- **22 January 1973** Roe v. Wade Supreme Court decision legalizes abortion
- **10 October 1973** Amid charges of corruption and scandal, VP Spiro Agnew pleads no contest to income tax evasion and resigns from office.
- **6 December 1973** Gerald Ford, congressman from Michigan, becomes the new vice president.
- **1974** Economy in worst recession in 40 years.
- **9 August 1974** Ford becomes the thirty-eighth president after Richard Nixon, facing impeachment charges, is forced to resign.
- **1975**—United Nations declares International Year of the Woman.
- **30 April 1975**—South Vietnam falls to Communist forces of North Vietnam.
- **4 July 1976**—The country commemorates the 200th anniversary of the Declaration of Independence with a spectacular bicentennial celebration.
- **1978**—Residents of Love Canal, NY, evacuated due to dangerous toxic chemicals buried in the area.
- **19 November 1978.**—American religious cult leader Jim Jones and 900 People's Temple followers die in mass suicide in Jonestown, Guyana.
- **28 March 1979**—Radioactive leak at Three Mile Island nuclear power plant.
- **4 November 1979**—Iranian militant students seize the U.S. embassy in Tehran capturing 66 hostages and setting off an intense standoff that lasted 444-days.

PEOPLE

Cesar Chavez—Organized farm workers to demand higher wages, health insurance, and other benefits for migrant workers in California.

Shirley Chisholm—First African-American woman elected to the U.S. House of Representatives; ran for the office of President of the United States in 1972.

Patty Hearst—Granddaughter of newspaper mogul, William Randolph Hearst, kidnapped by the SLA, and subsequently participated with the SLA in an armed robbery of a San Francisco bank.

Jesse Jackson—A leader in the civil rights movement who founded PUSH (People United to Save Humanity) in 1971.

George McGovern—The senator from South Dakota who was the Democratic Party nominee for President in 1972.

Karen Silkwood—An employee of the Kerr-McGee nuclear processing plant who was killed in a car crash on the way to a meeting with a New York Times reporter to reveal evidence of unsafe and illegal practices at the nuclear plant.

Benjamin Spock—A pediatrician, author, and social reformer whose permissive philosophy in his influential book, The Common Sense Book of Baby and Child Care, was blamed for a wide range of social problems in the 1970's.

George Wallace—Governor of Alabama; shot and paralyzed from the waist down while campaigning for the presidency in 1972 on an anti-bussing, law and order platform.

Andrew Young—First African-American voted into the U.S. House of Representatives from the deep South since 1898

Wade Rathe—Founder of ACORN. enlisted civil rights workers and trained them in a program (at Syracuse University) patterned after Saul Alinsky's activist tactics.

Nixon, Ford and Carter were presidents.

Chapter 40

Theodore Takes Two Trips

In the 70's Theodore took on some heavy issues. Ireland and the British had always been at odds; the Catholics vs the Protestants. It was coming to a head again in the 70's. Theodore, just like his father J.P., had animosity for the British and compared what was happening in Northern Ireland to Vietnam and the United States. Theodore sided with the socialist democrats or the SDLP, which was formed in the 1970's and which were part of a larger group called the Party of European Socialists. The SDLP was first and foremost a party representing Catholic interests, with voters concentrated in rural areas and the professional classes, rather than a vehicle for Irish nationalism. They were interested in a social democracy. Theodore O'Mera was their greatest American supporter.

In 1971 to get away from those who were constantly criticizing him, Theodore took a short vacation to Hawaii and then went on a 10 day trip on a safari in Kenya. But when he returned, he was a different man, all geared up to begin again on the issues that were important to him. One of which was his lifelong campaign for National Health Insurance, but the President at that time butted heads with Theodore over the cost of his program. Many still were bitter towards him for his role in the death of the young girl in New York. Many had lost a great deal of respect for him. He got very little support from his colleagues. They were up for reelection and enough time hadn't passed since Theodore's indiscretion. Much of the public were sickened at the lack of his remorse or punishment—besides there was already enough pork in the President's programs.

Chapter 41

The Story of Anah II
~daughter of Jemeya
~granddaughter of Nora

Anah wrote her mother about the fun she would have when she and Fred would often go to a park where she would play with this younger little boy, Otango, who was at the park with his grandfather, who was white. You could tell that the little boy was part white because he was so light skinned. His grandmother and grandfather had come from Kansas, around the area where Fred Davidson had also grown up.

She met the little boy when he had just returned from Indonesia where he had been living for several years with his mother and her husband. Fred had told Anah that it was the little boy's father that had advised his mother to return him to the United States. His father met him at the airport when he arrived. His father went back home a few weeks later. That is how he came to live with his grandparents.

Anah wrote to her mother that she had visited Otango's home once with Fred Davidson and it was rather messy with many magazines lying around, dishes that hadn't been washed and a smoky smell caused by the heavy cigarette smoking by the boy's grandfather. She overheard Fred Davidson and the little boy's grandfather discussing the little boy's mother. His grandfather had been drinking. He was arguing with Fred and blaming him for the rift between his daughter and himself. She had wanted an abortion when she found out that she was pregnant, but Fred had convinced his friend that she should not have an abortion. He pointed out to his friend that abortions were illegal and stressed that he wouldn't regret encouraging her to keep the baby.

Abigale, the boy's mother, was planning on attending the University of Washington with her friends from High School. She and her parents had moved to Hawaii right after graduation. She did not want this baby. However, her father insisted she marry the father of her child and keep the baby. She ended up dragging the baby to Washington with her. Her husband stayed back in Hawaii to finish his degree. Abigale had always told her friends that she never really wanted to get married or have children. So when she appeared in Seattle with a child, they were quite surprised. She stayed for only a short time. Having trouble as a single mother, she returned to Hawaii, got a divorce from the baby's father and managed to finish her degree in Archeology with the help of Fred and her parents. She never used her degree during those drifting years.

She became an atheist and dabbled in crafts which seemed to be the career path of many who were part of the hippie generation. Her specialty was weaving. She married an Indonesian, and when he wanted to return to his home country, being the free spirit that she was, she followed. She tried to get her parents to take care of her son, but they said that the boy was her responsibility. She angrily left the house and didn't speak to them again until after she heard from the boy's father, who instructed her to return their son to the states. Otango's father would go to the states and get him settled with her grandparents. Fred Davidson encouraged his friend into taking the boy in upon his return to the states. In fact he tried to get him to take the boy in before Abigale left. But he had already listened to Fred about Abigale's right to an abortion. He was not going to pick up those pieces. Her anger with her father subsided somewhat when he offered to let the little boy return and live with them.

Anah wrote her mother asking her what she thought about women having abortions.

Jameya had written back to Anah telling her that she really didn't approve of abortions. She wrote that it was probably because if Beth had encouraged Jemeya's mother to get an abortion, she wouldn't be here and if she had gotten an abortion, Anah wouldn't be here. But everyone has their opinions and she wasn't one to judge.

Jemeya inquired more about Fred and his friend's family. She encouraged Anah to keep her informed of what went on and if she had any questions, she shouldn't hesitate to write her.

Anah was 6 years older than the little boy, who had a funny name, Otango. They shared the same birthday. He often joked with her about the red doodle on her neck. Anah had told him it was a birthmark, so that if she got lost her mother would be able to recognize her. Otango commented that his father also had a birth mark, but it was a large red patch, starting at the base of his chin, winding half way down his neck. He was proud that he was named after his father.

When they were at the park, Anah played with him while Fred and the white man talked. Anah wrote her mother that the two would get in rather heated discussions, but she wasn't really interested, so she didn't know what they were talking about.

Sometimes the little boy would come over to the Davidson's and they would hang out together. Fred would read Otango his poetry or discuss "blackness." In a letter, Anah asked her mother if it was true that she would never fit into a white society. She heard Fred tell Otango that no matter how we try by going to a white man's school, doing white man's work, and using white man's speech, we will always be looked at as black. Jemeya wrote back to Anah asking her what was wrong with being looked at as black. What did that mean?

Soon after Anah met Otango, a black man came to the park with Otango and his white grandfather. She remembered the day because it was her birthday, August 4, the same as Otango's. The man was Otango's father who had been divorced from his mother when the little boy was barely two. He had been named after his father and even though Otango hadn't seen his father for quite some time, Anah could tell that the little boy adored him. He was proud to be Otango Jr. She remembered that when Otango's father was around, he would have nothing to do with her. Otango's father joined them at the park several times, then one day a man from the mainland joined them. Fred always called the other states, the mainland. Anah and Otango Jr. played for a long time that day.

Jemeya got a letter at least every other week from Anah. She missed her mother very much, mainly because Fred's wife had a grudge against Anah and she didn't know why. She tried very hard to make Fred's wife like her.

That same year, 1971, Anah experienced something that would change her life. It was October 31. Anah had been out trick-or-treating earlier in the evening. Fred and his wife had one of their parties and invited several men and she thought she heard Otango's father. Anah had gone to bed as she always did when the Davidson's had their party and she had trouble falling asleep because she could hear their loud voices booming all the way in her room. The more they drank, the louder they became and the discussions became more heated. She heard them throwing around insults against the continental U.S. Her mother had always taught her to respect America. Anah's mother's belief was that in time, as blacks became educated, they would not be discriminated against. Anah, at times, had a hard time believing all that her mother was saying, but she had never felt the anger that these men felt that night. Around 1:00 A.M., all of the people had left but Fred and one other man, whom she thought was Otango's father. They were about as inebriated as one could get without passing out. As they came upstairs to go to bed, Fred's wife, who had also been involved in the heated discussions and who had drunk as much as Fred, taunted Fred to have a little fun with Anah. She heard Fred's wife say to Fred that she dared him and the other man to have a little threesome with Anah. She accused Fred of being this little girl's grandfather. She wanted to know why was it so important that she had come to live with them and why had he been so involved with Jemeya all of these years. She wanted him to prove to her that she was wrong. After all Anah was just like all of the other young girls they had often picked up to bring home to their parties. It was dark when the two men entered Anah's room.

Fred and his wife had told Anah that what she thought happened to her was only a dream. She must have heard them outside her door talking about an incident that had happened to a young acquaintance of theirs and that because she was half asleep, she must have dreamed the rest. However, when she found out that she was pregnant, she knew it was not a dream. She confronted Fred and his wife. Anah said she was going to tell her mother. They told Anah her mother would never believe such a story. They immediately sent a letter to Jemeya hoping to get to her before Anah.

Fred wrote to Jemeya that Anah had gotten pregnant by some boy she barely knew and they thought it would be best for Jemeya if Anah had an abortion. And if that wasn't an option they could put the baby up for adoption. Jemeya would have nothing to do with either an abortion or adoption. After the baby was born, she wanted Anah and the baby to return to the states to be with her.

Fred sent Anah to a home for unwed mothers. He knew a lot about these places where many girls were sent when they were pregnant and the families didn't want their daughter exposed to the type of chastisement that came with becoming pregnant out of wedlock. He was a proponent of abortions and was involved with the new movement to make abortions legal. He often had young students picket in front of these homes for unwed mothers, garnering coverage for pro-abortion supporters. Abigal's father questioned Fred why he was so concerned about Abigale keeping her baby when he fought for other girl's rights. He said that Abigale's plight was different. He left it at that.

Jemeya's health had not gotten any better by the time Anah had her baby, a girl she named Bella. Fred had agreed that maybe Anah could live with a family that he knew until Jemeya got better and then she and the baby could go back to Kansas. Anah was so distraught and wanted nothing to do with Fred Davidson or his friends, but the couple showed true concern about Anah and so she agreed to stay until she could go back to the mainland. They returned home in 1974, when Bella was 2.

Anah continued to live with Jemeya taking care of her daughter Bella. Anah was privileged to be able to stay home while Jemeya would care for them both, but Jemeya insisted that Anah finish high school. Jemeya was happy to have them living with her and she wanted to make up to Anah for the terrible things that had happened to her because she had sent her to live in Hawaii with Fred Davidson.

Chapter 42

The Story of Bella
~daughter of Anah,
~granddaughter of Jemeya,
~great granddaughter of Nora,
~great, great granddaughter of Tera
~great, great, great granddaughter of Sudra

Bella was born April 5, 1972, at the Catholic Home for unwed mothers and later she and her mother moved into the home of Fred's friends, the Jordans. Fred had told them the same version he had told Jemeya. He had told the Jordans what Jemeya had decided—Anah would keep the baby and return home as soon as Jemeya had gotten better. As soon as Anah's mother recuperated, she would be going back to the mainland. Anah and Bella moved in with the Jordan's and lived with them for the next two years.

Anah and Bella returned to the United States in 1974, when Bella was 2. Jemeya's health continued to improve after her kidney operation. The doctors reassured Jemeya that as long as the cysts didn't return, she could lead a normal life. She went back to work. She encouraged Anah to go to college after she finished high school, but Anah informed Jemeya she would hear nothing more about college. She wanted to stay home to take care of Bella. Anah knew how lonely she was when her mother had been gone so much. She didn't want Bella to feel as lost and lonely as she had.

Times were changing for blacks in America. Schools were no longer segregated. However, it did not change the anger that so many blacks still had. They thought the new Civil Rights Act would change their lives over night. But Jemeya knew that until many blacks realized that education would be their ticket to a life without so much anger, there would be much discontent in the black community. She never thought it was just the black community that was angry, it also came from whites who lived in poverty. Education brought a good job and with a good job brought home ownership and with home ownership brought a community and a community brought good family values and the cycle would begin all over again. Jemeya didn't want to break the cycle that she had started for her future generations. But Anah insisted that she would go to college after Bella had grown. And she would make sure that Bella would get a college education. She wanted to keep Bella from the hurt that she and her mother had experienced. Jemeya said that she had never felt betrayed. It was her decision to keep Anah's birth from her father. She said that when she began thinking about telling Anah about her father, he was reported missing in Vietnam. Anah told Jemeya that maybe someday she would learn more about her father's family, but maybe the time wasn't right just yet.

Anah had told her mother about what had happened the night she was raped by both Fred Davidson and a man she believed was also her friend Otango's father from Kenya. Jemeya couldn't believe her ears. Jemeya had always suspected that maybe Fred Davidson was her father and that he may have suspected the same himself. It just didn't seem like he would rape his own granddaughter. Anah told Jemeya that she had overheard the dare that his wife had made to him and that he was in such a drunken stupor he may have lost all comprehension of who it was and what he was doing. For this seemed a common practice for both he and his wife at many of their parties. Jemeya was beside herself. It was because of her that Anah had an experience that ruined the rest of her life.

Anah told Jemeya that both of them needed to get beyond the hurt and concentrate on Bella's life. How would they tell Bella and what would the knowledge do to her? They both agreed that they would tell her the truth when she asked and hoped that it would be when she was the age that she could understand. It worried Jemeya and Anah that Bella would not be able to understand what love between a man and a women would look like. Sudra learned it from Beth and Jonathon. Tera had learned of it through Sudra. Nora never had the chance. And Jemeya had experienced it, but only for a short time. And Anah saw love through the distorted relationship of Fred and his wife. Jemeya remembered the book that she had found in the safety deposit box where Beth had stored things to give to Nora. She had not read the book of poems by Elizabeth Barrett Browning, but maybe now might be the time. She went to the safety deposit box and brought the book home for Bella.

Jemeya continued to work as a journalist, supporting Anah and Bella. Anah stayed home, helping Bella with her school work and encouraging her with her music, for she had shown an interest in music at a young age. Jemeya had kept the piano that Beth had left in the house. Because Jemeya had always been shipped off to boarding schools, she was never encouraged to pursue music, even though she loved listening to Fred when he visited. Thinking of Fred disgusted her.

By the time Bella entered primary school, she was reading very well and playing the piano like a professional, at least a young professional. Anah read to Bella every night before she went to bed. She attended meetings at her church for single parents. She was determined to be a good parent.

The 70's were a trying time. Many of the books published in the 70's revolved around a general theme of man's alienation from his spiritual roots. But nothing in these books could compare to what had transpired in the lives of Nora, Jemeya and Anah. The times of the 70's were not going to influence Bella. Anah was going to make sure of that. The church she belonged to was a safe haven for parents who wanted to bring up their children outside the moral decay they found around them. She was not going to be angry; she was going to move forward, showing Bella the beauty that could be found in nature and most of all in books and poetry. She read Elizabeth Barrett's poems to Bella so much that as Bella got older she could repeat many of them by heart. Anah had also instilled in Bella a curiosity that gave her a love for learning, but in the end, it kept her from experiencing the friendship of others. Bella retreated into her books and music.

1980's

- **1980** The U.S. hockey team stuns the world by winning the gold medal during the Winter Olympics.
- **1981, August 1** MTV airs its first music video ("Video Killed the Radio Star").
- **1981** Sandra Day O'Connor becomes first woman on U.S. Supreme Court.
- **1984** Apple Computer® launches its Macintosh computer.
- **1986** The Space Shuttle Challenger explodes 74 seconds after liftoff.
- **1986** Chris Van Allsburg's *The Polar Express* wins the Caldecott Award.
- **1987, October 19** The stock market loses 22.6 percent of its value on "Black Monday."
- ***1989*** *Driving Miss Daisy* wins the Academy Award for "Best Picture."
- **1989** The Berlin Wall came down

FACTS about this decade.
Population: 226,546,000
Unemployed in 1980:
National Debt: 1980—$914,000,000,000   National Debt: 1986—$2,000,000,000,000
Average salary: $15,757
Life Expectancy: Male 69.9 Female 77.6
Minimum Wage: $3.10
BMW was $12,000; Mercedes 280 E was $14,800
Attendance: Movies 20 million/week
Presdients: Jimmy Carter and Ronald Reagan

Chapter 43

Celia

In 1987, during a more friendly administration, Willy returned to Washington D.C. to continue his lobbying. This time he wanted to push his agenda of teacher reform. People were growing weary of all the educational reforms and were in favor of approaching education by reforming the way teachers were hired. Enough money had been spent on revamping math and reading programs, never achieving any improvements and the history books were being rewritten all too often. Willy found that change was not going to be easy. Dealing with the teacher's unions would be his most challenging obstacle.

That same year, his aunt Celia, who was a retired politician from Indiana invited him to attend a summer lecture at the Chautauqua Institute in lower New York state. Upon returning from Dallas, Texas, in 1946, to Des Moines, Iowa, Celia married a man from Indiana. That is how she ended up spending most of her married life there.

This Chautauqua institute has been a place of intellectual pursuits since the last part of the 19th century. Famous people from all over came there to give lectures; discussions evolve around these lectures with audience participation. Celia had been going to Chautauqua for years and owned a condo there. She had invited any member of her family to come during those summer lectures; Willy was the first to accept her invitation.

He took John Dickerson and John's 18 year old son, Tommy, with him. After John married in 1969, he and his wife decided to make their home in Des Moines, Iowa. She had been born and raised there. His adoptive parents had died soon after he married in a tragic fire in their home in Dallas, Texas. Since John had no siblings, he felt that his wife's family was his family and settling in Des Moines near them was the logical thing to do, especially if he would be in Washington a good deal of the time. He was now working as an educational advisor to President Reagan. He was the inside man, passing on suggestions coming from his good friend Willy, the educational lobbyist. His son would be entering the University of Iowa on a football scholarship in September.

The fall of the Berlin Wall was the theme for the week that Willy and John were there. The vice President was the guest speaker. It was a wonderful experience for both of them. It was also a welcomed opportunity that Willy got to know his Aunt. He hadn't seen her since he was a young boy. Since she was so nice to open her home to them, Willy and John decided they should spend as much time with Celia as they could. Celia was quite interested in hearing all about John Dickerson and his son. Willy felt a little left out of the conversation and excused himself around 11p.m. Celia, John and Tommy continued talking until early morning. Since Celia had been born and grew up in Des Moines, they had a lot to talk about. She commented to John and Tommy that she had a brother named Tommy who died from meningitis when he was twelve. She mentioned to Tommy that she had a really good friend who also played football in Iowa and had won the Heisman trophy in 1939, but he had died off the Gulf of Paria in Venezuela in World War II. Tommy asked Celia if it was Nile Kinnick. Tommy was excited that she had known Nile Kinnick. He wanted to hear more, but Celia thought it was late and time to call it a night

Chapter 44

The Story of Anah III
~daughter of Jemeya
~granddaughter of Nora

In the summer of 1980, Anah came down with the same symptoms that her mother had in her early life. She assumed it was the same disease, but now there were medications that she could take that would shrink the cysts that formed on the kidneys; however, it had not been in existence long enough to know for how long a person could take the drug. Anah was part of the group using the experimental drug. It seemed like the drug was working as Anah's chronic kidney infections seemed to occur less often.

In 1982, when Bella was only 11, Bella's teacher applied to the school of music at the prestigious Julliard School in New York City to enroll Bella in their children's summer program. The school offered dormitories for their students, but Anah was afraid to have Bella in New York by herself. Bella had never really developed many friendships at school; she was too busy with her music. Sending her off to live with other girls her age seemed like a cruel idea. Unfortunately, she hadn't acquired the social skills she might need living with girls her age. It was as if Bella had skipped her childhood. Anah had felt that maybe she had been a little over zealous in her protection of Bella and the need for her to succeed. But because Bella's music overtook her life and it made her so happy, Anah was just grateful that Bella wasn't a typical adolescent. Anah decided she would go to New York with Bella and attend a college there herself. They left for New York in 1983.

Jemeya had replaced the money that she had borrowed from the safety deposit box, which was originally set up for her mother, The money had given Jemeya the chance for an education and a career. Now it was to be used for Anah and Bella. The money wasn't actually put back in the deposit box, but was invested in stocks. Jemeya hadn't really followed her investments, but she had heard that the 70's were not a good year to sell stocks. The Dow entered two long downturns in 1970 and 1974 and remained flat until 1982 when the market started to recover under a new president. Confidence was restored to the stock market. Since she was still working, she would try to help pay for Anah and Bella while they were in New York—leaving the original $125,000 in the market.

Anah and Bella left for New York, staying in a little apartment not far from Julliard. Anah noticed that Columbia University was only a few miles from the Julliard and so she looked into the possibility of taking a summer coarse in writing. While she was staying home in Kansas with Bella, Anah had gone to the library to attend some writing courses. Jemeya found some of the poetry that Anah had written and was very impressed. It was at her suggestion that Anah take a writing course at some institution in New York while Bella was busy all day.

Bella left early in the morning, and even though Anah didn't have a class until later in the day, she left with Bella, dropping her off at the school and then going on to Columbia. She would go to the library, either working on her day's assignment or just reading.

One day when Anah was working on one of her poems in the library, she noticed a young man that kept looking at her. She noticed he was there several mornings when she was at the library and each time he seemed to stare at her. One day he came over to Anah and said that he had noticed her several times in the library and that she seemed familiar to him. They introduced themselves. Anah couldn't believe it. This was Otango, the same little boy she had played with in Hawaii many years ago. He said he recognized the "paint" on her neck. They both laughed. However, the smile disappeared from her face. She remembered it was his father who she thought had participated in the rape that took place at Fred Davidson's house and that had gotten her pregnant. Could his father be Bella's father?

She decided that she would try to find out as much as she could about his father. Where he was. What he was doing. Would he be seeing him soon. She didn't want to be too inquisitive, so she thought she would encourage their friendship and gradually ask some of the questions that needed answering. Whenever he came to the library they would talk. He seemed eager to talk about his father. He had no one else to talk to that knew him.

This was his last year before graduating. She found out that he had kept in touch with his father, except for the short time that he was in Jakarta, Indonesia living with his mother and her new husband. In 1971 he returned to Hawaii. He reminded Anah, that it was the same year that she had met him at the park when she came to the park with his grandfather's friend, Fred Davidson. Otango said that he and Fred Davidson had become good friends and Fred became his mentor. He said it was Fred who had shown him that his blackness would always be with him. He could either accept it or continue to be in limbo, between being white and being black. It was because of Fred that he chose to be part of the black community.

He reminded her that it was that same year she had met his father. He told her that he and his father had always kept in touch. He seemed proud of his father but there was a sense of sadness when he talked about him.

He said that his father tried to be involved in the politics of Kenya, but in 1965 he had written a paper entitled "Problems Facing Our Socialism," published in the *East Africa Journal.* This paper harshly criticized the blueprint for national planning, called "African Socialism and Its Applicability to Planning in Kenya," which had been produced by his father's friend Tom Minoya's Ministry of Economic Planning and Development. His paper was in opposition to the views of the government at that time.

He criticized the government for not better defining "African Socialism." Otango recited to Anah parts of his father's paper that he felt were outstanding:

"...the African tradition is fundamentally based on communal ownership of major means of production and sharing of the fruits of the labours, so expended in production, to the benefit of all; yet the blueprint for national planning advocates land title deeds and private ownership of land." "These two conflicting factors had to be reconciled." "...If one says that the African society was classless as the paper (blueprint) says, what is there to stop it from being a class society as time goes on?"...But we need to eliminate power structures that have been built through excessive accumulation so that not only a few individuals shall control a vast magnitude of resources as is the case now. It is a case of cure and prevention and not prevention alone." "...Theoretically, there is nothing that can stop the government from taxing 100 per cent of income so long as the people get benefits from the government commensurate with their income which is taxed." (Problems Facing our Socialism)

Otango got excited talking about his father's paper and said he understood his father's dilemma. Kenya was in such poverty and his father felt that Socialism would be an easy sell to the populace because they didn't know about land ownership. Those in power in Kenya wanted to change that structure by allowing the populace to own their own land and giving them more incentive to work. Otango's father wondered how the government could ward off building a class structure with such an arrangement. Otango said that any possible political career for his father ended with that paper.

His father had a spiral down turn, drinking and partying and ended up dying a drunk. He said that he once talked to a friend of his fathers and found out that there were two sides to his father and that maybe this dichotomy lead to his drinking. His friend said that his father never felt part of the village that his father moved to. He felt like a *Jooko*. His father loved living the good life, drinking the best liquor, driving the finest cars, smoking the best cigars and dressing in the most stylish clothes and being accompanied by a woman on his arm, often a wealthy one who could contribute to his luxurious life style. Yet in his paper he chastised the bourgeoisie lifestyle; the same lifestyle he enjoyed.

He then told Anah that his father had just died in a car accident this year. He regretted that he had not gotten to see him before he died. There were so many questions that had gone unanswered. However, he said that he often reads the paper that his father wrote because it was written in his father's own hand and were opinions that Otango never got to hear in his father's own words, and many that he agreed with. He felt that this paper explained his father's dream for Kenya—a dream that never happened in his father's life time.

One day while they were talking in the library, a man came to see Otango. He asked to speak with him privately and they went to another table, but not so far that Anah could not hear some of what they were saying. The man, looking quite serious, told Otango that he had made plans for him to work in New York while he finished up his degree. Otango had his heart set on going to Harvard just as his father had done. But his grades were not good enough to get into that prestigious law school. Harvard always gave students a chance to reapply after a few years, if they cleaned up their record by serving in the military, doing community work or taking courses to bring up one's average. He told Otango, that he needed to stop drinking, smoking pot and behave himself from now on. The conversation was short and Otango returned to the table. He told Anah that the man he was visiting with was quite an interesting fellow. He had been with the weather underground in the 60's, and had been accused of killing several people in a riot that had taken place in defiance of the Vietnam War, but because of some legality he was never charged with any crime.

He told Anah that this man and Fred Davidson had been a great influence in the decisions he was making and felt honored to have each man in his life. Anah asked Otango how he could respect a man who had actually been involved with a violent organization that would justify such actions, no matter what the reason. Anah didn't get her answer that day. She had to go to class.

As he said goodbye, he suggested they meet one last time, and suggested they meet outside the library and she should bring Bella along. Anah wasn't sure that would be a good idea, but she thought if she ever did tell Bella, she had the right to know that this boy might be her half-brother. They decided to meet at a small restaurant called The West Inn Bar, which happened to be a common meeting place for his father and his

Kenyan friends who also attended colleges on the East Coast in the 60's. It was not far from Colombia. They were to meet him at 6:00 for dinner. They waited until 7:00 and he did not come. However, as they were leaving the restaurant they noticed him coming down the street with his arm around a woman that looked like he might have picked up off the street. He was obviously very drunk and smoking a cigar. He slurred his apologies as we walked by. Like father like son, Anah thought to herself. She was disappointed; she was starting to like this young man. She was determined to follow his life to see if he pulled himself together as he was instructed by the man he met at the library.

Bella's 8 week course was over and Anah had completed her class. They had taken advantages of all the sights in New York, but what Anah enjoyed the most was Bella's solo piano performance at the Lincoln Center. She didn't want it to end. She couldn't have been more proud of Bella or any happier.

Even though they each had a wonderful time in New York, both Anah and Bella were excited to get back home and tell Jemeya all about their adventures. Seeing Otango brought up memories in Anah that she had allowed herself to forget. Bella was going on thirteen and she knew that soon she would be asking questions about who her father was. When she did, Anah would tell her all that she knew.

Chapter 45

The Story of Bella II
~*daughter of Anah*
~*granddaughter of Jemeya*

When Bella was going on ten, in 1981, she listened to a television production of the celebration of the 90th year of the founding of Carnegie Hall. Ruth Laredo, who was considered the prima dona of female American pianists, was one of five pianists selected to perform. Bella was mesmerized and completely paralyzed with Ruth Laredo's performance. From that day forward Bella wanted to be just like Ruth Laredo. Bella's concentration and practice of the piano took over her life. That Christmas, Jemeya and Anah bought an LP record that Ms. Laredo made in 1970 on which she recorded two pioneering and acclaimed sets: the entire Scriabin piano sonatas, and the complete solo repertory of Rachmaninoff. Bella listened to that LP record over and over. Her greatest interest was that of Rachmaninoff, because of the passionate and expressive tone of his works. She felt in another world when she played his pieces. Bella had learned to play the piano because she could play by ear. She learned to play Rachmaninoff by just listening to Ms. Laredo's LP record. Bella's teacher was very impressed, but she also told Bella that she could never be a great pianist without learning to read music and she would never be accepted into a music program unless she learned how. Bella found it extremely hard to concentrate on reading music because it was necessary that she play the music as it was written. Her teacher would not let her listen to the music first, she had to play while reading the notes on the sheet of music. However, with the enticement of going to the Julliard, Bella spent hours learning how to read music.

That next year, 1982, when Bella was 11, her music teacher at school nominated Bella for a youth summer scholarship at the Julliard School of Music in New York City. Her teacher recorded Bella's rendition of one of Rachmaninoff's concertos and presented it to Julliard when she nominated Bella. Bella was accepted. In 1983, she and her mother set off for New York.

Bella played Rachmaninoff's Rhapsody on a Theme of Paganini, Op 43 as her solo when the summer students were presented at the Lincoln Center. She received a standing ovation. Bella was the youngest student to ever play at the Lincoln Center from the Julliard School of Music. To the dismay of the teachers at Julliard, when Bella got on stage, she played her own rendition as she heard it on the LP record she had at home. But when she got the standing ovation, what could Julliard say. However, Bella did learn that she needed to develop her own style and not rely on the composition of others. It wasn't enough to play pieces as other's played them, she needed to compose her own renditions.

1990's

- In **1990** the average American's income per year was $28,970.00. By 1999, it had risen to $40,810.00, and influence of the new dot.com.
- **1992** Stephen King's *Dolores Claiborne,* John Grisham's *The Pelican Brief,* and Danielle Steel's *Mixed Blessings,* are Bestsellers.
- **1993**, February A 51-day standoff in Waco, TX, begins when agents from the Bureau of Alcohol, Tobacco, and Firearms attempt to arrest Branch Davidian leader David Koresh.
- **1995** Matthew Broderick is awarded the Best Actor Tony Award for his role in the musical "How to Succeed in Business Without Really Trying."
- **1996** Celine Dion's *Falling Into You* wins the Album of the Year Grammy.
- **1997**, August 31 Diana Princess of Wales dies in a Paris car accident, August 31, 1997.
- **1998**, October 29 At age 77, John Glenn becomes the oldest astronaut in space.
- **1999**, March 29 The Dow Jones Industrial Average closes above 10,000 for the first time.

Population: 281,421,906 (2000 Census)
Unemployment: 5.8 million, or 4.2% (Sept 99)
National Debt: $5,413.1 Million (1997)
Average Salary: $13.37/hr (1999)
Teacher's Salary: $39,347 (1998)
Minimum Wage: $5.15/hr (1997)
Life Expectancy: Male 73.1 Female 79.1(1997)
Auto Deaths: 49,772 (1997)
George Soros broke the bank of London (1992)

Presidents: George Bush, William Clinton

(George Soros Aside 6a)
("dot-com boom/bubble" and the "Y2K" Aside 7)

Chapter 46

A False Security

Just as in other booms the economy appeared robust, people were spending, charging on their credit cards, buying or refinancing a house. Business taxes filled the government coffers, so that it appeared that we had a surplus economy. The government, as were many people, rich on paper. 401 investments tripled as the market soared. As people spent more, using their credit cards as money, the economy kept growing. America seemed to be at a good place. We were not involved in any big war. However, there were rumblings from outside and a few inside:

In 1993, we had the first World Trade Center bombing; in 1995, there was an attempted crashing of a plane on the White House; in 1995, there was the Oklahoma City bombing; in 1996, there were the Khobar Towers, an enclave for Americans who worked in Saudi Arabia, was bombed; in 1998, the U.S. Embassy was bombed in Tanzania, Kenya; in 2000, the USS Cole was bombed in Yemen. None were played up by the press and were dismissed as isolated incidents by the Clinton administration. Life seemed good to the average American.

Because of the .com boon and the "Y2K" fix at the end of the decade, taxable salaries increased as the stock market took off and people cashed in on their fortunes. Computer companies had to hire more techs to handle the conversion from 20th century to the 21st century. The "Y2K" fix generated over 300 Billion U.S. dollars. Then the personal taxes and new business taxes created a surplus for the government. However, by the beginning of 2000 the boom was ending, and the business generated by the "Y2K" fix was subsiding, the tax revenue decreased, but the spending continued.

Willy was going on 65 and was thinking about retiring from his law practice. He could devote more time campaigning for his Presidential choice in the upcoming elections. Even Theodore was slowing down. He became enthusiastic about the new kid on the block—a state senator from Chicago. It was as if he was passing the torch on to this young man. Theodore virtually disappeared, except when he could be out front, usually during elections.

Chapter 47

The Story of Jemeya V
~daughter of Nora
~granddaughter of Tera

Jemeya had retired several years ago and she had a good retirement pension. Bella had graduated from high school and was attending the Julliard. Anah had gotten her own place while working full time at the library. Even with the expenses of Bella's schooling, she did not need to dig into the savings that was left in the safety deposit box. She had always been thankful for that money. She would take it out when she needed it, but had always put it back. Somehow its existence was reassuring and she always wanted Anah and Bella to have that security. The original sum had gone from $250,000 to over $400,000 and she had left the stock certificates in the safety deposit box. The envelope with the twenty ten dollar bills tucked in the sleeve of the book of poetry had never been touched.

When Bella had left for the Julliard and had not taken the book with her, Anah had put it back into the safety deposit box and had returned the envelope to its proper place. Jemeya had gone to the bank and brought home the box. For some reason she was wanting to travel down memory lane. Maybe it was because Bella was gone and Anah was at the library working and doing her research. She was a little lonely and her weekly dialysis was taking its toll on her health. She decided she would finally get around to reading the poems of Elizabeth Barrett Browning. She sat back in her rocking chair and began reading. Why had she waited so long.

Bella and Anna came to visit Jemeya that very day. They found her in her chair. The book lay open on her lap.

My Heart and I

ENOUGH ! we're tired, my heart and I.
We sit beside the headstone thus,
And wish that name were carved for us.
The moss reprints more tenderly
The hard types of the mason's knife,
As heaven's sweet life renews earth's life
With which we're tired, my heart and I.

II.
You see we're tired, my heart and I.
We dealt with books, we trusted men,
And in our own blood drenched the pen,
As if such colours could not fly.
We walked too straight for fortune's end.

III
We loved too true to keep a friend ;
At last we're tired, my heart and I.

III.
How tired we feel, my heart and I !
We seem of no use in the world ;
Our fancies hang grey and uncurledAbout men's eyes indifferently ;
Our voice which thrilled you so, will let
You sleep; our tears are only wet :
What do we here, my heart and I ?

IV.
So tired, so tired, my heart and I !
It was not thus in that old time
When Ralph sat with me 'neath the lime
To watch the sunset from the sky.
'Dear love, you're looking tired,' he said;
I, smiling at him, shook my head :
'Tis now we're tired, my heart and I.

V.
So tired, so tired, my heart and I !
Though now none takes me on his arm
To fold me close and kiss me warm
Till each quick breath end in a sigh
Of happy languor. Now, alone,
We lean upon this graveyard stone,
Uncheered, unkissed, my heart and I.

VI.
Tired out we are, my heart and I.
Suppose the world brought diadems
To tempt us, crusted with loose gems
Of powers and pleasures ? Let it try.
We scarcely care to look at even
A pretty child, or God's blue heaven,
We feel so tired, my heart and I.

VII.
Yet who complains ? My heart and I ?
In this abundant earth no doubt
Is little room for things worn out :
Disdain them, break them, throw them by
And if before the days grew rough
We once were loved, used,—well enough,
I think, we've fared, my heart and I. (Elizabeth Browing)

2000's

• **2001** Tiger Woods becomes the first golfer to hold all four major golf titles simultaneously by winning the Master's tournament in April 2001.

• **2001, September 11** Hijacked airliners crash into the World Trade Center, the Pentagon, and a field in Shanksville, PA.

• **2003, February 1** The Space Shuttle Columbia breaks apart during reentry, killing the seven astronauts onboard.

• **2005** Monty Python's *Spamalot* opens on Broadway in 2005

• **2005, August 29** Hurricane Katrina, the costliest hurricane in U.S. history, hits southeast Louisiana.

• **2007, July** Author J.K. Rowling publishes the final installment of her Harry Potter series, *Harry Potter and the Deathly Hallows.*

• **2008, November 4** Senator Barack Obama elected president on November 4, 2008.

• **2009** Super Bowl XLIII is the most watched television broadcast in history with 151.6 million viewers.

US population 281,421,906
President: George W. Bush

Chapter 48

Bad Times Ahead

Both Willy and John campaigned for George W. Bush. Theodore pressed forward for his support of Vice President Al Gore. Gore had been in politics his whole life as were his father and grandfather. He was of the same mold as Theodore. Many said that Gore had been primed to be president. Some complained about Bush's connections, but no one ever said that he was primed to be President; those opposing him said if he were being primed, those doing the priming would have done a better job. However, Bush was elected.

The elections of 2000 was highly contentious, with the outcome having to be decided by the Supreme Court. The new president hadn't been in office more than a few months before the attack on the Twin Towers in New York City on September 11, 2001, referred to as the attacks of 911. What had been brewing for the last ten years finally took place on American soil. The new president, who had gotten off to a rocky start, brought the American people together with his empathy and concern. The election had been a very dirty political race. The new president entered the office with a conservative, but socially responsible, agenda: However, with the bombing of the Twin Towers by Islamic Extremists, the President's agenda changed. With a democratic congress to appease, the social agenda seemed to take center stage and the cost of the war added to the deficit. This was an agenda that was not acceptable to all of America. There were those who have never felt we should enter a war again, no matter the circumstance, and there were those who felt war was inevitable to deter something like this from happening again, and then there were those who were somewhere in between.

But one person who developed a deep hatred of Bush was George Soros, who was determined to destroy him. He made that known throughout the entire campaign in 2000, but more in 2004. His money supported MoveOn.org, a liberal web site that was influential in the politics of 2004 and 2008.

The economic boom had come to a dramatic halt and the expenses of the war were taking a toll on the government coffers.

Most of the first part of the decade was a recovery from the tech bust. But the recovery was slow and not very reliable. Obviously, Americans had not learned from previous speculative investments which preceded both the stock bust of 1893 and that of 1929. By the middle of 2008, the market took a tumble, possibly with the help of outside forces. There were those who had studied the market and who knew toying with the market could cause a reverse and who could pull out just in time. It seemed strange that the market dropped so much just before the 2008 election.

Not only was the stock market teetering, but so was the housing market. Low interest rates, instituted by Alan Greenspan, Chairman of the Federal Reserve, opened up the housing market and also created a market where prices kept rising beyond anyone's dreams. The Congress and the Senate had also been influential in creating an atmosphere where banks were obligated to offer low interest, low or zero down-payment loans to people who couldn't ordinarily purchase a house. After the housing market took at tumble on the back of the .com bust, and credit card companies had deluged their customers with numerous credit cards at high interest rates, the western world turned topsy turvy with so much debt, there was no way for the average person to pay all that they owed. But all was not realized until it came to a head in 2008, when there was no more money to lend and the housing market became oversaturated. Houses that people purchased with mortgages at full price were not worth the amount left on their mortgages. Many people walked away from that mortgage, leaving the banks with their homes.

By late 2008, unemployment was up to 6.5% and many banks looked like they were on the verge of collapsing. In retrospect this was not something out of the ordinary; we have always had ups and downs in our markets and in the 30's unemployment was in the 30% range; we have often been in the 10% range. But the way this downturn was handled was different.

Because news was 24/7, the media created a panic and then the government added more fuel to the fire when the Treasury Secretary Paulson, with the support of Ben Bernanke, new Chairman of the Federal Reserve, advised President Bush that the economy would collapse without TARP money for bank bailouts. Most believed that Bush was ill advised. It did seem strange that a previous executive of Goldman Sachs would be making decisions which might favorably affect that same company, especially now that Sachs had become a "holding company" instead of an "investment company." Willy wondered how many people were involved in this American Experiment he had heard it mentioned so often. Did it include the Federal Reserve as well? After all it was a private entity, and not part of the Federal Government. It was all sounding like a conspiracy theory and he wasn't really interested in being a part of it. But he couldn't help wonder.

****

In November of 2008, Celia, William's last child died.

On Christmas Eve, 2008, John Dickerson, Willy's friend, received a package. It contained the book *Hero Perished*, a collection of letters of an All-American Heisman Trophy winner who had a political career all laid out for him until he lost his life in 1943 fighting in World War II. In the package there was a brief note: "I am so glad that I was able to meet you and Tommy, and I am so sorry I never got to hold you or Tommy in my arms and be the mother and grandmother you both deserved. The time was never right. Keep on fighting for your beliefs." John immediately called Willy.

Chapter 49

The Story of Anah IV
~daughter of Jemeya
~granddaughter of Nora

Anah couldn't get him out of her mind. The more she thought about him, the more she wanted him to fail. This wasn't like Anah. She had let it all go when she was raising Bella, but now it all began to surface. Bella was in New York and her mother was gone. Her thoughts turned to a sadder time. That day she saw him drunk walking down the street with a cigar in his mouth with his arm around that women and an air of arrogance made her think of his father. When she was working in the library she would search the magazines for anything she could find that was written about him. He was becoming easier and easier to follow because more and more was being written about him, often glowingly. That even made her angrier. She couldn't figure it out. It was as if he came out of no where.

First there was a big write up that he was the first black editor of the Harvard Law Review. Then the library learned that his memoirs would be coming soon. Why the big announcement? But as she searched a little deeper, she found out that the original $125,000 advance for his memoirs from a prominent publishing company had been rescinded. He had failed to come up with any kind of outline or rough draft of his book, and they were worried about the quality because there was nothing available for them to see that he had ever written, not even anything from the Harvard Law Review. Then a lesser known press company did give him a $44,000 advance to publish his book after he presented a rough draft of the first few chapters. She thought it seemed arrogant that someone who hadn't accomplished much would think he should write his memoirs. But then she thought, after reading the book, that there was definitely an agenda developing.

One day Anah picked up the Chicago Tribune and spotted his bio. He was running for a seat in the State Senate. It gave a rundown of his accomplishments. He had become a Civil Rights attorney and was teaching a course at a Law School in a University in Chicago. He was also involved in community organizing. Anah called it "saber rattling."

It mentioned that this young man had great oratory skills and as an aside, said he dressed impeccably. A few months later, Anah read that he had eliminated any competition for his senate seat by revealing some damaging information about his opponents. Anah was on a mission. She was going to follow this young man's every move.

One day in 2004, she opened the paper and saw the announcement that he would be giving the keynote address at the Democratic National Convention which was being held in Boston, MA. It was at the suggestion of Theodore O'Mera that he be given this opportunity. Later Anah read the accolades about this new rising star in the Democratic party. Not soon after he was serving as US senator.

To get Anah interested in something other than following the politics of Odanko. Bella knew her mother had been upset when her friend dismissed her by failing to show up for their last get-together, but this had gone to far. Bella suggested to her that she should pick something that she was avid about and help fight for that cause. Bella reminded her of Jemey's interest in bettering the education system. She suggested that Anah become involved with something to do with education. Anah picked right up on that suggestion. There had been a notice in the library advertising an educational forum to be given by a prominent attorney from Omaha, Nebraska. His name was Willy something or other, she couldn't remember his last name. It was entitled "Hidden Agenda in our Educational System." Anah decided to go. This speech was very enlightening and frightening. She had decided to use some of her time at the library when she was working to see if what the speaker said was true or whether he was just speaking in half-truths, like politicians tend to do.

It was hard finding out much about this hidden agenda, but she goggled "Educational Forums." She thought this might be a good place to start because forums are usually places where people discuss certain topics. The first topic listed was World Education Forum, 2006. She went to that web site. On this web site were pictures of guest speakers and it also showed the speeches that were given by them. Anah was taken aback. She recognized the picture of one of the speakers. She thought it was the same man that had come to the library at Columbia University to speak to her long lost friend. She checked this man's bio and he had been in New York in 1983 working on his Education degree. That was the same date that she was in New York with Bella and the same year that she had seen her friend in the library.

President Hugo Chavez, Vice-President Vicente Rangel, Ministers Moncada and Isturiz, invited guests, **comrades***. I'm honored and humbled to be here with you this morning. I bring greetings and support from your brothers and sisters throughout Northamerica. Welcome to the World Education Forum!* **Amamos la revolucion Bolivariana!**

This is my fourth visit to Venezuela, each time at the invitation of my comrade and friend Luis Bonilla, a brilliant educator and inspiring fighter for justice. Luis has taught me a great deal about the Bolivarian Revolution and about the profound educational reforms underway here in Venezuela under the leadership of President Chavez. We share the belief that education is the motor-force of revolution, and I've come to appreciate Luis as a major asset in both the Venezuelan and the international struggle—I look forward to seeing how he and all of you continue to overcome the failings of capitalist education as you seek to create something truly new and deeply humane. Thank you, Luis, for everything you've done...

On my last trip to Caracas I spoke of traveling to a literacy class— Mission Robinson—in the hills above the city along a long and winding road. As we made our way higher and higher, the talk turned to politics as it inevitably does here, and someone noted that the wealthy—here and everywhere, here and in the US surely—have certain received opinions, a kind of absolute judgment about poor and working people, and yet they have never traveled this road, nor any road like it. They have never boarded this bus up into these hills, and not just the oligarchy or the wealthy—this lack of first-hand knowledge, of open investigation, of generous regard is also a condition of the everyday liberals, and even many of the radicals and armchair intellectuals whose formulations sit lifeless and stifling in a crypt of mythology about poor people. Everyone should come and travel these roads into the hills, we agreed then—and not just once, but again and again and again—if they will ever learn anything of the real conditions of life here, surely, but more important than that, if they will ever encounter the wisdom and experience and insight that lives here as well…

I walked out of jail and into my first teaching position—and from that day until this I've thought of myself as a teacher, but I've also understood teaching as a project intimately connected with social justice. After all, the fundamental message of the teacher is this: you can change your life—whoever you are, wherever you've been, whatever you've done, another world is possible. As students and teachers begin to see themselves as linked to one another, as tied to history and capable of collective action, the fundamental message of teaching shifts slightly, and becomes broader, more generous: we must change ourselves as we come together to change the world. Teaching invites transformations, it urges revolutions small and large…

The woman in the poem—just like the students in Mission Robinson—is living out a universal dialectic that embodies education at its very best: she wrote her name, she changed herself, and she altered the conditions of her life. As she wrote the word, she changed the world, and another world became—suddenly and surprisingly—possible….(Bill Ayers)

After Anah read his entire speech, she immediately got out the Senator's book. She was sure that the writer of this speech was the author of the Senator's book. Anah immediately told her friends at the library, who skeptically listened. Anah said that she would prove it. Her friends were willing to go along with Anah, only because they had heard from the journalistic grape vine that this man had helped the Senator write the book. Some even suggested he wrote it entirely. However, no one knew this for sure, but that several years later when this individual published his own book, the syntax used was very similar.

They all sat around the table comparing several of the passages from the speech and the memoirs. The head librarian had heard that writers often give speeches or interviews in the same tone and cadence in which they often write. The only samples they had were the speech and interview from the World Education Forum and the Senator's memoirs.

World Education speech:

"I walked out of jail and into my first teaching position—and from that day until this I've thought of myself as a teacher, but I've also understood teaching as a project intimately connected with social justice. After all, the fundamental message of the teacher is this: you can change your life—whoever you are, wherever you've been, whatever you've done, another world is possible. As students and teachers begin to see themselves as linked to one another, as tied to history and capable of collective action, the fundamental message of teaching shifts slightly, and becomes broader, more generous: we must change ourselves as we come together to change the world. Teaching invites transformations, it urges revolutions small and large."

Interview:

"Well, that's true of all societies, and it's as true of ours as any other. Go to the schools in the inner city. Go to the schools in the privileged suburbs and see what you see. To separate progressive education from the savage inequalities of our schools, from the drill and kill, from the sort and punish, it's like a fantasy world. You're not changing anything if you don't address the social inequities out there."(Bill Ayers)

Senator's book

"...He spoke of the wild animals that still roamed the plains, the tribes that still required a young boy to kill a lion to prove his manhood. He spoke of the customs of the Luo, how elders received the utmost respect and made laws for all to follow under great-trunked trees. He told us of Kenya's struggle to be free, how the British had wanted to stay and unjustly rule the people, just as they had in America; how many had been enslaved only because of the color

of their skin, just as they had in America, but that Kenyans, like all of us in the room, longed to be free and develop themselves through hard work and sacrifice."

Senator's interview:

"One of the things I think I can bring to the presidency is to make government and public service cool again. There's such a hunger among young people for some outlet for their idealism. That's why you see these movements around Darfur or climate change. You don't see it expressed in terms of people wanting to serve in the Justice Department or the foreign service. Why should they, when the core missions of those agencies have been gutted?"

They were very surprised to see how similar the interview remarks were to the Speech given at the World Education Forum. But the Senator's interview was not similar to the way he writes. Even though it did seem that there might be a connection., no one, except Anah, thought it mattered. She didn't get it. Why didn't they care.

Anah just couldn't give it up. She said that she was going to write a letter to one of the talk-show-hosts who had been investigating the association of this man and the Senator. She thought she could also tell them a thing or two about Fred Davidson also. The obscenities that the Senator's preacher ranted sounded similar to the rantings of Fred Davidson all those nights when Anah lie awake in bed, trying to block out all the shouting.

All of this bitterness began to take a toll on Anah's health. And it looked like she was beginning to become immune to the medicine that she had been taking to help her kidneys resist growing more cysts. She was starting to have recurring kidney infections and when she had gone in for her checkup, the doctor noticed that she had several cysts about the size of quarters. He suggested that she be operated on to have them removed. He also told her, that one of her kidneys wasn't working as well as it should. In time she might have to have one kidney removed. They would know more about it when they got in to remove the cysts. He had even gotten Anah's permission to remove the kidney if he thought it should be removed. Anah did not tell Bella the seriousness of the operation. She didn't want her to miss her recital at the Kennedy Center. It was to be her first solo appearance.

Before Anah went in for her operation, she decided that she should write a note for Bella to read someday that would explain what happened to her, who might be her father and something about both of the men who raped her that terrible night in Hawaii. She would put it in the safety deposit box that Jemeya had kept that contained the letter to Nora.

Anah died on the operating table. That same day the New York Times had an article in the paper stating that Bella Porthouse was the next Ruth Laredo.

Chapter 50

Chautauqua Revisited

The Presidential election seemed like it had been going on for years. In 2006, the democratic nominee had already made the news by going to the village of Kogelo in Kenya to visit his relatives. This was the village of his father who he hadn't seen since his visit to Hawaii when he was ten. He spent two weeks there getting to know his relatives and looking around the homestead where his father had lived.

This nominee officially threw in his hat only two years after he was elected senator. At first it seemed like he would not have a chance of winning the primaries, but his celebrity status increased with every speech he gave and every state he visited. He offered change. He had personality, he was young, he had a lovely wife and young children, he had a well-managed campaign and a media who got "goose bumps" whenever he spoke. After the election, everyone, even those who had not voted for him, were hoping that he would bring the country together. But with his election came a majority in the house and the senate. Bi-partisanship went out the window. The same would have happened if the Republicans had won both houses and the presidency. A balance of power is always achieved if the power is shared. If one party has all of the power, they view it as a mandate, forgetting about the other 45-50 percent of the populaces who are included in the citizenry.

To take a break from all the politics, Willy thought he would visit Chautauqua one last time in memory of his Aunt Celia. John wanted to go with him. Chautauqua usually has a weekly theme and all the guest speakers lecture on that theme. This particular week was "education" so Willy was especially interested. The President of a University in Chicago was going to speak on the new education curriculum for teachers which was being developed by a professor at their school. Intellectuals that come to Chautauqua always get together to discuss books that they may have read related to the theme for that week. One book that a professor from this University had mentioned was entitled *Putting the Movement Back into the Civil Rights*, by Deborah Menkart. He mentioned that it was now a book listed on the NEA's website. It was recommended reading for teachers. Willy had heard that this was a controversial book. He immediately went to a computer and looked on the NEA web site. There it was. He read the synopsis.

"As one of the most commonly taught stories of the struggle for social justice, the Civil Rights Movement has the capacity to help students develop a critical analysis of U.S. history and strategies for change. By putting the "Movement" back into civil rights teaching, students can find their connection to history and their place in fighting injustice today. This book includes interactive, interdisciplinary lessons, readings, photos, primary documents and interviews, with sections on education, economic justice, citizenship and culture."

Someone in the small discussion asked if this was part of the American Experiment that Theodore O'Mera kept talking about when he was in closed circles. No one ever knew what he was referring to because his interest was always in Health Care. Willy had heard this phrase before, but not in the context of education. He and John tried to enter into this discussion, but as those in the group realized who they were, they changed the subject.

It wasn't long after the President took office that he went to the "Meeting of the Americas" where he met with the Cuban president, dined with the Brazilian ambassador and shook hands with and was presented a scathing book about the U.S. by Hugo Chevez, the president of Venezuela. It reminded Willy of the speech that the President's friend had given at the World Education Forum in Venezuela in 2006. He had heard it was this same friend who was involved with developing this new curriculum at the University in Chicago.

After that trip, when Willy was present at the President's 2nd address to the nation, he saw over in the corner his Chicago mentors: Chief of Staff and his two senior advisors looking nervous. After the speech, Willy overheard the President's senior advisor say. "I think he can pull it off" if he just keeps to the teleprompter." Following that speech, Barney Frank and Jose Serrano introduced a bill before Congress to repeal the 22nd Amendment so the new President could serve more than 2 terms. It was tabled.

In July, 2009, the President visited Uganda on his way home from the G8 summit in Italy. He gave a very inspiring speech directed at the people in Africa, telling them that they would see better times ahead.

However, in America, his speeches were not as inspiring. By the end of 2009, rumblings from outside the government were being instigated by many Americans who said they had voted for the President because he offered change. They were now just discovering what the new change was and they were not happy. The takeover of the car manufacturing business and banks, the changes in several health guidelines, the threat of internet regulations, the discussion about a fairness doctrine, the introduction of a Healthcare Bill and a Cap and Trade bill were all changes that many felt tampered with their freedoms.

Chapter 51

Non-violent Demonstrations

"People who are hungry and out of a job are the stuff of which dictatorships are made."(F.D. Roosevelt)

A non-violent movement called "The Tea Parties" surfaced very quickly. The tea bag was the symbol that began the Revolutionary War in 1776. This group became the platform for those who didn't like the sudden reverse of our country, those who thought their freedoms were being taken away.

Willy and John Dickerson were two of those "tea baggers." They participated in these non-violent demonstrations. Willy said that he was following the footsteps of his great, great, great grandfather Joseph Peairs who fought in the Revolutionary War. Many people stood alongside Willy and John, bringing signs to offer their opinions. One upset mother whose child's school had just canceled Valentine and Halloween celebrations in the school brought her sign: **"Keep our traditional Holidays, first went Christmas, now its Valentine's Day and Halloween."** Another person was just fed up with the government in general: **We would rather die on our feet then live on our knees**.

However, the mainstream media wasn't interested in letting this group be heard. They referred to those who participated in these demonstrations as loonies and as President Clinton called them "tea baggers"—a rather bigoted remark considering what the meaning of a "tea bagger" is. (One who has a job or talent that is low in social status or a person who is unaware that they have said or done something foolish, childlike, lame, or inconvenient.) Inconvenient maybe, but foolish no.

When in 2010 it was suggested that the Federal government partner with the newspaper organizations, the tea parties took on a whole new dimension.

Around September of that year, just before the 2010 elections, Tommy, John Dickerson's son, reinvented the tea party concept that had sprung up throughout the country. Tommy had just finished his last tour of duty in Iraq. He had signed up for three previous duties, but decided to make this his last. Being in the service had opened up his eyes to the freedoms he had always taken for granted. Upon his return in 2009, he felt these freedoms were being taken away from him. He felt convinced that his calling was to begin a movement that would at least let those whose voices that were now being left out of the government be allowed to have a forum in which to be heard and to learn ways to fight back.

Tommy had admired the opposing parties community organizing that appeared to fight for the rights of those that felt disenfranchised. He felt they needed a voice. But he didn't think they should be used in order to achieve a goal that he thought was misdirected—a goal that kept those same disenfranchised beholden to the government.

Because Tommy Dickerson had been an outstanding quarter back in Iowa, parts of the media were suddenly paying attention. And even though the main stream media, T.V. and front page news stories didn't publicize this movement, it did begin appearing in the sports section of well known newspapers. Tommy decided that he would start holding educational academies for the public in different parts of the country. Instead of recruiting lecturers, he would recruit moderators who would moderate round table discussions. Those that had signed up for these academies would be given questions before hand to do research. All of those with similar questions would participate at one of the round table discussions which had a moderator who was knowledgeable in that particular topic. These one day academies became very popular and the best part of these academies was that fresh ideas from the common man were injected into the problems that needed to be solved, and people always came away with some new knowledge.

One question that seemed to get the best traction for discussion was: How can our economy ever recover when the people's debt from credit cards is over $950 billion. One small business owner who attended one round table discussion said he had to use his credit card to make payroll. Another participant said that he had 10 credit cards and they were all maxed out. He had always been a staunch believer that we were responsible for ourselves, but when you can't find a job and you are losing your home and you need to put food on the table, government help sounds good.

Another participant had suggested that if the government paid all the credit card debt of $950 billion, individuals and many small businesses would be out of debt and the banks that held that debt would be able to put that money back into the system, and then individuals and small businesses might be less beholden to the government.

Another pointed out that this government might prefer that the citizens are beholden.

One person pointed out that the only caveat with this suggestion was: would those who had gotten their debt removed pile it on again. Maybe that's when the banks needed to step in and take up the responsibility of not letting that happen.

On top of the problems of the economy in 2010, the trial of the mastermind behind the terrorist attack of 911 which was to began in New York was postponed until the beginning of 2011. But many were still asking why would the President allow this to take place in a public court and not a military court? Many feared that this terrorist might be exonerated because of a technicality, such as not receiving his Miranda rights. Was there outside pressure on the President?

In April of 2009 it was understood that Soros was the instigator behind the Commission on Accountability, which was a conglomeration of Human Rights groups who signed a petition to be given to the President. The push was part of a vindictive campaign to pay back the architects of the War on Terror for making a good faith effort to defend America. Soros had not given up on his Bush vendetta. The President and Congress were not going to order an investigation. **Alternative plan**: Try the terrorist in an American court.

Willy was wondering if maybe this man wasn't also supporting the "American Experiment" about which he heard so much.

Chapter 52

The Story of Bella III
~daughter of Anah
~granddaughter of Jemeya
~great, granddaughter of Nora,

Bella's mother had insisted that Bella finish high school before going to the Julliard. She continued her piano lessons with a professor of music that came to their house every other day after school, and practiced several hours a day as well. When she graduated from high school, she moved to New York to attend the Julliard. She didn't have to worry about socializing; Julliard's intense study did not leave time for that. For two years she attended the Julliard and instead of joining an Orchestra when she completed her studies, she just traveled to different orchestras that invited her to perform. She didn't have the personality to be with a large group of musicians. She preferred to be alone. She always got wonderful reviews, whether it was her solo with the Philharmonic Orchestra or the London Symphony.

The love of poetry of Elizabeth Barrett Browning that Bella had known by heart had now been replaced by her music. She didn't even take the book with her. She had no time for a personal life. Her mother was her best friend. Bella was always so excited to see her mother in the audience when she would perform—her body would become erect and her passion would explode.

All of that changed when Anah died. Bella became extremely depressed. She had not been there for her mother before she died. She was too involved with herself. Critics began to comment on the lack of passion Bella had in her performances, and the orchestras stopped inviting her to play. Her agent suggested that she see someone about her depression, so in 2014 after not doing much of anything for a year, she visited a woman psychiatrist that had been recommended to her by a violinist who had lost his wife of 30 years. She realized after discussing her life with the psychiatrist, that her music had taken the place of any passion she could have in life, and that now that her mother was gone, the passion of music had turned to anger over the death of her best friend. She had no one. The therapist told Anah that she had to find out who she was. She needed other people in her life. She had always played so passionately for her mother. That love was gone. She need to find out where she got her musical talent, her love of books, or her deep passion when playing her music.

In 2014, she boarded a plane in Kansas City to begin her search for her roots. She had come to a dead end in the United States. She knew it would be impossible to get any DNA from the young man who her mother had said might be her half brother. Fred Davidson might be her father, but he was probably already in her DNA because she was fairly sure he was her grandfather. Before ruining the families of Fred Davidson, she had to rule out the possibility of the other black man who raped her mother that night in Hawaii. Besides Fred Davidson had become a celebrated black author being read by college students all across America. Who would believe her. A respected person does not rape their own granddaughter.

When Bella arrived in Cape Town, she kept running into an American woman who was somewhat older then her mother would have been. She ran into her at the train station and then again at the hotel where she would be staying. When she had gone down for dinner, the American woman invited her to dine. A friendship grew between the two women. Bella confided in her more then she thought she could. It felt good to have a friendship with another person, something that Bella never really had. It might have helped that the older woman reminded Bella of her own mother, in a special way. Over time, after spending a day in Durban, time in Mombasa, and several days in Nairobi, the two had found a common thread in their destination—the two men who were central to their travels. Both would be traveling to the village of Kogelo to visit the Jo-Alego tribe and so would her friend.

Bella knew exactly what family she was looking for. She knew that Otango's father had died in 1982 and his grandfather in 1971. There was sure to be someone related to Otango's father in this village. Bella didn't know exactly where to begin. She was the only person alive that knew about the rape of her mother by Otango Sr. However, all she really wanted to do was get a DNA sample of a close relative. If it matched, Otango would be her half-brother; if it didn't match, she wasn't sure what she would do.

Chapter 53

More Change

The President's health care reform passed the House and the Senate by the first part of 2010. Because the President and Congress had been successful in passing the Health Care Reform Bill and because the President's personal ratings were still quite high, Barney Frank and Jose Serrano again reintroduced to Congress a constitutional amendment to repeal the 22nd Amendment, which limits presidents to two terms. This would allow the present President to run for a third term in 2016. The passage of the O'Mera Health Care Bill (named after Theodore O'Mera) proved the President's mandate. The amendment passed allowing the President to seek a third term in 2016. This new amendment gave the media something to talk about other than health care reform.

However some couldn't get off the topic of health care, especially the seniors. Medical care was getting so complicated for seniors with restrictions on kidney dialysis, transplants, Cat Scans, MRI's, heart procedures, etc. One of the ways Congress finagled the costs of the Health Care Reform Bill was to lower Medicare costs for seniors. Age limits on certain procedures made it almost impossible for anyone over 62 to have access to good medical care, especially since so many of the doctors were opting out of taking Medicare patients because of the limited pay scale. Lists of who gets what, when were increasing every year.

Health care rationing had become a reality. One of the first procedures to go was mammograms for women. The government would not pay for mammograms for women under 50 or over 70, unless at extreme risk. Seniors over 64 weren't allowed H1N1 flu shots—reason being that age group was already immune. Seniors thought it a coincidence that the magic age was 64, the year before Medicare kicked in. All of this took place before the new Health care program had been put in force. That was to happen in 2014.

It was right after the Health Care Reform Bill passed that many businesses started to move out of the country, some to India, but many to Kenya. This was particularly prevalent among medical and pharmaceutical companies. Even though the bill didn't take effect until 2014, taxes were immediately going to be increased to cover the bill's cost.

Willy's concern was not with the financial situation or health initiatives, he was going to leave those concerns to Tommy Dickerson, but he was concerned with the educational reforms that the new administration was trying to incorporate. Willy had fought during the campaign to bring to the attention of the media his concern of the democratic candidate's affiliation with an activist who taught in the Education department at the University in Chicago . The same man who had spoken at the World Education Forum in Venezuela. A man who had studied the teachings of Saul Alinsky and who taught a college education course for teachers called 'Improving Learning Environments' saying prospective K-12 teachers need to "be aware of the social and moral universe we inhabit and…be a teacher capable of hope and struggle, outrage and action, teaching for social justice and liberation." (Bill Ayers)

Willy really was worried. His party was now in the minority. The democrats had reached their 60 majority in the Senate. The new Secretary of Education also came out of this same Chicago mold. He was a good friend of the presidents from his days in Chicago. This man had been the Chicago Schools CEO. Like the President, this man was Harvard-educated, and his Chicago roots ran deep. The school's chief grew up in the city's Hyde Park neighborhood, where the President had lived. He went to the same private school the President-elect's daughters attended.

He graduated from Harvard with a sociology degree. His senior thesis, for which he took a year's leave to do research in Kenwood, in inner-city Chicago, was entitled *The values, aspirations and opportunities of the urban underclass.* Within short order, he was garnering national attention for starting an innovative public school, Ariel Community Academy. He was tapped by Chicago Mayor Richard Daley to run the city's schools in 2001 because of the success of that academy.

Both these men worked with the President while he was a community organizer in Chicago, to raise funds to promote their educational ideology.

Willy started giving speeches pertaining to this hidden agenda. As word got out he was asked to come to communities to have town forums. Willy compared this agenda to little moles that had incorporated a certain ideology in English classes by selecting certain books that should be read, in History classes by the history that should be taught, left out or interpreted and in the civics lessons of social justice in social studies. In 2009 the Federal Government had put money in the stimulus package requiring teachers to be reeducated in history (a new view of history?) because the Federal Government thought they had not been adequately prepared.

Now they wanted a "science pedagogy framed around social justice where concerns can become a medium to transform individuals, schools, communities, the environment, and science itself, in ways that promote equity and social justice. Creating a science education that is transformative implies not only how science is a political activity but also the ways in which students might see and use science and science education in order to transform our way of thinking in business and the power structure."(Social justice web site.) There is also a textbook on teaching math for social justice.

Soon after Willy starting giving these speeches, he was approached by the FBI. They had learned about his "no birth" birth certificate. They knew about the Australian "death certificate" issued after the car accident; they were interested in having proof of his identity. Because of the incursion of terrorists into the country, they said that they were looking into all who had "no birth" birth certificates. While investigating, they ran across the death certificate. Willy had two months to come up with an explanation.

Willy had already researched his parent's involvement with the author Egon Kisch. In 1935, Kisch had addressed a crowd of 18,000 in Sydney warning of the dangers of Hitler's Nazi regime, warning of war and concentration camps. However, Egon Kisch was a communist. Willy understood through his research that a small segment of his supporters were not communist, but were a group who supported his reporting about Hitler's monstrosities. There was not enough being reported at that time about Hitler and his dictums. This group decided to go underground because of the Australian's left party's desire to run Kisch out of the country. He thought his parents left the country to start a new life in the US and to maybe carry on the plans of this underground organization. They had gotten in the car accident on their way to visit Eva. Maybe it was an accident or maybe not. The Australian government had listed them all dead. Willy felt that the Australian government was covering their tracks by telling Willy's mother that they were in a witness protection program and that it might be best if everyone thought Willy was dead also. Witness protection programs hadn't even been put in place in most countries until 1970. Willy told this story to the FBI. At the time they seemed to accept his explanation. After all, he was a baby when it all happened. But he did wonder why all of this was surfacing now.

By 2011, these education reforms had already taken root in several community schools in Chicago, Boston, San Francisco and one in Denver. Willy had visited several of these schools. He liked the idea that small class numbers were now being implemented, but what he didn't like was the social agitation that came up all day whether it be Science, Math or Literature and even at recess and PE. Children couldn't come away from their studies without feeling either guilty or persecuted, depending on their parent's status in life. Willy was determined to fight this reform.

Talk of the American Experiment was becoming more pervasive. No one could quite put their finger on it, but it seemed more and more people were using that term when discussing progressive programs.

After the elections of 2010, the Republicans did not pick up the number of seats that they wanted. Unemployment had increased, people still had their debt, which was even greater now because the value of the dollar was less. The Feds couldn't make money fast enough. The cost of things kept rising. The people needed help and the Democrats promised that help. It was a given that taxes would be raised, but when one doesn't pay taxes, which includes over 90% of the people, with another 15 to 20% getting tax credits where they receive money, why would you vote against all that.

The Republicans could not sell their program: keep Bush's tax cuts, cut business taxes to help create more jobs for small businesses, reduce spending. The average Joe just wanted more money in his pocket and that is what it seemed like they were getting from the government. The situation had not improved and all of this carried over into the 2012 election. The President won again in a land slide.

Chapter 54
2014
The New Bella

Bella and I found a nice hotel in Kisumu, however, we didn't leave for Kogelo for a few days because Bella wasn't feeling well. It was then that I found out that Bella did have a kidney disease and that even though she had a portable dialysis machine, it only allowed her to partially empty her kidneys, thus causing flare ups of kidney infections. After a few days of medication, she would be ready to go.

In that time Bella and I would rest, sitting around reading and making small talk. Suddenly one evening, Bella said that she wanted me to tell her everything about my life. It was as if her whole life had passed by and she needed to catch up by listening to my story. There was so much to cover— 60+ years. I told her it is important to look back every once in a while in order to see how we got from there to here, and then decide where you want to go. This was a good exercise for me. I told her about my childhood in a small town, my college years, my teaching years, my years in Okinawa, the adoption of a Korean baby, the birth of my 3 daughters and the years I owned and operated a Bistro. I told her about my loss when my mother passed away at the age of 96, 24 years after my father, who died when he was 72. I wanted her to know that I understood her loss.

To give Bella an insight into how our small community looked out for each other, I told her about an experience I had as a fifteen year old. My parents had always encouraged my siblings and me to get a part time job after we turned 15 or 16. My first job, at fifteen, was at the Franklin dime store. My job was to empty the cash register and reconcile the money with the day's receipts. There were many evenings that I spent hours trying to get them to reconcile, often needing the help of the manager. After many painful days of doing this, I was offered a job by a man who ran a small clothing store. He offered me a higher hourly wage. I turned in my resignation to the dime store manager, telling him I had gotten an offer with better pay. It wasn't until I was older and wiser that I realized these two men had gotten together and had come up with this scheme to get me out of the job in which I was having so much trouble without feeling embarrassed or a loss of self confidence. I am forever grateful to these two men. It left a lasting impression with me. I hope I have "passed it along."

She wanted to hear all about my brothers, my father and Willy. She had never had a male figure in her life. The stories I told her about Willy seemed to intrigue her. She wondered what he was planning next. He was hoping to convince Tommy Dickerson to run for President in 2016. Willy had thought that the 2012 elections was the wrong path for our country. He was hoping that the path could be changed in 2016.

Every time I tried to get Bella to talk, she begged me to go on. Her head was no longer lowered; her eyes met mine; her body leaned toward me, making sure she missed nothing. I found it a little embarrassing. Finally I just told her I was tired of listening to myself talk about myself.

Chapter 55

Kogelo

After Bella's health improved, we headed out to Kogelo to visit members of her family who were of the Jo-Alego tribe. A lot of time had passed since my grandfather had met with the ruoth of that tribe and I doubted I would get any more information about him, but maybe there were a few stories handed down between fathers and sons. . This town was very modern. We had heard from our driver that we would be surprised when we entered Kogelo. In the early 2000's, there was no electricity, water was hauled from a well and there was no T.V., only radio transmissions. Today it looks like a modern American city. He said it was because of the increased tourism that has taken place in this part of Kenya.

He took us to the little town hall where one could learn about the culture of the village and the people who lived there, especially where the relatives of the President lived. They had a lot of information about the President. It was if he had lived there. I could see why they were proud.

Bella acted as if she didn't know much about her ancestors, and she wasn't interested in my helping her out. She suggested that I look around town and go into a few pharmacies that we saw when driving into the village.

I spotted this one pharmacy that included a little museum inside; there was a display in the window showing the evolution of medicine, from herbal leaves to elixir bottles to prescription pills. There was a bottle just like the one I had at home and that I had seen in the museum in Nairobi. The curator, as she was called, but more of a clerk checking out customers on the cash register, said she would get me a brochure that explained the display which was located at the back of the store. I wanted to talk to someone, not read a brochure.

When I walked to the back of the store, there was a young gentleman looking at the array of instruments and paraphernalia used in early witch craft. We began talking about the display and how Kenya was becoming the mecca of medical technology in such a short time. To him it seemed like only yesterday that he was having such a hard time getting patients to trust him without killing a goat first. He was a doctor in this village and was very interested in its history. I told him that I was the granddaughter of the man who had first introduced that elixir bottle to the Jo Alego clan. He was a very blunt individual as I learned. Instead of being pleased that he had met someone associated with that medicine bottle, he looked rather distraught and asked me if my grandfather was the white man that brought disgrace to a woman of his tribe.

When I questioned further, he suggested that my grandfather impregnated her and left her here with nothing. I resented the attack on my grandfather. I told him that I couldn't believe that my grandfather would be that man. He was a gentleman in every way and his total respect for every human being would not have been compromised for a roll in the hay. I asked him who this woman was and how did he know this. He went on and told me that it was a well-known story in the Jo-Alego tribe. A woman named Tera, who was the second wife of the ruoth, had a mother named Sudra who had worked for a white family on a plantation. Because my grandfather had come to the village introducing medicine to the clan in 1894, the same year Sudra was with child, and because her child Tera had such light skin, they assumed that he was probably her father. However, Sudra's family always told people that William was not Tera's father. They never admitted that Tera had a white father, but her light skin said otherwise. They were quick to get Tera married off when she was thirteen. That is how Tera began to live with the Jo Alego clan. The people of the village knew Tera was the President's grandmother. After he became President they were all curious if he knew the truth about his grandmother's birth. Maybe he was told when he visited the village in 1987.

I told the doctor a story that my mother told me about my grandfather's miracle in Kenya. My grandfather often jokingly referred to the cough elixir that he had given to the wife of a tribal ruoth as the miracle that opened up his market in that part of the world. He had given Turko's first wife some medicine to help cure her cough. Nine months later she gave birth to a long-awaited baby boy. Turko called this a miracle because all three of his children were girls. We both laughed, loosening up the conversation. My grandfather had kept in contact with Turko until he died in 1916.

The doctor went on to tell me how much my President was doing for Kenya. The new businesses coming into his country had created many jobs for their youth. He felt sending aid was always so demeaning. And now instead of doctors like him moving out of the country, many are deciding to stay put. He mentioned that he was also thankful for our last President; the large contribution he allocated during his tenure to fight Aides in Africa has helped reduce the number of deaths by ½, especially the deaths of children infected with aides at birth.

After the doctor left, I noticed a stand that had a registry where you could sign your name, your home town and the date that you had visited the museum. The museum had been started in 1965 and displays had been added over the years. The last few years the museum had expanded because new displays were being added exponentially. I have always had fun going through registries wherever they had them. I signed this one and started looking back over the years. Starting with 2010 there had been tens of thousands of Americans every year who had stopped at this village and visited the museum. I thumbed back over the years. The President had visited there in 1987, which I had known. His father was from this village. There were no more Americans going back in time until I reached October 28, 1971, which listed the name of Theodore O'Mera, a senator from Massachusetts. Going back even further, I could not find another

American who had visited this village in Kenya. I was sure that thousands of Americans had gone to Kenya on safaris, but I guess they had not visited this small village near Lake Victoria. Why had Theodore O'Mera visited this village in 1971?

When we met up later, Bella said that she had run into this young gentleman, who seemed to be very knowledgeable about this community. He had overheard Bella's name and wondered if she was the famous pianist he had heard in Washington D.C. at the Kennedy Center. They began talking and she discovered that he was the Economic Czar for Kenya in the Presidents administration. He preferred living in Kogelo, the village where he was born, instead of Nairobi, the capital of Kenya and where official business is done. He noted that the drive to Nairobi wasn't a long drive and even faster by train. At the end of the conversation he invited Bella to dinner.

When we got to the American café, Bella spotted the young man and she introduced him to me. His face had an expression of surprise, which made me think that maybe Bella hadn't told the gentleman that I would be joining them. We had dinner and made small talk. Noticing that I was an extra, I decided to excuse myself because it had been a long day. Bella appeared relieved and also excited.

It seemed like Bella had given up on her search for her roots, as she now had a new interest. She was spending all of her time with this new young man. She was falling in love for the first time. I hadn't realized that we were going to spend this much time in Kogelo, but I didn't mind because there was so much to learn about their culture and everyone was so eager to visit with me.

One night when Bella returned from an evening with Jushro, she was very distraught, would not explain herself and began packing. She said she would be leaving in the morning. That was not like Bella. She was always waiting for someone else to take charge. I knew something was terribly wrong, but now was not the time to discuss it. We left early the next day. Bella was in a hurry to get back to the states.

Chapter 56

The Story of Bella IV

Bella wanted to stay at the town hall herself, so she suggested to her friend, Catrina, that she go to the pharmaceutical museum that they saw as they drove into the village. While Bella was waiting to talk to the clerk, she overheard several men standing around talking about their visits to the US. One of the gentlemen gazed at her and smiled. It embarrassed her and she looked away. Then she noticed a family tree donning one whole wall. There was the family she was looking for. It listed the date of birth, date of death, dates of marriages, children etc. The President's father was born June 12, 1936, death was November 13,1982, Hussein, his grandfather, was born 1895, death was October 29, 1971, Tera, his grandmother, was birth August 13, 1895, death was June 12, 1936. Bella thought she must have died in child birth.

When it was her turn, she approached the lady sitting at the widow that would help tourists coming into the village. They had over a thousand visitors a week, so they were prepared to give the tourist any information that they needed. When Bella told the woman who she was looking for, the woman was stunned. No one had ever thought they could personally see or talk to any of the relatives of the President. Only certain people were allowed a visit with his immediate family. Bella had thought that this was just a small little village who had ties to an important American. Because she never read or heard much about this village or the American's family, she thought they were just living a life that they lived before the American became President of the United States. She was so disappointed. It must have shown on her face. The man who was talking about the United States and who had smiled at her, approached her, introduced himself and asked her for her name. When he heard her name, he recognized it as the famous pianist he had heard at the Kenedy Center several years ago. He tried to make small talk with Bella, but she seemed to be in a hurry. He told her he was honored to meet her, and as she was walking away, he asked her if he could take her to dinner at the American Café down the street next to the utility company. For the first time in her life, Bella was excited to be in the company of a man, even though she didn't act like it. She didn't know how to act. But there was a feeling in her that she had never felt. As she walked out the door she told him she would be there at six. . All of a sudden the poems of Elizabeth Barrett Browning flooded her consciousness. She couldn't wait to tell Catrina of their plans for dinner that evening.

They met Jushro Hudrom at an American café, which was one of many American cafes that had sprouted since the President had been elected. When Bella and her friend, Catrina, walked in, Jushro's face looked a little disappointed. Bella had been so excited, but now Jushro didn't seem as excited about being with her. But when they sat down his smile returned. They had a nice dinner and made a lot of small talk before Bella's friend excused herself. Bella was actually pleased that her friend had decided to go back to the hotel.

Bella found it so easy talking with Jushro. He loved classical music and actually studied music when he had gone to England for his first year in college. However, his father wanted him to study economics so he switched to a school in the United States. They talked about their favorite symphonies and the types of classical music they both enjoyed. Jushro knew that Bella loved playing Rachmaninoff for she always included one of his sonatas in her performances. The evening ended by his walking Bella back to the hotel and asking her if they might spend the next day together. He thought she might like looking around the countryside and that he might be able to help her with her search for her relatives. Bella had not told him exactly who she was looking for.

They spent the next several days together, talking and driving around the country side. Bella never mentioned her search for her family. They laughed and talked all day, every day. They had so much in common even though they were from two different cultures.

She found out that he had never married; he had never found anyone that he could share his love for music, especially classical music, and he had always been too busy traveling, not staying in one place long enough to develop any kind of relationship. After spending several days together, Jushro told Bella that he thought he might be falling in love with her. Bella was flattered and she knew that Jushro had created feelings in her that she had never felt before. He kissed her and surprisingly she kissed him back, feeling a little awkward not knowing exactly what to do. But it all came so naturally with Jushro. She loved being with him but she knew so little about him.

The last evening before he had to travel to Nairobi for business, during dinner she asked him how he got the job as Czar, and he seemed surprised that she didn't know, but then how could she have known. Not everyone was that interested in the Kenyan Czar to the United States. He told her that he thought the President of the United States had appointed him Ambassador because he was his relative. Bella was beside herself as he kept on talking about his family and his connection to the President. . She had fallen in love with a relative of her half-brother, whom she thought was the President. She excused herself, and headed for the lady's room where she regained her composure and returned to the table, only thinking about getting a DNA sample from this man. She saw him take a drink from his wine goblet. She interrupted Jushro as he continued to talk about his family. She said that she had forgotten that she was suppose to meet her friend, Catrina at the hotel at 7:30 because they only had one key. Jushro went to the restroom before paying the bill. Bella asked the waitress for a to-go-container and a bag and then she slipped Jushro's wine goblet into the bag and left the to-go-container on the table, so Jusnro would think she was in the restroom. She hurried out the door before Jushro returned. Bella never saw Jushro again while she was in Kenya.

Chapter 57
2014
Sudden Departure

We left for the states the next day, flying from Nairobi to Cape Town, London and then to New York. Bella had decided to stay in New York. I would fly on to Florida. We were to stop over in Cape Town and take the flight the next day to London, but we were able to catch an earlier flight to London. Bella did agree that we could stay the night in London and catch the flight the next day for New York. I had agreed to move up my flight home to accommodate Bella. In her state of mind, I did not want to leave her on her own. When we got to our hotel in London, Bella told me the whole story about how her mother was raped by two men, both black, one from Hawaii and the other from Kenya. The one from Kenya was the one that brought her on this search. That was all that she told me, except that the man she had fallen in love with may be related to the man who had raped her mother. I asked her why she hadn't told him about her fears. She said she was too embarrassed and what good would it do. Nothing could come out of it if she had told him.

When I got back to Florida, there was a call on my answering machine from Jushro. He said that he had remembered my name and where I was from and found my telephone number on the internet. He said he was sorry to bother me, but would I call him when I returned. He asked me not to tell Bella that he had called. I didn't know if I should talk to Bella and ask her what I should do. I didn't think it would hurt to see what he wanted.

When he answered the phone, I wasn't sure how the conversation was going to go. He had asked me why Bella had disappeared so suddenly? What had he said or done? He was in love with her. He had finally found his soul mate and would do anything to get her back. I didn't know what I could say to him. It didn't seem like their relationship could work out. But I had decided that I would tell him what Bella had told me, about her mother being raped when she was young and that Bella was the product of that rape and that he, Jushro, might be related to the man who had raped her mother. After I heard myself talking, I realized that this wasn't something I should be telling him. Bella had confided in me. It was too late. Jushro told me what he had said to Bella that night. He asked me if Bella was talking about the President. I was speechless. I told Jushro that I had probably said too much. I told him it would be best if he left Bella alone. After I got off the phone I was in shock; could I have been traveling with the President's half-sister?

Chapter 58

The Story of Bella V

When Bella returned to New York, she returned to the condo that she had bought when she began playing piano professionally and which she had left several years ago when she became so depressed. Her main goal now was to find out who her father was and to get back at the person who ruined her life. She had fallen in love and now that was taken away from her. Bella had become a different person. Her once passive personality suddenly became aggressive. She had fallen in love with a man that could be her relative.

She looked in the phone directory under DNA and found only one lab that could perform the test. Bella took the wine goblet that should have the fingerprints and saliva of Jushro to the lab not far from her condo. She had been careful to put the goblet in a plastic bag when she took it out of the paper bag at the hotel in Kojello. She did not want to contaminate the DNA. When she got to the lab, there was no one at the desk. She waited impatiently, ringing the bell at the desk several times. Finally a young woman, chewing gum and taking her time, asked if she could help Bella. Bella sharply asked the woman what kind of operation were they running here that they could take so long to help someone. The woman had told her that they were short on employees with the number of DNA samples that came into the lab every day. She said that since the government had begun running the labs, the paperwork had increased threefold.

DNA forms, explaining the reason for the requests, had to be sent to a designated government screening office that reviewed them. There was usually a two week waiting period before the requests could be honored. Bella could leave the goblet there if she wanted and risk contamination or take it home with her. She needed to fill out the request form. Bella wondered what she should put on the request form—that she was trying to determine whether or not the President of the United States was her half-brother because his father had raped her mother. This might not be the best explanation. She decided that she would just put down proof of sibling relationship between a young man and young girl. They had been separated at birth and had just found each other. Bella filled out the form, but chose to take the goblet with her. They would call her to tell her whether or not her request had been accepted.

Bella had decided to begin playing the piano again. Many who heard her play were surprised at the intensity at which she played. She changed her whole style playing Chopin and Braham, picking their more light hearted Scherzos. The notes are played quickly and sharp, but to the audience it seemed like pieces that Bella wanted to hurry through. Because of her past reputation, she was still receiving invitations to play solos with other symphonies around the country, but as time went on, she wasn't getting the ovations she had received before when her mother was still living.

After a month, the lab called Bella and said that her request had been approved and that she could come in to get her blood drawn, and they reminded her to bring the goblet with her. After she had her blood drawn and she gave them the plastic bag with the goblet, she wanted their reassurance that the goblet would not be contaminated or broken. They reassured her. She should have the results in less than a week.

Bella was counting the days. When the test came back negative, Bella was excited in one respect but repulsed in another. There were only two men who raped her mother and Joshro, the President's relative, did not have a DNA match with Bella. She found out that she was not related to Jushro, so the President was not her half-brother. Could it mean that her great-grandfather was also her father. She ran out of the laboratory into the ladies room and vomited. Her mother had told her in the letter that whatever she might find out, she must not let it destroy her life.

Anah had been a good example for Bella, for she had allowed herself to move on with her life, putting all of her energies into creating a good life for Bella, and letting go of what had happened to her. But Bella had no "Bella" in whom to put all of her energies. But thinking of her mother did allow Bella to compose herself and go home. On the way home, she thought of what would she do next. What kind of man would knowingly rape his own granddaughter?

After Bella,s initial reaction of disgust and revenge, she became excited and ecstatic. She was not related to Jushro. How can she repair the damage that she had done that last night. She had torn up anything that she had that reminded her of him. She did not have his telephone number and she couldn't remember his last name, for she had never had the opportunity to use it, except that one night when she introduced him to her friend. She did know it was not the same last name of the man she had thought had raped her. She was in a panic. She decided to look on the Internet to see if she could get his number. The government web page did have a contact number for him. But when she called it and asked for his personal phone number they said that they could not give out that information. Did she want to leave a message? Jushro was out of the country, but he would get the message when he returned to the states. Bella left a message for Jushro to call her. But now all she could think of was to call Catrina.

Chapter 59
2014
The Analysis

After I returned home, I decided to reread the President's memoirs. I had always been curious about this new President. I so desperately wanted to know more about his life; the media only told us bits and pieces of his life. No one knew much about him except what he told us in his first book about his family. I had read it before, but now that I had actually visited the village that his father had lived, I decided to reread his book. I was so surprised at how poetic it sounded. The flow of the words just didn't sound like him. After reading the book again, I couldn't envision his ever having goose bumps when he heard the Star Spangled Banner. I couldn't imagine his sitting by a campfire with other boys his age, playing in the high school marching band, delivering newspapers, fishing on a summer day, or climbing trees in his back yard. I could only see an angry little boy, sitting beside a bitter black man discussing injustices.

His mother was a hippie and an atheist who dabbled in Archeology, spending much of her life trying to find herself. Her parents had moved to a city near Seattle just so she could attend a newly formed high school with far left leaning ideology with teachers who taught radical beliefs. He was left by his parents to live with grandparents who obviously wanted their daughter to learn about an ideology that was contrary to what our country held true. His father, from a foreign country, left him when he was two. His mentor was an angry man who hated America. Hawaii had only been a state for a few years before he was even born. Most of the citizens of Hawaii hadn't been part of the birth of the United States; hadn't fought for the liberties that we have; hadn't been a part of the celebrations and turbulence that occurred over the years. How could such a person be a president of a country that had been founded from an ideology contrary to that of his mother, his father, his grandparents and possibly the state in which he grew up. We are what are parents are. We learn to love what they love and be proud of what they are proud. Visiting the village of his father and seeing a culture which was foreign to me, made me realize that there would be no way in which I could step into their world and love it like they do.

Chapter 60

Love Rekindled

Before I left for New York, Bella called to tell me that she and Jushro were not related. It was then that I told her that he had called and what he had said. She did not know his phone number or his last name. She said that she had left her name with his contact person here in the states, but she didn't want to wait that long. What could she do. Then I remembered that I had his telephone number in my phone.

Jushro and I arrived at the Condo at about the same time. The excitement between the two was overwhelming. I took my cue and went down to the corner coffee shop for a latte and to read the daily paper. When I returned, both Bella and Jushro were asleep in each other's arms; the book of poems by Elizabeth Barrett Browning lay open in Bella's lap.

And yet, because thou overcomest so,
Because thou art more noble and like a king,
Thou canst prevail against my fears and fling
Thy purple round me, till my heart shall grow
Too close against thine heart henceforth to know
How it shook when alone. Why, conquering
May prove as lordly and complete a thing
In lifting upward, as in crushing low!

And as a vanquished soldier yields his sword
To one who lifts him from the bloody earth;
Even so, Belovèd, I at last record,
Here ends my strife. If thou invite me forth,
I rise above abasement at the word.
Make thy love larger to enlarge my worth.
(Elizabeth Barrett Browning)

Chapter 61

The Story of Bella VI

Bella called her friend, Catrina, after she left a message at the Embassy for Jushro to call her. She told her friend all about Jushro and the lab results. She told Bella about her conversation with Jushro and gave Bella his cell phone number so she could contact him. When she called his cell phone and she heard his voice, those feelings she had felt when she was with him, shot through her body. She told him she would tell him everything. Could he come soon. He would grab the first plane and be in New York by the next evening.

He arrived around 8:00 P.M., the next evening. They spent little time talking and just enjoyed the warmth of each other's company. They had the rest of their lives to sort out Bella's past and to plan their future.

After a night relishing in their love for each other, Bella confided in Jushro about what happened to her mother and about the black man who she now assumed was her father and grandfather. Bella was resigned that Fred Davidson was her father,

Getting a DNA sample from family members of Fred Davidson wouldn't prove who was Bella's father; she was fairly certain that he was her grandfather. She already had his DNA.

Bella had remembered that she and her mother stayed with a family that had been friends of the Davidsons. Her mother became very fond of the couple and had written to them several times when she first returned, after a few years it was only at Christmas that she heard from them. She thought she could still find their names in her mother's address book. Bella had not thrown out much of her mother's things. She just couldn't bring herself to do it. After reading the letter her mother had left her, she thought that to throw everything out might destroy any proof of her existence.

She contacted the Jordons and they were excited to hear from her. She wasn't sure what she would learn by talking to the Jordons, but it might clear up that foggy night in October. Maybe there were others involved. She didn't want it to be her grandfather.

Bella and Jushro flew to Hawaii to see the Jordons, the couple that had been so nice to her mother and her in the few years she lived with them. When they got to the address that she had found in her mother's old address book, an older couple answered the door. They were in their late sixties. Bella introduced herself and Jushro. The couple was overjoyed to see Bella. After a few pleasantries and a hardy meal, Bella asked the couple if they knew about her mother's rape and who might be her father. Bella told the couple about the letter her mother had left her. The couple looked at each other and hesitated, but then told Bella they didn't know anything, only that the Davidsons had asked them to take in Bella and her mother. The four of them chatted a while longer and then Bella and Jushro left for their motel. When they returned to the motel, there was a message for Bella. The Jordons, the family Bella had just visited, wanted them to come back. When they returned Bella was told the whole story of that night her mother was raped.

Anah had come home from trick-or-treating around 9:00 and had gone to bed. The Davidsons had been partying all night with some younger men from the college. Fred was trying to recruit some college men to participate in a strike that would take place at the National Hawaiian Pineapple Association's headquarters that next week. He was willing to pay the young men to participate in this strike. Tom Jordon was one of those college recruits. He described himself as a rather lost young man who had been mesmerized by the verbosity and admiration of Fred Davidson. Fred was well-respected in the community, both black and

Hawaiian, for his oratory and writing skills. Everywhere he went he was recognized. Tom said whenever he was with Fred Davidson, he became part of his world. That night there had been much drinking and discussion about the black plight in the mainland, Some of the students didn't like what they were hearing and chose to leave. Tom Jordon said that Fred Davidson had brought out that anger of blackness that he often tried to repress. It felt energizing.

The three of them continued to drink into the evening. Bella asked what three was he referring to. He said Fred, his wife and himself. He went on to tell Bella that he had participated in the rape with Fred Davidson. Bella looked at Jushro stunned. Jushro took over the conversation from there. He asked Mr. Jordon if he might be Bella's father. He answered yes, he had always thought it was a possibility. Jushro asked if he would be willing to have a DNA test. He said he would. Mr. Jordon was sobbing. He was happy to see Bella after all this time, thinking she may be his daughter, but feeling so distraught over what he had let pass for so many years. His wife never knew the story, but said she always wondered why her husband was such a changed man after Bella and her mother left. He quit drinking, finished college and became a respected sociology professor at the University of Hawaii until retiring several years ago. Once Bella had taken in all of this information, she had a few of her own questions. Did he know that Fred Davidson was her great grandfather? No he did not. What did he think of the stature that Fred Davidson had today? He said that he had been against his writings being introduced into the curriculum at the University, mainly because of his character flaws, but then if we eliminated all works of writers with character flaws from being studied, there would be little to read.

Bella and Jushro had made reservations to return to the states the next day. They took a saliva sample of Mr. Jordon with them to do a DNA test. They would contact him with the results.

When Bella and Jushro returned to the states, they immediately sent the sample to the lab, following the same procedure Bella had done before, so Bella knew it would be at least a week to get approved and one week more for the results.

A few days after Bella returned from Hawaii, she came down with a high fever and terrible stomach pains and Jushro took her to the hospital. Her liver had become inflamed because of the continuous medication that she had been taking. It was suggested that she stop the medicine and go on dialysis for a few days to see if they could clear up her liver. The doctor suggested that she may need a transplant. She had known this for some time, but hated to face the reality of it. It was nearly imposable to get a transplant unless from a relative. The list for transplants was long and the number of doctors doing them were few.

On the second day that Bella was in the hospital, when Jushro went into her room early in the morning, he noticed that Bella's dialysis machine was not running and Bella was not awake. He ran out of the room and contacted the nurse. They were so surprised that her machine and the alarm had been disconnected. Someone must have tripped over the cord, but how did the alarm get disconnected. Jushro instructed the nurses to remain in the room in the evenings. He would always be with her when she was sleeping during the day.

Chapter 62
2014
Closer to the Puzzle

I had not yet told Bella about my visit with a man at the museum, because I didn't want to bother Bella with it while she was sick. One day when I was visiting Bella, Joshro and I went down to the cafeteria for coffee and a sandwich. Jushro told me about their visit to Hawaii. I told Jushro about my talk with a doctor at the Kenyan museum I visited. We decided to make a time line of Bella's ancestors—when they were born, when they died and who they married and the names and dates of all the children that they knew. Jushro did know that Marna Kendo Hudrom, his grandmother, was the sister of Hussein Kendo, the President's grandfather. Bella's DNA was not compatible with Jushro's.

However, one thing did seem strange. Tera's first husband died in 1916 and she didn't have Nora until 1917. She did have a daughter Sebrinko in 1909 with Turko Kendo, her first husband, and this daughter was given in marriage in 1916 to Odato, as a convenience to join the two clans, even though Sebrinko was only 7. Tera didn't marry Hussein, the President's grandfather until 1935 when Tera was 40. Hussein hadn't returned to the village where Tera was living until 1930. Then who was Nora's father? I had read that often if an African woman was still able to bear children after her husband died, she would most likely be impregnated by another unrelated male member and the child becomes the child of the dead husband, taking his last name.

Jushro said that Turko did not have any brothers, he was the only male child and Jushro's DNA didn't match Bella's. The only male member living in the household at that time was Sebrinko's husband Odato, who had moved into Kendo's homestead because there was no other male in the family to help run the homestead. Odato was probably Nora's father. This also explained why Jushro was not related to Bella. The President and Bella were not closely related, but still related. Tera was Bella's great, great grandmother and the President's grandmother. Their common line was not through the Kendo line, but through Tera. They had decided not to tell Bella until they were sure the president was related to her.

Just to prove the blood line from Tera to Bella and the President, Jushro had decided that he would see if the President's DNA would be a match with Bella's, but he wasn't sure how he could get a sample from the President. He was always welcome to visit the President when he was in the states. In fact the President loved having him visit. He loved talking about his father to Jushro. Every time he visited the President, after he had a few drinks, he would whip out the last article his father had written and ask Jushro if he had read it. Jushro always read it again to satisfy the President. Jushro thought that it was so strange that the President had such a love for a father that had deserted him.

When Jushro returned from his visit with the President, he brought with him the cocktail glass that the President had used. He said that as he came near the President's office, he was stopped by his Chief of Staff and was asked how was his little girl friend doing. Obviously, this person knew about his relationship to Bella and that she was sick. The President had also been well-informed of his relationship with a young woman who had been in Kenya snooping around about his relatives. He also knew of her kidney disease and her need for a transplant.

Bella and I were surprised that he could take a goblet from the President so easily. Jushro said that the President often started drinking in the morning. It seemed like the President had lost his enthusiasm for the Presidency. Much of the presidential work was always done by his advisors; he had made so many appearances over the years that the people just sort of stopped listening, and his continual use of the teleprompter made his speeches seem impersonal. He didn't have much to do these days and he turned to drinking. By the time Jushro got there around 12:00, he had several empty glasses sitting around the oval office. When he was in the restroom, he just slipped one into his pocket that was lined with a plastic bag. Jushro immediately took the President's glass and a saliva sample from Bella to the same lab that Bella had taken Mr. Jordon's. He did use his influence as Czar, thinking that this would speed things up and pass through the routine without much checking. He hated using the word. Czar. It sounded so autocratic. He was recognized and the lab didn't make him wait In fact the lab didn't make him wait the week for approval; they took both samples on the spot.

After just three days, Jushro was called by the lab with the results. Bella's DNA was a match with the President's.

When Jushro brought the news to Bella, she was stunned. How could she be related to the President but not to Jushro. Was there an error in Jushro's testing or with that of the Presidents. Just as Jushro was going to explain the relationship to Bella, he got a call on his cell phone from the President's secretary and she said the President wanted to see him immediately.

Jushro left to see the President. He was gone for quite a long time. In the mean time, Bella and I were discussing her family tree. I said that I had meant to ask Bella if she had ever found out why her great, grandmother Nora's skin was so light. She said that Tera, Nora's mother, was the product of a white man and her mother, named Sudra. I told her about my encounter with the doctor I had met at the museum. I told her that he had accused my grandfather of impregnating Sudra in 1894, when my grandfather visited the plantation that same year. I told him that I resented his implication because I knew that my grandfather would not have taken advantage of a young woman like that. I told Bella that my grandfather traveled with Theodore O'Mera's grandfather to Africa in 1894. There were three white men at the plantation other then my grandfather. If it had been Jonathon Porthouse, he and his wife would have probably been run off the Plantation by the English government. The other man was Primrose whose livelihood depended on his friendship with the Kenyan tribes in that area. I don't think it could have been him. And the stories I have heard about all the O'Mera men, including the one who traveled with my grandfather, would point in his direction. If this is the case then Theodore O'Mera would also be related to the President. I also mentioned that Theodore had been in the village October 28, 1971, the same month that Otango Sr's father died, which was October 29, 1971. I had seen O'Mera's name in the registry at the museum.

When Jushro returned from his visit with the President, Bella and I had told him about Theodore O'Mera. Jushro would not believe any of it. It sounded like another one of those conspiracy theories being passed around on the Internet. But I told him that I was sure it was Theodore O'Mera's grandfather who had traveled with my grandfather to the plantation.

Jushro explained to Bella that she was related to the President through Tera, his grandmother. He told her about Nora's father. Jushro also had told Bella that the President's father was always bragging about his son's report card and his great athletic ability, and told everyone in the village that there were forces propelling his son into great things. Jushro told us that when he was received by the President, he must have been drinking for some time, because he was rambling. He said that he was not Bella's half-brother. The lab was in error. This would be the end of it. So Jushro said he tried to appeal to the President's reputation, saying the American public would think he was courageous to acknowledge this distant relative of his. He said definitely not. What would that do to my father's image? I tried to explain to him that it would do nothing to the reputation of his father. I tried to explain to him that his father was not Bella's father, but he wasn't listening. He just poured himself another drink and sat down in his chair with his hands in his face, sobbing. Jushro didn't know why the President had asked him to come. Maybe he was asking for my help. When he saw I wasn't going to help, he asked me to leave.

Jushro told Bella he could not protect the President any longer. He wondered who he could trust with the information. Bella knew about Willy and Tommy Dickerson, because Catrina had told her about him when they were traveling together. Then he would tell everything to Willy and Tommy Dickerson.

Both of them agreed to meet Jushro at the airport to catch a plane to Nairobi. Once in Nairobi, they rented a car to go to Kogelo. When they got to the village where Otango Sr. grew up after leaving the village where he was born, Jushro told Willy that it was customary for a baby's placenta to be buried near the vicinity of the homestead where a baby is born. These small areas are usually marked. It is proof that a man was born in this village in case his family has left the homestead many years before and the man wished to return. Once a man can prove that he was born in that village, he becomes a part of that village and is not a *jooko*.

Jushro took Willy to the place where he thought he would find Odinko's placenta. Since the two were from the same family, their placentas were buried side by side, on the right side of the home under the fig tree; they both were born under the same Asian birth sign. The wide branches on each side of the fig tree with its smaller ones huddled in the center looked like an Ox, which would corresponded to the Asian birth year of 1961 and 1973. Since there are always many placentas buried under the tree, there are small markers in the ground with the name and birth date inscribed on the top. They found Joshro's, but next to his, the marker was missing and the ground disturbed, with remanents of a broken urn. Someone who recognized Jushro pointed at the water ditch that was several hundred yards from the homestead. There was the the marker lying face up in the water and parts of the broken urn. The inscription on the marker had been scratched out.

Epilogue
2015

~Bella received a kidney from her biological father, Mac Jordon, and lives part of the year with her husband Jushro in Kogelo, the same village where the ex President and his family live. He was welcomed into the village with open arms. He was not considered a *jooko*. DNA tests confirmed it. Bella spends part of the year in New York, playing with symphonies around the country. The only possession she really needed was her book of poems by Elizabeth Barrett Browning that she could read to her three newly adopted children from the village where her great, great, great grandmother Sudra had taught other women in the village that through books they could see the possibilities of another kind of life.

~George Soros, was now 83, and had already moved to Nairobi in 2013.

~The ex-President's mentor is now teaching at the University of Kenya in Nairobi.

~Tommy Dickerson is running for President in the next election. His book, *Finding my American Hero*, is on the New York Time's Best Seller's list. Willy is his campaign managers.

~A whistle blower had come forward and implicated the White House in the attempted murder of Bella when she was in the hospital. After the American Experiment was discovered, the deaths of Minoya and Hussein

Kendo were being investigated. There were even some who wanted an investigation into the tragic death of an American Hero who perished in the Atlantic Ocean in 1943.

~Theodore O'Mera died July 4, 2015. Several days before he died he called Tommy Dickerson and Willy to his bedside. Since the President had already resigned and because there were so many rumors floating around about the American Experiment, he thought he owed it to the American public to know the whole story. It was up to them to decide whether "the end justified the means."

It all started in 1946 when Theodore's father, J.P. O'Mera confided to Saul Alinsky and Fred Davidson about his father's child back in Kenya, a daughter born in 1895 because of his father's love affair with a Kenyan woman. Her name was Sudra. Their daughter's name was Tera. In 1935 she married her second husband, Hussein Kendo, late in life. She had a son by him, named Otango, and she died in child birth, leaving her husband to raise the young boy.

J.P., Theodore's father, began the first step of the American Experiment. In 1947, when the young boy was eleven, he anonymously sent a large sum of money to Hussein Kendo, Otango's father, with a note instructing him to enroll his son into the finest schools he could find. From that day on, this boy's destiny, as was his son's, was planned by the three who had met that day in Chicago in 1946.

Otango attended the finest schools in Kenya and then came to the United States on a scholarship set up by Minoya, at the request of Fred Davidson. Fred Davidson had already moved to Hawaii. and had enrolled him in the University.

Because Hawaii didn't frown on mixed marriages, their plan was to introduce this young man to the daughter of Fred Davidson's friend from Kansas, hoping he would impregnate her—an easy request. In her high school years, her parents had sent her to a school in Seattle that instilled in her the same ideology similar to the three. She was white, was young, an atheist and a product of the 60's, probably fertile, lacked moral boundaries and full of defiance of all things that appeared to be an injustice. Just as planned; she became pregnant and married the young man

Theodore said that he found out about his grandfather's affair with Sudra when he met with Minoya in 1969. In 1971 Theodore visited Hawaii when it came to his attention that this young man, Otango Sr., was there visiting his son, who at that time was ten years old.

It was at this meeting in the park with Otango Sr. and Fred Davidson that he found out about the "Great American Experiment." They discussed the next part of the plan which would be two prong: Creating an individual who would be a good president and creating an environment conducive to receiving their ideology. The making of a President was easy. That was started in 1947 and was coming along fine. The most challenging was convincing society that change was needed. Orchestrating the plan was done through incremental steps over several decades.

Theodore's visit to the village of Hussein, Otango Sr.'s father, October 28, 1971, confirmed the story he heard from Minoya in 1969. Otango Sr. had always intended to return to Kenya to help his country become part of the modern world. It was his hope that his son would someday return to his homeland. That is why Otango Sr. insisted that Abigale give birth in his home country and his placenta buried in the ground on the homestead. When his son returned, he would not be a *jooko* *(outsider)*, as Otango always felt he was because he had moved away from his birthplace and grew up in another village.

Until Davidson's health started to decline in1984, unbeknownst to the future President, Fred Davidson had controlled all aspects of his life: his birth, his ideology, the college he would attend, the subjects he would take, and the people with whom he should associate. When Fred Davidson realized that he was dying, he passed his mentorship onto a man to whom Fred had confided in when he had gone to a meeting in the 70's of the Weather Underground. This man moved to New York in 1983 where Odinko was finishing up his last year at school.

Because the President's grades from Columbia weren't good enough to enter Harvard right out of undergraduate college, he worked in New York for two years while his new mentor received his advanced degree in Education. The future President moved to Chicago and worked with a local community organizer, preparing for the next step, and his mentor took the position of educator at the University.

After several years of working as a community organizer, the president reapplied and was accepted into Harvard law school, the same college that his father had attended; his new mentor used that time in Chicago to pave the way for a new community leader, who would continue the work of Saul Alinsky. He used this time to find the president a suitable wife who was intelligent, had a similar ideology and who could be a silent force in this young man's life; he also worked on an autographical book that would introduce this young man to the public. Their goal: the 2008 elections.

The Chicago political machine did the rest. In 2008, the President was elected.

"come from outside the government and enter the government like a mole" Saul Alinsky

The history of our grandparents is remembered not with rose petals but in the laughter and tears of their children and their children's children. It is into us that the lives of grandparents have gone. It is in us that their history becomes a future.

~Charles and Ann Morse1

Appendix

1 Charles and Ann Morse are the authors of the book *Whobody there?*

All of the following information was found on the internet, that wonderful tool that allows anyone and everyone to express their points of view, search topics that piques one's curiosity, find lost friends and keep in touch with loved ones. It is important that this tool remains open with no controls. A free society is the only way this can happen.

Aside 1

Historical Events

The past often repeats itself but always advancing forward building on what has happened before.

1773, December 16 The Boston Tea Party. After the troubled British East India Company passed the Tea Act, which created a monopoly on the tea exported to the American colonies, 60 men boarded the ships carrying tea cargo and dumped the entire shipment of tea into the harbor. It was one of the key events leading to the American Revolution. The colonies were being taxed but had no representation.

July, 1776 United States formed one nation and Congress issued the Declaration of Independence.

October, 1781 The war ended.

1783 Treaty of Paris The formal British abandonment of any claims to the United States.

1800 Washington, D.C. becomes the capital of the United States, a new city located at the junction of the Potomac and Anacostia rivers. Major Pierre Charles L'Enfant (1754–1825) designs an imposing plan modeled on the radiating arteries of Versailles with grand public spaces and spacious avenues centered on a domed Capitol.

1801-1809 Jefferson President

1802 The American Academy of the Fine Arts is founded in 1802 in New York by Mayor Edward Livingston (1764–1836) with the help of his brother Robert R. Livingston (1746–1813), U.S. minister to France, who sends a collection of sculptural casts from Paris.

1803 President Thomas Jefferson) purchases the French territory of Louisiana for about $15 million from Napoleon, doubling the size of the nation with the addition of the vast region between the Mississippi River and the Rocky Mountains. Jefferson sends his personal secretary Meriwether Lewis (1774–1809) and army officer William Clark (1770–1838) to explore the region in the years 1804–06.

1808 Congress prohibits importing African slaves

1809-1817 James Madison President

1817-1825 James Monroe President

1820 The Missouri Compromise allows Maine to enter the union as a free state and Missouri to enter as a slave state, maintaining a sectional balance between southern and northern states in the U.S. Senate and setting boundaries for slavery in the lands of the Louisiana Purchase.

1820 Fed offers land @ $1.25 an acre.

1821 Missouri Compromise *

1823 Monroe Doctrine**

1825 The Erie Canal opens in 1825 from Albany to Buffalo and Lake Erie. The canal connects the Hudson River cities of Albany and New York with the vast interior of the nation, the growing farming communities of upstate New York and the Great Lakes Region, allowing New York merchants to turn their city into the economic center of the nation.

1825 A group of artists led by the painter Samuel F. B. Morse (1791–1872), later the inventor of the telegraph, establish the National Academy of Design, an art school and exhibition venue for contemporary arts.

1825-1829 John Quincy Adams President

1829-1837 Andrew Jackson President

1829 Introduction of the Spoils System***

1830 The Indian Removal Act of 1830 attempts to remove the Cherokee and other "Civilized Tribes" living in the southwestern states (Creeks, Choctaws, Chickasaws, and Seminoles) to federal land west of the Mississippi. The Supreme Court ruling in *Worcester v. Georgia* (1832) declares that the state of Georgia's claim of state law over Cherokee land is unconstitutional, but President Andrew Jackson (1767–1845) ignores the decision. In 1838, his successor Martin Van Buren (1782–1862) sends the army to march the remaining 18,000 Cherokee people to Oklahoma; 4,000 die on the "Trail of Tears."

1831 The Mount Auburn Cemetery opens in Cambridge, Massachusetts, outside Boston. The first "rural landscape" cemetery addresses problems with older burial practices, and provides city dwellers and tourists with an experience of nature. The naturalistic landscaping accentuates the rural character of the site, while large sculptural monuments celebrate the lives of the deceased.

1836 Ralph Waldo Emerson (1803–1882) publishes his essay *Nature*; he becomes the central figure in a circle of radical thinkers and writers known as the Transcendentalists, who share a belief in a higher reality than that found in the experiences of the senses or achieved by human reason. Henry David Thoreau (1817–1862) publishes *Walden, or, Life in the Woods* (1854), his effort to put these philosophical ideals into practice in the real world.

1837 The Panic of 1837, the culmination of a speculative boom, causes a six-year depression with numerous bank failures and widespread unemployment.

1837-1841 Martin Van Buren President

1839 The daguerreotype, invented by Frenchman Louis-Jacques-Mandé Daguerre (1787–1851), is introduced into the United States by artist and inventor Samuel F. B. Morse (1791–1872). The light-sensitized metal plate becomes an early form of photography.

1841 William Henry Harrison President (Died after 32 days in office)

1841-1845 John Tyler President

1844 Dry-goods merchant A. T. Stewart (1803–1876) begins building his grand "Marble Palace," the first department store, in New York.

1845-1849 James K. Polk President

1846 The Mexican War begins when General Zachary Taylor (1784–1850) crosses the Rio Grande into Mexico. General Winfield Scott (1786–1866) seizes Mexico City in September of 1847. The United States receives Texas, New Mexico, and Alta California from Mexico in the Treaty of Guadalupe Hidalgo (1848)

1848 Workmen discover gold in the Sierra Nevada foothills at the mill site of German immigrant John Sutter. News reaches the east coast and President Polk confirms the discovery in his annual address to Congress. In 1849 alone, more than 80,000 migrants, known as "forty-niners," arrive. California becomes a state in 1850.

1849-1850 Zachary Taylor President (Died 16 months after being elected.)

1850 The Compromise of 1850 averts a sectional crisis. California enters the union as a free state but the balance is broken between free and slave states in the U.S. Senate. Territories acquired as a result of the Mexican War are allowed to enter the union by the principle of popular sovereignty. The Fugitive Slave Act puts federal authority and officials behind the return of enslaved people who have escaped to freedom.

1850-1853 Millard Fillmore President

1852 Harriet Beecher Stowe (1811–1896), the most successful novelist of the antebellum era, publishes the antislavery novel *Uncle Tom's Cabin*, which sells 350,000 copies in its first year.

1853 Commodore Matthew C. Perry (1794–1858) sails into Tokyo Bay and succeeds in signing a full commercial treaty with Japan.

1853 The New-York Exhibition of the Industry of All Nations opens with the commemoration of its central exhibition hall, the Crystal Palace, an iron and glass structure that features displays of manufactured goods and artistic achievement. This first world's fair on U.S. soil is modeled after the 1851 London Crystal Palace.

1853-1857 Fredlin Pierce President

1854 Republican party formed for abolition of slavery

1857-1861 James Buchanan President

1857 Dred Scott Decision****

1858 The Greensward Plan for a pastoral park in the center of Manhattan is completed by Fredrick Law Olmsted (1822–1903), the park's superintendent, and Calvert Vaux (1824–1895). The 843-acre Central Park is the first large landscaped public park in the country.

1861-1865 Abraham Lincoln President

1862 Congress enacted the first income tax law. It was the forerunner of the present income tax based on the principles of graduated or progressive, taxation and withholding at the source.

1861–65 The United States Civil War, a military conflict between the Union and the Confederacy, begins in April 1861 when Charleston's Fort Sumter is fired upon. The conflict lasts four years, takes more than 600,000 lives, and emancipates 4 million enslaved people.

1865, 3 March, The Freedmen's Bureau Bill, which created the Freedmen's Bureau, was initiated by President Abraham Lincoln and intended to last for one year after the end of the Civil War. Passed on March 3, 1865, by Congress to aid former slaves through education, health care, and employment, it became a key agency during Reconstruction, assisting freedmen (freed ex-slaves) in the South. The Bureau was part of the United States Department of War. Headed by Union Army General Oliver O. Howard, the Bureau was operational from June 1865 to December 1868. ****1

Lost Cause of the Confederacy hindered the Bureau's agents in carrying out their duties to enforce their authority.****2

1865-1869 Andrew Johnson President (a Northern War Democrat and selected as Lincoln's VP. Had sympathies for the pro-slavery policies of the Southern Democrats.)

1865, January 1 Lincoln's Emancipation Proclamation*****

1866 The Civil Rights Bill is enacted by Congress. Johnson vetoes the bill, but Republican Congress overrides his veto. The Act gave blacks the rights and privileges of full citizenship. It counteracts Black Codes.

1866 The 14th Amendment to the Constitution is proposed by Congress. It provides blacks with citizenship and guarantees that federal and state laws should be applied equally to black and white citizens. It also rejects the placement of the Southern old guard to positions of government.

A black cavalry and regiment are created by the U.S. Army. Emancipation is celebrated at the U.S. capitol by 15,000 people

1867 The first, second and third Reconstruction Acts are passed. The time known as "Radical Reconstruction" begins. Congress provides that Southern states will not be readmitted to the Union until they ratified the

14th Amendment. All of the states, except Tennessee, refused to do so. All of the southern states, with the exclusion of Tennessee, are divided into five military districts.

1867 Howard University with the funds allocated to it by Congress. It was named after the commissioner of the Freedmen's Bureau, General Oliver Otis Howard. The university is located in Washington, D.C. and is composed of a predominately black student body. Federal funds are allocated to Howard University every year—2008 was $233.9 million.

1868 The 14th Amendment is ratified. All persons born or naturalized in the United States, and subject to the jurisdiction thereof, are citizens of the United States and of the state wherein they reside. No state shall make or enforce any law which shall abridge the privileges or immunities of citizens of the United States; nor shall any state deprive any person of life, liberty, or property, without due process of law; nor deny to any person within its jurisdiction the equal protection of the laws.

South Carolina, North Carolina, Georgia, Alabama, Arkansas, Florida, and Louisiana each ratify the 14th Amendment and are readmitted to the Union.

A black majority is elected to the South Carolina legislature.

A fourth Reconstruction Act is passed.

1869 Ulysses S. Grant is elected President.

In Tennessee, an all white Democratic "Redeemer" government is created.

The Transcontinental Railroad is completed when a golden spike is driven at Promontory Point, Utah Territory, linking the Union Pacific and the Central Pacific railroads.

1870 The 15th Amendment is enacted. to the Constitution granting African American men the right to vote by declaring that the "right of citizens of the United States to vote shall not be denied or abridged by the United States or by any state on account of race, color, or previous condition of servitude."

Hiram Rhoades Revels is the first black elected to the U.S. Senate and Joseph Hayne Rainey becomes the first black elected U.S. Representative.

Virginia, Mississippi, Texas, and Georgia are readmitted to the Union.

Virginia and North Carolina form "Redeemer" governments.******

1871 Georgia forms a "Redeemer" government.

The Ku Klux Klan Act is passed. It gives the federal government power to punish violators of civil rights laws.

1872 Eliminated Income tax (again taxed distilled spirits, tobacco)

1872 The Freedmen's Bureau is terminated.

Yellowstone Basin of the Wyoming Territory becomes the first national park after the Hayden Expedition of 1871 with the artist Thomas Moran (1837–1926) convinces many that the wilderness area needs to be set aside and preserved from development.

1871 Stanley was sent out to find Livingston

The Amnesty Act is passed. It removes the restrictions placed on Confederate office-holders.

1874 Arkansas and Alabama form "Redeemer" governments.

1875 Mississippi forms a "Redeemer" government.

The Civil Rights Act is passed. It gives blacks equal access to public accommodations.

1876 National league of baseball was formed

1876 Alexander Graham Bell (1847–1922) invents the telephone, uttering the famous first words to his assistant: "Mr. Watson—come here—I want to see you."

The Centennial Exposition or "International Exhibition of Arts, Manufactures, and Products of the Soil and Mine," opens in Philadelphia as an anniversary of U.S. independence and celebration of scientific and industrial progress (1996.95). Thomas Eakins' *Gross Clinic*, rejected by the Exposition's art jury, is exhibited instead in the medical section, inciting much controversy over its uncompromising realism.

1877 Republican Rutherford B. Hayes becomes president. The Compromise of 1877 allows for the withdrawal of federal troops from the South.

Reconstruction ends.

The last federal troops leave South Carolina and effectively end the federal government's presence in the South, bringing the Reconstruction era to a close.

1877-1881 Rutherford Hayes President

1879 Woman lawyers permitted to argue before the Supreme Court

1879 Thomas Alva Edison (1847–1931) builds the first incandescent electric light with a carbonized cotton thread filament.

1881 James Garfield President (Shot 6 months after taking office)

1881-1885 Chester Arthur President

1882 The Chinese Exclusion Act is passed by Congress and bars the further entry of Chinese laborers into the United States.

1883 Civil Service established*******

1883 The Brooklyn Bridge, after fifteen years of construction, is completed, a giant suspension bridge that links Brooklyn and Manhattan and is a new symbol of functional architecture.

1885 Mark Twain (1835–1910) publishes *The Adventures of Huckleberry Finn*, a comic novel of Huck, a boy who flees his father by rafting down the Mississippi River with a runaway slave, Jim.

1885 Chicago's Home Insurance Company building is completed. Architect William Le Baron Jenney (1832—1907) designs the first skyscraper with a load-bearing structural frame of steel, inaugurating the skyscraper age.

1886 The Statue of Liberty is dedicated in New York harbor to commemorate the friendship of the United States and France. Sculptor Frédéric-Auguste Bartholdi (1834–1904) and engineer Gustave Eiffel (1832–1923) collaborate on the pedestal and statue.

1888 The amateur photography craze is launched with the invention of the Kodak #1 camera by George Eastman (1854–1932).

1889-1893 Ben Harrison

1890 AFL founded

1890 Sherman Antitrust Act*******

1893-1896 Grover Cleaveland President

1896 Supreme Court separate but equal legal

1897-1901 William McKinley

Footnotes to Time Line

*The Missouri Compromise "A Balance of Power" March 3, 1820

The institution of slavery had been a divisive issue in the United States for decades before the territory of Missouri petitioned Congress for admission to the Union as a state in 1818. Since the Revolution, the country had grown from 13 states to 22 and had managed to maintain a balance of power between slave and free states. There were 11 free states and 11 slave states, a situation that gave each faction equal representation in the Senate and the power to prevent the passage of legislation not to its liking. The free states, with their much larger populations, controlled the House of Representatives, 105 votes to 81.

In February 1819, New York Representative James Tallmadge proposed an amendment to ban slavery in Missouri even though there were more than 2,000 slaves living there. The country was again confronted with the volatile issue of the spread of slavery into new territories and states. The cry against the South's "peculiar institution" had grown louder through the years. "How long will the desire for wealth render us blind to the sin of holding both the bodies and souls of our fellow men in chains?" Asked Representative Livermore from New Hampshire.

The South's economy was dependent upon black slavery, and 200 years of living with the institution had made it an integral part of Southern life and culture. The South demanded that the North recognize its right to have slaves as secured in the Constitution.

Through the efforts of Henry Clay, "the great pacificator," a compromise was finally reached on March 3, 1820, after Maine petitioned Congress for statehood. Both states were admitted, a free Maine and a slave Missouri, and the balance of power in Congress was maintained as before, postponing the inevitable showdown for another generation. In an attempt to address the issue of the further spread of slavery, however, the Missouri Compromise stipulated that all the Louisiana Purchase territory north of the southern boundary of Missouri, except Missouri, would be free, and the territory below that line would be slave.

**The Monroe Doctrine was a United States policy introduced on December 2, 1823, which said that further efforts by European governments to colonize land or interfere with states in the Americas would be viewed by the United States of America as acts of aggression requiring US intervention.[1] The Monroe Doctrine asserted that the Western Hemisphere was not to be further colonized by European countries, and that the United States would not interfere with existing European colonies nor in the internal concerns of European countries. The Doctrine was issued at the time when many Latin American countries were on the verge of becoming independent from Spain, and the United States, reflecting concerns echoed by Great Britain, hoped to avoid having any European power take Spain's colonies.[1]

***In the politics of the United States, a spoil system (also known as a patronage system) is an informal practice where a political party, after winning an election, gives government jobs to its voters as a reward for working toward victory, and as an incentive to keep working for the party—as opposed to a system of awarding offices on the basis of some measure of merit independent of political activity.

****Dred Scott was the name of an African-American slave. He was taken by his master, an officer in the U.S. Army, from the slave state of Missouri to the free state of Illinois and then to the free territory of Wisconsin. He lived on free soil for a long period of time.

When the Army ordered his master to go back to Missouri, he took Scott with him back to that slave state, where his master died. In 1846, Scott was helped by Abolitionist (anti-slavery) lawyers to sue for his freedom in court, claiming he should be free since he had lived on free soil for a long time. The case went all the way to the United States Supreme Court. The Chief Justice of the Supreme Court, Roger B. Taney, was a former slave owner from Maryland.

In March of 1857, Scott lost the decision as seven out of nine Justices on the Supreme Court declared no slave or descendant of a slave could be a U.S. citizen, or ever had been a U.S. citizen. As a non-citizen, the court stated, Scott had no rights and could not sue in a Federal Court and must remain a slave.

At that time there were nearly 4 million slaves in America. The court's ruling affected the status of every enslaved and free African-American in the United States. The ruling served to turn back the clock concerning the rights of African-Americans, ignoring the fact that black men in five of the original States had been full voting citizens dating back to the Declaration of Independence in 1776.

The Supreme Court also ruled that Congress could not stop slavery in the newly emerging territories and declared the Missouri Compromise of 1820 to be unconstitutional. The Missouri Compromise prohibited slavery north of the parallel 36°30′ in the Louisiana Purchase. The Court declared it violated the Fifth Amendment of the Constitution which prohibits Congress from depriving persons of their property without due process of law.

Anti-slavery leaders in the North cited the controversial Supreme Court decision as evidence that Southerners wanted to extend slavery throughout the nation and ultimately rule the nation itself. Southerners approved the Dred Scott decision believing Congress had no right to prohibit slavery in the territories. Abraham Lincoln reacted with disgust to the ruling and was spurred into political action, publicly speaking out against it.

Overall, the Dred Scott decision had the effect of widening the political and social gap between North and South and took the nation closer to the brink of Civil War. (http://www.historyplace.com/lincoln/dred.htm)

****1 The Freedmen's Bureau spent $17,000 to help establish homes and distribute food, established 4,000 schools and 100 hospitals for former slaves. This Bureau also helped freedmen find new jobs.

At the end of the war, the Bureau's main role was providing emergency food, housing, and medical aid to refugees, though it also helped reunite families. Later, it focused its work on helping the freedmen adjust to their conditions of freedom. Its main job was setting up work opportunities and supervising labor contracts. It soon became, in effect, a military court that handled legal issues. By 1866, it was attacked by former Confederate leaders for organizing blacks against their former masters. Although some of their subordinate agents were unscrupulous or incompetent, the majority of local Bureau agents were hindered in carrying out their duties by the opposition of former Confederates, the lack of a military presence to enforce their authority, and an excessive amount of paperwork[1]. (See Lost Cause of the Confederacy).

President Andrew Johnson vetoed a bill for an increase of power of the Bureau, supported by Radical Republicans, on February 19, 1866.

****2 Many white Southerners were devastated economically, emotionally and psychologically by the defeat of the Confederacy in 1865. White Southerners sought consolation in attributing their loss to factors beyond their control and to betrayals of their heroes and cause. Many Southerners felt that their way of life had been disrupted by the North.[2]

The term *Lost Cause* first appeared in the title of an 1866 book by the historian Edward A. Pollard, *The Lost Cause: A New Southern History of the War of the Confederates*.[3] However, it was the articles written for the Southern Historical Society by Lt. Gen. Jubal A. Early in the 1870s that established the Lost Cause as a long-lasting literary and cultural phenomenon.

Early's original inspiration for his views may have come from General Robert E. Lee himself. When he published his farewell order to the Army of Northern Virginia, Lee spoke of the "overwhelming resources and numbers" that the Confederate army fought against. In a letter to Early, Lee requested information about enemy strengths from May 1864 to April 1865, the period in which his army was engaged against Lt. Gen. Ulysses S. Grant (the Overland Campaign and the NK"http:// en.wikipedia.org/wiki/Siege_of_Petersburg"\o"SiegeofPetersburg"Siege of Petersburg). Lee wrote, "My only object is to transmit, if possible, the truth to posterity, and do justice to our brave Soldiers." In another letter,

Lee wanted all "statistics as regards numbers, destruction of private property by the Federal troops, &c." because he intended to demonstrate the discrepancy in strength between the two armies and believed it would "be difficult to get the world to understand the odds against which we fought." Referring to newspaper accounts that accused him of culpability in the loss, he wrote, "I have not thought proper to notice, or even to correct misrepresentations of my words & acts. We shall have to be patient, & suffer for awhile at least...At present the public mind is not prepared to receive the truth." All of these were themes that Early and the Lost Cause writers "gained wide currency in the nineteenth century and remain remarkably persistent today."

Lost Cause themes were taken up by memorial associations such as the United Confederate Veterans and the United Daughters of the Confederacy, helping Southerners, in some degree, to cope with the dramatic social, political, and economic changes in the post bellum era, including Reconstruction.

*****The Emancipation Proclamation

January 1, 1863

A Transcription

By the President of the United States of America:

A Proclamation.

Whereas, on the twenty-second day of September, in the year of our Lord one thousand eight hundred and sixty-two, a proclamation was issued by the President of the United States, containing, among other things, the following, to wit:

"That on the first day of January, in the year of our Lord one thousand eight hundred and sixty-three, all persons held as slaves within any State or designated part of a State, the people whereof shall then be in rebellion against the United States, shall be then, thenceforward, and forever free; and the Executive Government of the United States, including the military and naval authority thereof, will recognize and maintain the freedom of such persons, and will do no act or acts to repress such persons, or any of them, in any efforts they may make for their actual freedom.

"That the Executive will, on the first day of January aforesaid, by proclamation, designate the States and parts of States, if any, in which the people thereof, respectively, shall then be in rebellion against the United States; and the fact that any State, or the people thereof, shall on that day be, in good faith, represented in the Congress of the United States by members chosen thereto at elections wherein a majority of the qualified voters of such State shall have participated, shall, in the absence of strong countervailing testimony, be deemed conclusive evidence that such State, and the people thereof, are not then in rebellion against the United States."

Now, therefore I, Abraham Lincoln, President of the United States, by virtue of the power in me vested as Commander-in-Chief, of the Army and Navy of the United States in time of actual armed rebellion against the authority and government of the United States, and as a fit and necessary war measure for suppressing said rebellion, do, on this first day of January, in the year of our Lord one thousand eight hundred and sixty-three, and in accordance with my purpose so to do publicly proclaimed for the full period of one hundred days, from the day first above mentioned, order and designate as the States and parts of States wherein the people thereof respectively, are this day in rebellion against the United States, the following, to wit:

Arkansas, Texas, Louisiana, (except the Parishes of St. Bernard, Plaquemines, Jefferson, St. John, St. Charles, St. James Ascension, Assumption, Terrebonne, Lafourche, St. Mary, St. Martin, and Orleans, including the City of New Orleans) Mississippi, Alabama, Florida, Georgia, South Carolina, North Carolina, and Virginia, (except the forty-eight counties designated as West Virginia, and also the counties of Berkley, Accomac, Northampton, Elizabeth City, York, Princess Ann, and Norfolk, including the cities of Norfolk and Portsmouth[)], and which excepted parts, are for the present, left precisely as if this proclamation were not issued.

And by virtue of the power, and for the purpose aforesaid, I do order and declare that all persons held as slaves within said designated States, and parts of States, are, and henceforward shall be free; and that the Executive government of the United States, including the military and naval authorities thereof, will recognize and maintain the freedom of said persons.

And I hereby enjoin upon the people so declared to be free to abstain from all violence, unless in necessary self-defence; and I recommend to them that, in all cases when allowed, they labor faithfully for reasonable wages.

And I further declare and make known, that such persons of suitable condition, will be received into the armed service of the United States to garrison forts, positions, stations, and other places, and to man vessels of all sorts in said service.

And upon this act, sincerely believed to be an act of justice, warranted by the Constitution, upon military necessity, I invoke the considerate judgment of mankind, and the gracious favor of Almighty God.

In witness whereof, I have hereunto set my hand and caused the seal of the United States to be affixed.

Done at the City of Washington, this first day of January, in the year of our Lord one thousand eight hundred and sixty three, and of the Independence of the United States of America the eighty-seventh.

By the President: ABRAHAM LINCOLN

******Beginning in 1869, Southern states began to replace biracial Republican governments elected under Congressional Reconstruction with white-only Democratic ones.

*******In 1883 Congress passed and President Chester Arthur signed the Civil Service Act, sometimes referred to as the Pendleton Act, legislation that created the foundations of the American civil service system. The act established a merit-based system for filling certain classes of federal jobs. Instead of being awarded as political favors, these jobs would be filled through competitive examinations open to all citizens. The act also protected such employees from arbitrary dismissal, demotion, or coercion in any form for political reasons.

********The Sherman Act authorized the Federal Government to institute proceedings against trusts in order to dissolve them. Any combination "in the form of trust or otherwise that was in restraint of trade or commerce among the several states, or with foreign nations" was declared illegal. Persons forming such combinations were subject to fines of $5,000 and a year in jail. Individuals and companies suffering losses because of trusts were permitted to sue in Federal court for triple damages. The Sherman Act was designed to restore competition but was loosely worded and failed to define such critical terms as "trust," "combination," "conspiracy," and "monopoly.

(Johannesburg Aside 2)

The Witwatersrand Gold Rush was a gold rush in 1886 that led to the establishment of Johannesburg, South Africa.

There had always been rumors of a modern-day "El Dorado" in the folklore of the native tribes that roamed the plains of the South African high field, and the gold miners that had come from all over the world to seek out their fortunes on the alluvial mines of Barberton and Pilgrim's Rest, in what is now known as the province of Mpumalanga.

But it was not until 1886 that the massive wealth of the Witwatersrand would be uncovered. Scientific studies have pointed to the fact that the "Golden Arc" which stretches from Johannesburg to Welkom was once a massive inland lake, and that silt and gold deposits from alluvial gold settled in the area to form the gold-rich deposits that South Africa is famous for.

It is believed that it was a Sunday in March 1886 that an Australian gold miner, George Harrison, stumbled across a rocky outcrop of the main gold-bearing reef. He declared his claim with the then-government of the Zuid Afrikaanse Republiek (ZAR), and the area was pronounced open diggings. His discovery is recorded in history with a monument where the original gold outcrop is believed to be located, and a park named in his honor. Ironically, Harrison is believed to have sold his claim for less than 10 Pounds before leaving the area, and he was never heard from again.

Founding of Johannesburg

It did not take long for fortune-seekers from all over the world to flock to the area, and soon what was a dusty mining village known as Ferreira's Camp was formalized into a settlement. Initially, the ZAR did not believe that the gold would last for long, and mapped out a small triangular piece of land to cram as many plots onto as possible. This is the reason why Johannesburg's central business district streets are so narrow.

Within 10 years, the town was already the largest in South Africa, outstripping the growth of Cape Town, which was more than 200 years older. The gold rush saw massive development of Johannesburg and the Witwatersrand, and the area remains the prime metropolitan area of South Africa.

(Frederick Selous Aside 3)

Frederick Selous was born in 1851 in London, in an affluent and well structured family: his father was the chairperson of the prestigious London Stock Exchange and his mother was a poet.

Frederick Courtney Selous led a full and vibrant life. During his life not only did he pursue his interests in nature and hunting but also rubbed shoulders with many influential people, such as President Theodore Roosevelt. In fact in 1909, Theodore Roosevelt, after leaving his presidency, went to East Africa on a Safari, accompanied by Frederick Selous.

As president of the United States, Theodore Roosevelt made conservation a central policy issue of his administration. He created five National Parks, four Big Game Refuges, fifty-one National bird Reservations, and the National Forest Service. Roosevelt advocated for the sustainable use of the nation's natural resources, the protection and management of wild game, and the preservation of wild spaces. Considering America's landscape to be the source of American wealth and the American character, Roosevelt believed conservationism was a democratic movement necessary to maintain and to strengthen American democracy. It was this love for conservation, the outdoors and hunting that took him and his son on the safari trip to Africa with Frederick Selous.

Theodore Roosevelt was the first to visit Africa but for personal reasons. President William Jefferson Clinton was the second US President to visit Africa after over 75 years and the first to preside officially. Nothing constructive came out of that visit, except more aid.

(What is the Gold Standard Aside 3a)

Definition of the Gold Standard

An extensive essay on the gold standard on The Encyclopedia of Economics and Liberty defines the gold standard as "a commitment by participating countries to fix the prices of their domestic currencies in terms of a specified amount of gold. National money and other forms of money (bank deposits and notes) were freely converted into gold at the fixed price." A county under the gold standard would set a price for gold, say $100 an ounce and would buy and sell gold at that price. This effectively sets a value for the currency; in our fictional example $1 would be worth 1/100th of an ounce of gold. Other precious metals could be used to set a monetary standard; silver standards were common in the 1800's. A combination of the gold and silver standard is known as bimetallism.

A Very Brief History of the Gold Standard

If you would like to learn about the history of money in detail, there is an excellent site called A Comparative Chronology of Money which details the important places and dates in monetary history. During most of the 1800s the United States had a bimetallic system of money, however it was essentially on a gold standard as very little silver was traded. A true gold standard came to fruition in 1900 with the passage of the Gold Standard Act. The gold standard effectively came to an end in 1933 when

President Fredlin D. Roosevelt outlawed private gold ownership (except for the purposes of jewelry). The Bretton Woods System, enacted in 1946 created a system of fixed exchange rates that allowed governments to sell their gold to the United States treasury at the price of $35/ounce. "The Bretton Woods system ended on August 15, 1971, when President Richard Nixon ended trading of gold at the fixed price of $35/ounce. At that point for the first time in history, formal links between the major world currencies and real commodities were severed." The gold standard has not been used in any major economy since that time.

What Do We Use Today?

Almost every country, including the United States, is on a system of fiat money, which the glossary defines as "money that is intrinsically useless; is used only as a medium of exchange." We saw in the article "Why Does Money Have Value" that the value of money is set by the supply and demand for money and the supply and demand for other goods and services in the economy. The prices for those goods and services, including gold and silver, are allowed to fluctuate based on market forces. Next we'll look at how the monetary system used can change other variables in the economy.

The Benefits and Costs of a Gold Standard

The main benefit of a gold standard is that it insures a relatively low level of inflation. In articles such as "What is the Demand for Money?" we've seen that inflation is caused by a combination of four factors:

The supply of money goes up.

The supply of goods goes down.

Demand for money goes down.

Demand for goods goes up.

So long as the supply of gold does not change too quickly, then the supply of money will stay relatively stable. The gold standard prevents a country from printing too much money. If the supply of money rises too fast, then people will exchange money (which has become less scarce) for gold (which has not). If this goes on too long, then the treasury will eventually run out of gold. A gold standard restricts the Federal Reserve from enacting policies which significantly alter the growth of the money supply which in turn limits the inflation rate of a country. The gold standard also changes the face of the foreign exchange market. If Canada is on the gold standard and has set the price of gold at $100 an ounce, and Mexico is also on the gold standard and set the price of gold at 5000 pesos an ounce, then 1 Canadian Dollar must be worth 50 pesos. The extensive use of gold standards implies a system of fixed exchange rates. If all countries are on a gold standard, there is then only one real currency, gold, from which all others derive their value. The stability the gold standard cause in the foreign exchange market is often cited as one of the benefits of the system.

The stability caused by the gold standard is also the biggest drawback in having one. Exchange rates are not allowed to respond to changing circumstances in countries. A gold standard severely limits the stabilization policies the Federal Reserve can use. Because of these factors, countries with gold standards tend to have severe economic shocks. Economist Michael D. Bordo explains:

"Because economies under the gold standard were so vulnerable to real and monetary shocks, prices were highly unstable in the short run. A measure of short-term price instability is the coefficient of variation, which is the ratio of the standard deviation of annual percentage changes in the price level to the average annual percentage change. The higher the coefficient of variation, the greater the short-term instability. For the United States between 1879 and 1913, the coefficient was 17.0, which is quite high. Between 1946 and 1990 it was only 0.8.

Moreover, because the gold standard gives government very little discretion to use monetary policy, economies on the gold standard are less able to avoid or offset either monetary or real shocks. Real output, therefore, is more variable under the gold standard. The coefficient of variation for real output was 3.5 between 1879 and 1913, and only 1.5 between 1946 and 1990. Not coincidentally, since the government could not have discretion over monetary policy, unemployment was higher during the gold standard. It averaged 6.8 percent in the United States between 1879 and 1913 versus 5.6 percent between 1946 and 1990."

So it would appear that the major benefit to the gold standard is that it can prevent long-term inflation in a country. However, as Brad DeLong points out, "if you do not trust a central bank to keep inflation low, why should you trust it to remain on the gold standard for generations?" It does not look like the gold standard will make a return to the United States anytime in the foreseeable future.

http://economics.about.com

(One has to ask? If the depression of the 30's was prolonged in the US because of the inaction of the government to get off the Gold Standard earlier so that more fiat money could be made to pay for social programs then why did the depression of 2008-9 occur? We can't blame the gold standard. We haven't used that standard since 1971.)

(Life of a Coffee Bean Aside 4)

What we call a coffee bean is actually the seeds of a cherry-like fruit. Coffee trees produce berries, called coffee cherries, which turn bright red when they are ripe and ready to pick. The fruit is found in clusters along the branches of the tree. The skin of a coffee cherry is thick and bitter. However, the fruit beneath it is intensely sweet and has the texture of a grape. Around this fruit is the parenchyma, a slimy, honey-like layer, which helps protect the beans. The beans themselves are covered by a parchment-like envelope called the endocarp. This protects the two, bluish-green coffee beans, which are covered by yet another membrane, called the spermoderm or silver skin. The ripe berries are handpicked twice a year, with the main picking season from October until the end of the year while the second and smaller harvesting season runs from June to July or early August. The bean is then separated from the cherry by the use of a mechanical device. There are usually two beans in each cherry. Each day's harvest is sorted and processed separately into small boutique lots of green coffee beans. There is a common drop off area where the beans are sold and each farmer receives the same price for their crop according to the grade of their bean. The market governs the price of the raw green coffee bean,

The Coffee Board of Kenya established guidelines on standards for the beans. All coffee is graded after it is milled and Kenya AA generally means the largest beans while AB is next in size. The theory is that the larger beans will contain more of the special oils which give coffee its aroma and taste.

(World War I Aside 5)

The proximate catalyst for World War I was the 28 June 1914 assassination of Archduke Franz Ferdinand of Austria, heir to the Austro-Hungarian throne, by a Bosnian-Serb nationalist. Alliances had already been drawn. As an ally of Serbia, Russia mobiles her forces. Because of the Triple Entente, France and Britain entered the fray. The alliances of those two countries, Canada, Australia, and Italy, Japan, Italy entered the war. The Central Powers consisted of the German Empire, the Austrian-Hungarian Empire, the Ottoman Empire, and the Kingdom of Bulgaria. The name "Central Powers" is derived from the location of these countries. All four were located between the Russian Empire in the east and the French Third Republic and the United Kingdom in the west.

The United States declared war on Germany on the grounds that Germany violated American neutrality by attacking international shipping and because of the Zimmerman telegram which was a coded telegram dispatched by the Foreign Secretary of the German Empire, Arthur Zimmermann, on January 16, 1917, to the German ambassador in Washington, Johann von Bernstorff, at the height of World War I. On January 19, Bernstorff, per Zimmermann's request, forwarded the Telegram to the German ambassador in Mexico, Heinrich von Eckardt. Zimmermann sent the Telegram in anticipation of the resumption of unrestricted submarine warfare by the German Empire on February 1, an act which German High Command feared would draw the neutral United

States into war on the side of the Allies. The Telegram instructed Ambassador Eckardt that if the United States appeared likely to enter the war he was to approach the Mexican government with a proposal for military alliance. He was to offer Mexico material aid in the reclamation of territory lost during the Mexican-American War, specifically the American states of Texas, New Mexico, and Arizona. Eckardt was also instructed to urge Mexico to help broker an alliance between Germany and Japan. The Zimmermann Telegram was intercepted and decoded by the British cryptographers. The revelation of its contents in the American press on March 1 caused public outrage that contributed to the United States' declaration of war against Germany and its allies on April 6.

(World War Two Aside 6)

Causes

(Aside 4) World War Two began in September 1939 when Britain and France declared war on Germany following Germany's invasion of Poland.

Although the outbreak of war was triggered by Germany's invasion of Poland, the causes of the war are more complex.

Treaty of Versailles

In 1919, Lloyd George of England, Orlando of Italy, Clemenceau of France and Woodrow Wilson from the US met to discuss how Germany was to be made to pay for the damage world war one had caused.

Woodrow Wilson wanted a treaty based on his 14-point plan which he believed would bring peace to Europe.

Georges Clemenceau wanted revenge. He wanted to be sure that Germany could never start another war again.

Lloyd George personally agreed with Wilson but knew that the British public agreed with Clemenceau. He tried to find a compromise between Wilson and Clemenceau.

Germany had been expecting a treaty based on Wilson's 14 points and were not happy with the terms of the Treaty of Versailles. However, they had no choice but to sign the document.

The main terms of the Treaty of Versailles were:

1. War Guilt Clause—Germany should accept the blame for starting World War One
2. Reparations—Germany had to pay £6,600 million for the damage caused by the war
3. Disarmament—Germany was only allowed to have a small army and six naval ships. No tanks, no air force and no submarines were allowed. The Rhineland area was to be de-militarized.
4. Territorial Clauses—Land was taken away from Germany and given to other countries. Anschluss (union with Austria) was forbidden.

The German people were very unhappy about the treaty and thought that it was too harsh. Germany could not afford to pay the money and during the 1920s the people in Germany were very poor. There were not many jobs and the price of food and basic goods was high. People were dissatisfied with the government and voted to power a man who promised to rip up the Treaty of Versailles. His name was Adolf Hitler.

Hitler's Actions

Adolf Hitler became Chancellor of Germany in January 1933. Almost immediately he began secretly building up Germany's army and weapons. In 1934 he increased the size of the army, began building warships and created a German air force. Compulsory military service was also introduced.

Although Britain and France were aware of Hitler's actions, they were also concerned about the rise of Communism and believed that a stronger Germany might help to prevent the spread of Communism to the West.

In 1936 Hitler ordered German troops to enter the Rhineland. At this point the German army was not very strong and could have been easily defeated. Yet neither France nor Britain was prepared to start another war.

Hitler also made two important alliances during 1936. The first was called the Rome-Berlin Axis Pact and allied Hitler's Germany with Mussolini's Italy. The second was called the Anti-Comitern Pact and allied Germany with Japan.

Hitler's next step was to begin taking back the land that had been taken away from Germany. In March 1938, German troops marched into

Austria. The Austrian leader was forced to hold a vote asking the people whether they wanted to be part of Germany.

The results of the vote were fixed and showed that 99% of Austrian people wanted Anschluss (union with Germany). The Austrian leader asked Britain, France and Italy for aid. Hitler promised that Anschluss was the end of his expansionist aims and not wanting to risk war, the other countries did nothing.

Hitler did not keep his word and six months later demanded that the Sudetenland region of Czechoslovakia be handed over to Germany.

Neville Chamberlain, Prime Minister of Britain, met with Hitler three times during September 1938 to try to reach an agreement that would prevent war. The Munich Agreement stated that Hitler could have the Sudetenland region of Czechoslovakia provided that he promised not to invade the rest of Czechoslovakia.

Hitler was not a man of his word and in March 1939 invaded the rest of Czechoslovakia. Despite calls for help from the Czechoslovak government, neither Britain nor France was prepared to take military action against Hitler. However, some action was now necessary and believing that Poland would be Hitler's next target, both Britain and France promised that they would take military action against Hitler if he invaded Poland. Chamberlain believed that, faced with the prospect of war against Britain and France, Hitler would stop his aggression. Chamberlain was wrong. German troops invaded Poland on 1st September 1939.

Failure of Appeasement

Appeasement means giving in to someone provided their demands are seen as reasonable. During the 1930s, many politicians in both Britain and France came to see that the terms of the Treaty of Versailles had placed restrictions on Germany that were unfair. Hitler's actions were seen as understandable and justifiable.

When Germany began re-arming in 1934, many politicians felt that Germany had a right to re-arm in order to protect herself. It was also argued that a stronger Germany would prevent the spread of Communism to the west.

In 1936, Hitler argued that because France had signed a new treaty with Russia, Germany was under threat from both countries and it was essential to German security that troops were stationed in the Rhineland. France was not strong enough to fight Germany without British help and Britain was not prepared to go to war at this point. Furthermore, many believed that since the Rhineland was a part of Germany it was reasonable that German troops should be stationed there.

In May 1937, Neville Chamberlain became Prime Minister of Britain. He believed that the Treaty of Versailles had treated Germany badly and that there were a number of issues associated with the Treaty that needed to be put right. He felt that giving in to Hitler's demands would prevent another war.

This policy, adopted by Chamberlain's government became known as the policy of Appeasement.

The most notable example of appeasement was the Munich Agreement of September 1938.

The Munich Agreement, signed by the leaders of Germany, Britain, France and Italy, agreed that the Sudetenland would be returned to Germany and that no further territorial claims would be made by Germany. The Czech government was not invited to the conference and protested about the loss of the Sudetenland. They felt that they had been betrayed by both Britain and France with whom alliances had been made. However, the Munich Agreement was generally viewed as a triumph and an excellent example of securing peace through negotiation rather than war.

When Hitler invaded the rest of Czechoslovakia in March 1939, he broke the terms of the Munich Agreement. Although it was realized that the policy of appeasement had failed, Chamberlain was still not prepared to take the country to war over "…a quarrel in a far-away country between people of whom we know nothing." Instead, he made a guarantee to come to Poland's aid if Hitler invaded Poland.

Failure of the League of Nations

The League of Nations was an international organization set up in 1919 to help keep world peace. It was intended that all countries would be members of the League and that if there were disputes between countries they could be settled by negotiation rather than by force. If this failed then countries would stop trading with the aggressive country and if that failed then countries would use their armies to fight.

In theory the League of Nations was a good idea and did have some early successes. But ultimately it was a failure.

The whole world was hit by a depression in the late 1920s. A depression is when a country's economy falls. Trade is reduced, businesses lose income, prices fall and unemployment rises.

In 1931, Japan was hit badly by the depression. People lost faith in the government and turned to the army to find a solution. The army invaded Manchuria in China, an area rich in minerals and resources. China appealed to the League for help. The Japanese government were told to order the army to leave Manchuria immediately. However, the army took no notice of the government and continued its conquest of Manchuria.

The League then called for countries to stop trading with Japan but because of the depression many countries did not want to risk losing trade and did not agree to the request. The League then made a further call for Japan to withdraw from Manchuria but Japan's response was to leave the League of Nations.

In October 1935, Italy invaded Abyssinia. The Abyssinians did not have the strength to withstand an attack by Italy and appealed to the League of Nations for help.

The League condemned the attack and called on member states to impose trade restrictions with Italy. However, the trade restrictions were not carried out because they would have little effect. Italy would be able to trade with non-member states, particularly America. Furthermore, Britain and France did not want to risk Italy making an attack on them.

In order to stop Italy's aggression, the leaders of Britain and France held a meeting and decided that Italy could have two areas of land in Abyssinia provided that there were no further attacks on the African country. Although Mussolini accepted the plan, there was a public outcry in Britain and the plan was dropped.

The main reasons for the failure of the League of Nations can be summarized into the following points:

1. Not all countries joined the League.

Although the idea for the League of Nations had come from Woodrow Wilson, there was a change of government in the United States before the signing of the treaty and the new Republican government refused to join. As a punishment for having started World War One, Germany was not allowed to join and Russia was also excluded due to a growing fear of Communism. Other countries decided not to join and some joined but later left.

2. The League had no power.

The main weapon of the League was to ask member countries to stop trading with an aggressive country. However, this did not work because countries could still trade with non-member countries. When the world was hit by depression in the late 1920s countries were reluctant to lose trading partners to other non-member countries. 3. The League had no army.

Soldiers were to be supplied by member countries. However, countries were reluctant to get involved and risk provoking an aggressive country into taking direct action against them and failed to provide troops. 4. Unable to act quickly.

The Council of the League of Nations only met four times a year and decisions had to be agreed by all nations. When countries called for the League to intervene, the League had to set up an emergency meeting, hold discussions and gain the agreement of all members. This process meant that the League could not act quickly to stop an act of aggression.

In the 1930's the American people—having lost many young men in World War I—were very hesitant to involve themselves in another distant war. The isolationism of the American people was reflected in Congress, which led to the passage of the Neutrality Act of 1937, making it unlawful for the United States to trade with belligerents.

However, President Roosevelt wanted the U.S. to become involved in the European war. When the war broke out in 1939, he proclaimed a limited emergency and authorized increases in the size of the Regular Army and the National Guard. Congress also agreed to amend the Neutrality Act to permit munitions sales to the French and British.

Meanwhile, in the Pacific, Japan had invaded Manchuria. Roosevelt reacted by shutting off American trade with Japan. This made the

Japanese even more aggressive since they needed resources from abroad to feed their industries. Japan decided to invade the resource-rich British and Dutch colonies in Southeast Asia.

Japan viewed the U.S. as the most significant threat to their aggressive ambitions. The U.S. Pacific Fleet at Pearl Harbor was the only force capable of challenging Japan's navy, and American bases in the Philippines could threaten lines of communications between the Japanese home islands and the East Indies. Every oil tanker heading for Japan would have to pass by American-held PERLINK"http://www.WorldWar2History.info/Luzon/"Luzon. From these needs and constraints, Japan's war plans emerged.

Back on the European front, the rapid defeat of France and the possible collapse of Britain dramatically accelerated American defense preparations. Roosevelt directed the transfer of large stocks of World War I munitions to France and Britain in the spring of 1940 and went further in September when he agreed to the transfer of fifty over-age destroyers to Britain in exchange for bases in the Atlantic and Caribbean.

In March 1941, Congress repealed some provisions of the Neutrality Act. Passage of the Lend-Lease Act, which gave the President authority to sell, transfer, or lease war goods to the government of any country whose defenses he deemed vital to the defense of the United States, spelled the virtual end of neutrality. The President proclaimed that the United States would become the "arsenal of democracy."

In the spring of 1941 American and British military representatives held their first combined staff conferences to discuss strategy in the event of active U.S. participation in the war. The staffs agreed that if the United States entered the war, the Allies would concentrate on the defeat of Germany first. The President authorized active naval patrols in the western half of the Atlantic, and in July, American troops took the place of British forces guarding Iceland.

However, Roosevelt was unable to directly enter the war, since the American people were still in favor of neutrality. The Japanese took care of this in December when they attacked Pearl Harbor. The day after the attack, on December 8, 1941, the U.S. declared war on Japan and Germany. http://www.worldwariihistory.info/in/USA.html

(George Soros Aside 6a)

In 1956, Soros immigrated to the United States. He worked as a trader and analyst until 1963. During this period, Soros adapted Popper's ideas to develop his own "theory of reflexivity," a set of ideas that seeks to explain the relationship between thought and reality, which he used to predict, among other things, the emergence of financial bubbles. Soros began to apply his theory to investing and concluded that he had more talent for trading than for philosophy. In 1967 he helped establish an offshore investment fund; and in 1973 he set up a private investment firm that eventually evolved into the Quantum Fund, one of the first hedge funds, through which he accumulated a vast fortune.

"The Man Who Broke the Bank of England"
On Black Wednesday (September 16, 1992), Soros became instantly famous when, believing the Pound Sterling was overvalued, he speculated aggressively against it. The Bank of England was forced to withdraw the currency out of the European Exchange Rate Mechanism, and Soros earned an estimated US$ 1.1 billion in the process. He was dubbed "the man who broke the Bank of England." In 1997, under similar circumstances during the Asian financial crisis, former Malaysian Prime Minister Mahathir bin Mohamad accused Soros of bringing down the Malaysian currency, the ringgit.

Despite his carefully groomed media image, Soros is a controversial figure. Although he has become extremely wealthy as an international investor and currency speculator (his fortune in 2004 was estimated at US$ 7 billion), he freely acknowledges that the current system of financial speculation undermines healthy economic development in many underdeveloped countries.

"But it was in France that Soros got into trouble with the authorities. In 1988, he was asked to join a takeover attempt of a French bank. He declined, but he did buy the bank's stock. In 2002, a French court ruled that was insider trading."

"Soros denies any wrongdoing and says news of the takeover was public knowledge. Nevertheless, he was fined more than $2 million...roughly the amount French authorities say he made from the trades." Bill Moyers PBS

A global financier and philanthropist, George Soros is the founder and chairman of a network of foundations that promote, among other things, the creation of open, democratic societies based upon the rule of law, market economies, transparent and accountable governance, freedom of the press, and respect for human rights.

Soros was born in Budapest, Hungary, in 1930. His father was taken prisoner during World War I and eventually fled from captivity in Russia to reunite with his family in Budapest. Soros was thirteen years old when Hitler's Wehrmacht seized Hungary and began deporting the country's Jews to extermination camps. In 1946, as the Soviet Union was taking control of the country, Soros attended a conference in the West and defected. He emigrated in 1947 to England, supported himself by working as a railroad porter and a restaurant waiter, graduated in 1952 from the London School of Economics, and obtained an entry-level position with an investment bank.

Philosophy

At the London School of Economics, Soros became acquainted with the work of the philosopher Karl Popper, whose ideas on open society had a profound influence on his intellectual development. Specifically, Soros's experience of Nazi and Communist rule attracted him to Popper's critique of totalitarianism, *The Open Society and Its Enemies*, in which he maintained that societies can only flourish when they allow democratic governance, freedom of expression, a diverse range of opinion, and respect for individual rights.

Philanthropy

As his financial success mounted, Soros applied his wealth to help foster the development of open societies. In 1979, Soros provided funds to help black students attend the University of Cape Town in apartheid South Africa. Soon he created a foundation in Hungary to support culture and education and the country's transition to democracy. (One of his projects imported photocopy machines that allowed citizens and activists in Hungary to spread information and publish censored materials.) Soros also distributed funds to the underground Solidarity movement in Poland, Charter 77 in Czechoslovakia, and the Soviet physicist-dissident Andrei Sakharov. In 1982, Soros named his philanthropic organization the Open Society Fund, in honor of Karl Popper, and began granting scholarships to students from Eastern Europe. Bolstered by the success of these projects, Soros created more programs to assist the free flow of information. He supported educational radio programs in Mongolia and later contributed $100 million to provide Internet access to every regional university in Russia.

The magnitude and geographical scope of his philanthropic commitments, coupled with the core principle of fostering open societies, has allowed Soros to transcend the limitations of many national governments and international institutions. During the 1980s, Soros financed a trip by young economists at a reform-minded think tank in China to a business university in Budapest; he also established a grant making foundation in China to foster civil society and transparency. In 1991, he helped found the Central European University, a graduate institution in Budapest that focuses on social and political development. Soros spent $50 million to help the citizens of Sarajevo endure the city's siege during the Bosnian war, funding among other projects a water-filtration plant that allowed residents to avoid having to draw water from distribution points targeted by Serb snipers. Most recently, he has provided $50 million to support the Millennium Villages initiative, which seeks to lift some of the least developed villages in Africa out of poverty.

In 1993, Soros created the Open Society Institute, which supports the Soros foundations working to develop democratic institutions throughout Central and Eastern Europe and the former Soviet Union. His network of philanthropic organizations dedicated to building open societies has expanded to include more than 60 countries in the Middle East, Central Asia, Africa, and Latin America. Despite the breadth of his endeavors, Soros is personally involved in planning and implementing many of the foundation network's projects. His visionary efforts have produced a remarkable record of successful philanthropy, including efforts to free developmentally challenged people from life-long confinement in state institutions, to provide palliative care to the dying, to win release for prisoners held without legal grounds in penitentiaries in Nigeria, to halt the spread of tuberculosis and HIV/AIDS, to create debate societies, to promote freedom of the press, and to help resource-rich countries establish mechanisms to manage their revenues in a way that will promote economic growth and good governance rather than poverty and instability.

In 2003, Soros said that removing President George W. Bush from office was one of his main priorities. During the 2004 campaign, he donated significant funds to various groups dedicated to defeating the president. He started up Moveon.org in order to raise funds to defeat Bush. It is said that Bush's support of Israel was one of the areas in which he strongly disagreed with Bush.

Publications

In 2006, Mr. Soros published *The Age of Fallibility: Consequences of The War on Terror* (Public Affairs, 2006). His previous books include *The Bubble of American Supremacy* (2005); *George Soros on Globalization* (2002); *Open Society: Reforming Global Capitalism* (2000); *The Crisis of Global Capitalism: Open Society Endangered* (1998); *Soros on Soros: Staying Ahead of the Curve* (1995); *Underwriting Democracy* (1991); *Opening the Soviet System* (1990); and *The Alchemy of Finance* (1987). His essays on politics, society, and economics appear frequently in major periodicals around the world.

Soros has received honorary degrees from the New School for Social Research, Oxford University, the Budapest University of Economics, and Yale University. In 1995, the University of Bologna awarded Soros its highest honor, the Laurea Honoris Causa, in recognition of his efforts to promote open societies throughout the world.

(Dot.com Bubble and the Y2K Fix Aside 7)

The "dot-com bubble" was a speculative bubble covering roughly 1995–2001 (with a climax on March 10, 2000 with the NASDAQ peaking at 5132.52) during which stock markets in Western nations saw their value increase rapidly from growth in the new Internet sector and related fields. The period was marked by the founding (and, in many cases, spectacular failure) of a group of new Internet-based companies commonly referred to as *dot-coms*. Companies were seeing their stock prices shoot up if they simply added an "e-" prefix to their name and/or a ".com" to the end, which one author called "prefix investing."

A combination of rapidly increasing stock prices, individual speculation in stocks, and widely available venture capital created an exuberant environment in which many of these businesses dismissed standard business models, focusing on increasing market share at the expense of the bottom line. In 2001, The low interest rates in 1998–99 helped increase the start-up capital amounts. Although a number of these new entrepreneurs had realistic plans and administrative ability, many more of them lacked these characteristics but were able to sell their ideas to investors because of the novelty of the dot-com concept.

A canonical "dot-com" company's business model relied on harnessing network effects by operating at a sustained net loss to build market share (or mind share). These companies expected that they could build enough brand awareness to charge profitable rates for their services later. The motto "get big fast" reflected this strategy. During the loss period the companies relied on venture capital and especially initial public offerings of stock to pay their expenses. The novelty of these stocks, combined with the difficulty of valuing the companies, sent many stocks to dizzying heights and made the initial controllers of the company wildly rich on paper.

Historically, the dot-com boom can be seen as similar to a number of other technology-inspired booms of the past including railroads in the 1840s, automobiles and radio in the 1920s, transistor electronics in the 1950s, computer time-sharing in the 1960s, and home computers and biotechnology in the early 1980s in accordance with the Japanese economic meltdown.

"YK2" Fix The Year 2000 problem (also known as the Y2K problem, the millennium bug, the Y2K bug, or simply Y2K) was a notable problem for both digital (computer-related) and non-digital documentation and data storage situations which resulted from the practice of abbreviating a four-digit year to two digits. The total cost of the work done in preparation for Y2K is estimated at over 300 billion US dollars

Found on author's web site:
http://www.publishedauthors.net/cmaryfinn/index.html
Comments from the author
Questions good for book clubs
African Social Paper. Barak H. Obama Sr., 1965
Character family tree chart
Complete geneology of Peairs' line from Charlmagne to author.
Chart for National Debt from 1800's to 2010—Federal Debt % of GDP

"Marx's book *Capital* is about the transition from the Capitalist stage to the coming socialist stage—understanding the different stages of social history and how one stage is transformed into another.

Marx's book *Capital, 1867*, is an analysis of this specific kind of commercial society, and in particular a study of its dynamic, how it tends to develop and change. His practical purpose is to forecast the transition to the next stage, socialism, which is not yet clearly in existence but is already coming to existence within capitalist society, just as capitalism had developed within the social order that Adam Smith had described. The Capitalist stage is another phase of Adam Smith's "commercial society." You will recall that Adam Smith spoke of four stages of social development—the age of hunters, the age of herders or shepherds, the age of farmers and the commercial age."

(http://www.humanities.mq.edu.au/Ockham/y6406.ht)